MURDER AT WESTGATE BAY

Murder At Westgate Bay

CAROL M. CREASEY

UNITED WRITERS
Cornwall

UNITED WRITERS PUBLICATIONS LTD
Ailsa, Castle Gate, Penzance, Cornwall.
www.unitedwriters.co.uk

British Library Cataloguing in Publication Data:
A catalogue record for this book is
available from the British Library.

ISBN 9781852002091

Printed and bound in Great Britain by
United Writers Publications Ltd.,
Cornwall.

I dedicate this book to
Sarah and Vivienne,
the lovely ladies who own
Westgate Galleria,
and thank them for their
support with all of my books
since I joined them in 2019.

Chapter One

"But I don't want another doctor, I want Dr Jones!"

Elsie Thornton's voice was defiant. Her lips were pursed as Staff Nurse Harriet Wren tried to appease her. Harriet was aware that Dr Jones had been here since early this morning, and it was already past the time that he usually went home. He only worked one day a week at the hospital because he was part of a communal practice in Westgate-on-sea, but it was clear to see Elsie had taken quite a shine to him, which wasn't surprising, as he had such a nice bedside manner.

"It's OK, Harriet," he smiled, showing very even white teeth, and his face lit up. He pushed his very black hair away from his forehead, conscious of the fact that he needed a hair cut. He was always busy, and by the time he got home the hairdresser's were all shut. But he must make an effort before next week, he did like to look smart.

He spent a few precious minutes talking to his patient. She was an elderly lady, and just recovering from a hip operation. She was still in pain and, although Harriet had given her some painkillers, in her mind, Dr Jones had fixed her hip, so he was the person she needed right now. Eventually she knew it wouldn't hurt, so, through her eyes, he was the best.

She soon settled down once he spoke to her soothingly, and then he was able to make preparations for going home. He washed his hands again, and took off his white coat.

Harriet herself was not immune to the fact that, at forty-five years old, he was a good looking man. She was happily married herself, with a family, but there was no harm in secretly admiring him.

They were on first name terms, as was everyone in the hospital, although they did use more formal terms sometimes in front of patients. She had known Ian for about twenty years, and he was a totally dedicated doctor, as his father was before him. His patients always came first, and this probably explained the sad fact that his wife had left him and was now living in Margate with her boyfriend.

Not that Ian discussed his private life, but in Westgate, everyone was friendly with one another and news soon got around. Ian seemed to be a private man, he was polite, with excellent manners, gentle and kind with all the patients, and by far the most popular doctor in the hospital. Whatever pain he may have been feeling over losing his wife was carefully hidden. He only really got into discussions about his patients, so although she had known him for a long time, he definitely was not an open book; there was always a certain reserve about him. Harriet couldn't help thinking what a fool his wife had been to leave the beautiful Victorian house they lived in, and her handsome and well respected husband, to go and live in a couple of rooms in Margate with a man who looked as if he belonged on the dodgems at Dreamland. Not that she had seen him, but he had been described in that way to her.

Ian said goodbye to Harriet. As usual he was later than he intended, but he did have a day off tomorrow. Years ago his father had used the bottom floor of his home as a waiting room and surgery for the local patients, but in recent years Ian had realised he must move with the times, so he had joined a local practice which housed eight different doctors, with three receptionists who were always busy either on the phone or checking in patients for their appointments. Being part of a bigger practice meant that he was able to take a day off during the week and he had chosen Thursdays. He was also now only on call about one weekend in six.

He had made that move partly so that he could spend more time at home with Pamela without feeling he was neglecting his patients, but in the end it hadn't saved their marriage, because she had chosen to start a new life with Stewart Russell, who was ten years her junior. Not that Pamela looked forty-four. With her raven black long hair, clear skin and very expressive green eyes, she was startlingly beautiful, so he could hardly blame Stewart for falling in love with her. He knew it was his own fault for being a workaholic, and for a long time they had been growing apart. Their son Marty was away at university and doing very well, so it was a relief to know he had coped with the break-up. Marty was a happy natured young man with a calm disposition, unlike his mother who had always been restless. But he guessed it must have been his fault that she had been attention seeking because he had neglected her.

He had been so immersed in his reverie whilst he negotiated the traffic after leaving the QEQM hospital, that he suddenly found himself very close to the small town of Westgate. Most of his local shops were closed now, so he drove over the railway bridge and turned right, passing the local shops in Station Road with their distinctive canopies over the top which afforded them shade on hot days, and a certain amount of protection when it rained.

Not many cars were parked in the spaces outside the shops at this time of day. Unlike daytime, when this thriving local shopping centre was busy and it was sometimes difficult to get a parking space. Luckily there were local roads without yellow lines in them where shoppers could also park.

Ian drove round the corner at the end of the road and headed towards the seafront. His house was set back from the road, it had a large garden surrounding it, with panoramic views of West Bay. The drive stretching up to the front door was narrow and winding. There was a double garage at the side of the house, but he rarely put his car in it, as it was full of old furniture and gym equipment which Marty used when he was at home.

Most of the other houses were more modest, with much smaller gardens, and since the 1960s bungalows had been built; some of them were holiday homes, and the rest belonged to couples who had retired to Westgate to enjoy a quieter pace of life and also to benefit from the clean and healthy sea air. A couple of blocks of flats had also been added in recent years.

Ian drove slowly up the winding drive and left his car outside the front door. It was much wider there, so he parked the car pointing towards the sea. The basement of the house had now been converted to a self-contained flat which was used by Marty when he came home from University. There was plenty of room for him to do his own thing, and he often brought friends of either sex home with him during the holidays.

The stair cases were wide, and the ceilings high, and the house had always been maintained to a very high standard. When she had lived there, Pamela had been in charge of all décor and furnishings. Ian had been more than happy to indulge her, and she had created a home which was eye-catching. Even though Pamela had been brought up in a council house, she had middle class tastes. Beautiful draped velvet curtains hung at the windows, the finest wall paper graced the walls, and deep pile carpets were in every room except the kitchen.

Ian had been a junior doctor when he first saw her. She was a student nurse and, even with her nurse's uniform on, her big green expressive eyes had captured his heart. Pamela was equally entranced with this handsome, sleek dark haired doctor who oozed kindness and empathy. In the beginning it had been a perfect love match, and their happiest period had been when Marty was born.

But reality soon set in when Pamela found herself at home, bringing Marty up with Ian frequently being called out for emergencies. She found herself resenting other families where both parents were present, even though she had a comfortable life style. Ian tried to do his bit when he was there, and had a close bond with his son, who never appeared to share his mother's resentment that Ian was not always around.

Pamela had more free time when they employed a nanny, but once Marty started school, the nanny was not really needed, and Pamela didn't like the idea of another woman claiming her son's affection. She continued to enjoy the comfortable life that Ian had provided her with until Marty left home to go to university. Marty was the glue that held them together, but once the house was empty Pamela decided she was going to really live her life, so she started going to social clubs and enjoying a drink or two.

Ian could not feel any malice towards her, it wasn't in his nature. Like his father before him, he had grown up with an ability to help heal the sick. It was such a powerful force inside him, but he did not know how to balance his family life with his passion to help others. He blamed himself entirely for Pamela leaving him. He would probably always love his wife. She was the mother of his son, but now she was with Stewart, and soon she would be divorced from Ian. He had still left her half of everything in his will, but as she had a new relationship, Marty would have the other half. But he might have to alter his will again, he realised, now that Holly had come into his life. But there was no rush to call in the solicitor, he was forty-five, fit and healthy, so he didn't expect to be going anywhere.

He opened the front door to be greeted by a delicious aroma coming from the kitchen. The furniture gleamed and the floors were spotless. He wondered how he would cope if he didn't have Kate, his housekeeper. She had cleaned the house from top to bottom, put some tulips in the vase on the dining room table, and, after inspecting the oven, he saw there was a coq-au-vin meal simmering slowly, waiting for his return, and a bottle of Chardonnay in the fridge. Next to the Chardonnay, she had prepared him a small salad, and although he might eat it on a tray, she had laid a place at the table with a snowy white tablecloth.

Kate was such a reliable housekeeper. She did her job admirably, and she was tactful and discreet. She lived with her sister Lisa in an apartment further along the road, and they had lived there for about ten years. During that time she had been a godsend to Pamela, and even more to him now, since Pamela had left. When he had his own private practice, Lisa, who was a trained nurse, had helped him as a nurse, doing injections and health checks for patients, but she couldn't be more different from her sister. She was excitable, and not at all discreet, and the most embarrassing thing of all was her fixation about him. He couldn't help being aware of it, so it had been a welcome relief to close his own practice and join the group practice, because, as he had explained to Lisa, "He was only one doctor there, and couldn't make decisions about who to hire."

At the time Lisa had taken it badly. She was very angry, and he had almost thought she might be a bit psychotic. But then as quickly as it came, her anger had evaporated, making him wonder if he had imagined it. He didn't see her that often now, to his relief, and Kate had told him she now worked as a nanny.

Ian went upstairs, anxious to get out of his suit. He had a shower, and then changed into light cotton trousers and an open necked shirt. Whilst he was dressing he remembered that his brother David was coming round that evening. Glancing at the clock he reckoned he just had time to eat his dinner before David turned up. Of course, he knew why his brother was coming, and this time he would have to be strict with him; no more money. David had to stop gambling and get his life back, because Ian was tired of being his money pot! His support must stop now. Just because Ian was careful with his money, it didn't mean that David could gamble it all away. David would have to find a way to settle his own debts.

He went downstairs. The shower had revived him a bit, and now he was hungry. But he reckoned he had five minutes to enjoy a whisky before he sat down to eat. He picked up the whisky decanter and poured himself a measure, knowing that when the cool liquid slipped down inside him, it would wash away all the stress and tiredness after a busy day's work. As he took his first sip, the telephone rang, so he quickly downed the drink and picked up the handset.

David Jones was feeling very nervous. He had got himself into a right mess. He had felt depressed since Sandra had left him. Well, that is what he blamed it on, and his gambling had got worse. But he had been gambling for all his adult life. He didn't think of it as an addiction, there was nothing wrong with it, especially when he won, then it was fun. It wasn't fun when he lost, of course, but then that only made him all the more determined to win it back.

His brother Ian had suggested he get therapy, but then Ian was a stick in the mud who never took any chances in his life. He was also a workaholic. Ever since he could remember, David had always felt he was the black sheep of the family, the one who had never amounted to much. He had not inherited his brother Ian's looks or skills. He was short and stocky, with very ordinary brown hair. His long suffering wife had put up with his gambling for years, but at

12

the age of forty, she had left him, and since then he had lost his job, and ages ago his house had been repossessed, so now he rented a two bedroom bungalow further down the same road as his brother. But now, unless Ian could help him cover the rent, which was two months in arrears, he would be homeless, and when he had mentioned it to Ian, he had told him he must stand on his own two feet, and get himself a new job.

David didn't believe he meant it. Ian had said this before, but he was kind, he wouldn't see his brother homeless. He would promise him never to gamble again if he could have one more chance. He was planning to pop round and have a drink with him. Ian was always more amenable after a whisky or two.

He saw his brother's car drive up the road, a bit later than usual, and he decided not to go round immediately. Ian might want to eat and take a shower. At this time of the year it stayed light until almost ten o'clock. He had to use every bit of his charm to manipulate his brother into preventing him from being made homeless, and each minute that ticked by seemed like an hour.

He washed his face in cold water, the humidity was still there and maybe they would get some rain later. He reckoned that Ian had been home for about forty-five minutes now, time enough to eat a meal prepared by his housekeeper, Kate, whilst he, David had to exist on a cheap ready meal. He guessed Ian would have his kitchen door open whilst the weather was so humid, so he could go in that way. He tended not to use the front door a lot. It was a heavy oak door, but most of the visitors came past the little walled kitchen garden and knocked on the back door. Now David just wanted to get this over with, so, putting on his most ingratiating smile, he left his bungalow and walked up the road towards his brother's house.

Holly Wheeler had come to a decision; it had not been taken lightly, but now she wanted to put her plan into action. At the age of twenty-four she had found herself pregnant, and deserted, all at the same time. As soon as she told Dan he had gone. She didn't love Dan, and he clearly had not loved her, so he was no loss. She had got used to hardening her heart, it stopped it from being broken. Ever since she was a little girl, she had known that her sister Lola was their dad's favourite. Lola looked like him with her blonde hair and blue eyes, and Holly didn't. She told herself she was more like her mother, Rita, with mid-brown curly hair and interesting dark eyes. She had always felt close to Rita, who tried to make up for the fact that Kevin Wheeler showed no interest in his eldest daughter.

Holly had put an auburn rinse on her hair, and experimented with make-up. She might not be as beautiful as Lola but she was certainly very attractive, so she really didn't know why her father rejected her; and it hurt, destroying her self-confidence.

She felt heartbroken when her mother became ill with cancer, and although she had treatment, and appeared to recover just long enough to attend Lola's wedding, the dreaded disease came back again, and within a few short months her mother was moved into a hospice where she died at the age of just forty-five. The disease had taken its toll on her and, when she passed away, she had lost so much weight she looked about ninety-five years old.

But, before she died, she told Holly a secret she had held for all her life. Kevin was not her father. Rita had fallen pregnant by another student whilst at university, and his name was Ian Jones. Kevin had married her, and she had never told Ian Jones about the pregnancy. This explained many things that Holly had not understood, and with her mother now gone, she left home to make her own way in life.

She made it her mission to track down her real father. It wasn't that easy, so she hired a private detective to help her. When she found out he was the Ian Jones that everyone in the Kent area spoke so highly of, she actually felt quite proud.

Her next step was to leave London and move to Kent. So she rented a flat in Canterbury, and got herself a new job as a receptionist in a large car dealership there. The wages did not compare with London, but she had enough money to live and eat. And then she met Dan, who had been quite exciting at the time, but his reaction to her pregnancy killed any feelings she might have had for him stone dead.

When she met Ian for the first time, it was whilst she was still with Dan, and did not know she was pregnant. He was a quiet man,

14

kindness and empathy positively shone out of him, and she really did feel a connection to him. He had been very sad to hear about her mother's untimely death, and had even offered to give some money towards her funeral. But Holly had been left out of any funeral arrangements by Kevin, who only wanted input from Lola.

So Holly was now going to ask Ian for money for a termination. She didn't feel maternal, and she certainly did not want Dan's baby. She could not afford to leave work. She felt totally on her own. Even at the funeral, it was Lola who gave the speech about their mother, and Kevin had not even acknowledged her. Right now she felt ill;' severe sickness and tiredness were plaguing her. Her real dad was the only person she could turn to, so she texted his mobile saying she would pop round after eight this evening, as she had something important to share with him. Knowing how busy he always was, she told him only to reply if it wasn't convenient. In the absence of a reply, she got herself ready to see him.

Kate had been Ian and Pamela's housekeeper for ten years. Shortly after she had moved into the apartment at West Bay, she had heard that Dr Ian Jones and his wife were looking for a cook and housekeeper, and as it was something she knew she could easily do, she had applied for the job and got it. Soon after Lisa had moved in with her, and as she had nursing experience, when Kate heard that the nurse was leaving to join another practice, she put in a word for Lisa. But she had wished she hadn't, because Lisa had developed an unhealthy passion for the doctor, and in the end Kate had realised she had to leave. This coincided with Ian's decision to join a group practice, so it had been a huge relief to Kate when Lisa had a change of career, and became a nanny.

Kate had helped her to move on from the obsessive behaviour she had shown towards Ian, and she hoped that he was no longer on Lisa's mind. Now she was working for a family with a young daughter, so she didn't really come into contact with Ian any more.

Since his wife Pamela had left, Ian needed Kate's help even more, so Kate dutifully did her job, and kept herself to herself.

She had left him a casserole in the oven, but from her house she could see when his car came up the road, and tonight he was late. She was just thinking maybe she should go back and turn it off, but to her relief, his car appeared. Now she could relax.

Lisa had arrived home from work now. In contrast to Kate, she was like a whirlwind, rarely still, and always unpredictable, but that is what Kate loved about her. Their bond was so strong; neither having married. If people thought it strange that two women from the same family were both unmarried, then they didn't know about it. Kate had felt lonely when she first moved in after her mother's death, but when Lisa had joined her it felt right.

Lisa was glad to be home. Little Abby was a year old, and now walking, and she was a handful. But she loved that little girl, and often thought wistfully she would have liked to have a baby herself, even though there was no man in her life. But there could have been. She knew the way she felt about Ian had been over the top. He had shown no interest in her, but she had found herself stalking him, and going round to the house for any excuse. Her feelings had turned her life upside down; she had not realised that it could affect her so badly. It was self-destructive, so she had turned to Kate for comfort, then done the sensible thing, changed her career and become a nanny. Most of her days were now spent at Birchington, and she avoided going into Ian's house, because she knew if she did, it would bring back all that longing to be with him again.

Chapter Two

DCI Alan Clarke was finding this evening a bit hot and stuffy as he drove home from Canterbury police station. It was only May but the humidity was overpowering in Canterbury, where there were many shops and buildings close to one another.

He had the air conditioning going full blast, his suit jacket lay on the back seat, and he had taken his tie off. He couldn't wait to put his shorts on and take a trip to the beach. He had been lucky enough to get a transfer with his job, and he now worked at Canterbury Police Station, but selling their London flat had not been as easy as they had hoped. Several people wanted to buy it, but the chain kept breaking down, and after a few stressful months of showing people around, they had decided to leave it in the hands of the estate agent.

So with his wife Zoe also keen to leave the pollution and traffic in London behind them, they had rented a bungalow at Birchington on the Garden Estate. They both wanted their son Adam to grow up in the clean sea air, so they decided that, once the London flat had sold, they would look for a new family home.

Adam was just over a year old now, and had started to toddle around. Alan loved going home to his family. Sometimes he was called for an emergency, but Zoe never complained, she was used to it by now. She had gone back to work as a nurse, working part-time at the QEQM hospital at Margate. In the meantime they had a part-time nanny for the three days that Zoe worked. Her name was Helen, and she lived in Westgate-on-sea. She, too, had once been a nurse, but now she had decided to make a career looking after young children. When Alan and Zoe realised that she was thirty-eight, more mature than most of the young girls they had interviewed, and had the experience of caring for her own mother towards the end of her life, they decided she would have the experience to take good care of Adam. She had also produced very favourable character references from the hospital.

When they interviewed her she seemed bright and bubbly, and nothing was too much trouble. Adam smiled a lot when she was around, which was a very important reason why they chose her, as his happiness was paramount to both of them, and he seemed to like this vibrant lady who had a keen glint in her eye.

As Alan pulled into the drive of the bungalow, he spotted Helen's car parked on the concrete area in the front garden. That meant Zoe wasn't home yet, but he could take over. He loved his time spent with Adam; Alan Clarke the tough policeman became Adam Clarke's doting dad as soon as he entered the house.

Helen Hunter was sitting attempting to read Adam a story, but his son was doing his best to climb off her lap and carry on exploring, when he entered the lounge of the small bungalow.

"Hi everyone," he said genially, grabbing his son, and swinging him up in the air, which made Adam chuckle with excitement.

"Hi Alan." Helen smiled. She was a very striking looking young woman, with red gold hair, which cascaded around her shoulders, and tawny brown eyes. Today she had put her hair back in a ponytail, and Alan wondered idly why she had never married, she was certainly very attractive, and seemed to positively glow with energy. At her interview she had told Zoe she was "happily single," and could therefore devote her time and energy to Adam. That had impressed Zoe because one of her nursing friends was always complaining about her nanny always being on her mobile, and frequently breaking up and making up with her current boyfriend, and not always concentrating on her job.

"How has he been?" asked Alan, whilst his son continued to crow with laughter as he was swung up in the air.

"He's been great. I kept him out of the sun, but he had a splash in his paddling pool. Oh, and by the way, he's just had his tea, so maybe don't hold him upside down."

18

"Oh yes, of course." Alan hastily brought Adam down to ground level; he didn't want him throwing up all over his trousers. He grinned disarmingly at Helen, realising he had been a bit too exuberant.

"Would you like a cup of tea?" asked Helen, smiling. Her eyes barely left Adam. She clearly adored him, thought Alan proudly, but then who wouldn't?

"No it's fine thanks, I will get something cold from the fridge. You have done a great job, and now you can go. We'll be fine until Zoe comes in."

Helen smiled her thanks, and picked up her bag to go. Alan held Adam up, encouraging him to wave goodbye to her. This was his latest skill, but he wasn't having any of it; Adam would make his own mind up when he wanted to wave. He just stared with his big blue eyes as wide as saucers.

"Zoe's here, I best move my car," said Helen hurriedly. And as she went through the door, Adam could be heard chanting, "Byebye bubbub." Which made Alan beam with pride, even if Helen couldn't hear him.

When the two women met, there was a brief conversation before Helen went on her way. Zoe came in, and Alan moved towards her still holding Adam. "Here is your mum," he said to Adam, who chanted: "Mumum, bubba," and Zoe smiled, giving them both an affectionate brush with her hand. She scooped Adam up quickly for a cuddle, and Alan relinquished him, but the little boy wriggled, he wanted to go on the floor, so she put him down, and they both watched him toddling around. Adam was never still for a moment, and Zoe had remarked meaningfully that she knew who he got that from, which made Alan feel proud. Was Adam really like him? Zoe leaned over and kissed his cheek.

"If you want to go and get changed, I can watch Adam."

"But honey, you only just came through the door."

"That's OK, I can get changed after as well."

"If we wait a bit until it's cooler, we can pop down to Minnis Bay, and have our tea in the cafe," suggested Alan. "I am sure you don't want to cook tonight."

"Oh, that sounds lovely!" exclaimed Zoe. "I can't wait to get my shorts on."

An hour later, they put Adam into his buggy, the walk to the bay was about fifteen minutes.

They both felt refreshed after changing and Zoe had packed a small bag to take in case it was needed for Adam. But, as they went through the door, Alan's mobile rang. His heart sank. If it was an emergency, he would have to go. He answered it quickly. "Yes, Alan Clarke here."

"Good evening sir, I am afraid we have an emergency. A local doctor living in West Bay, Ian Jones, has been found dead in his home. We need you to visit the scene. He died last night."

Alan's face was showing concern. Zoe guessed what would happen next, but she was calm, this was what Alan's job was all about; she had always understood.

"What was the cause of death?"

"We have someone here now investigating that."

"OK, give me the address. I'll pick up Martha, and we'll be there soon."

An address in Westgate was given, and he quickly scribbled it down with the postcode. Zoe was lifting Adam out of his buggy, and he turned apologetically to her.

"Honey, I am sorry, there's been a death in Westgate. I have to go and see what's going on."

"It's OK, but you haven't eaten. Is it a murder?"

"Not sure yet, but don't worry, I can eat when I get back."

Zoe smiled, she knew when Alan had a new case he often forgot to eat, but she would make sure there was something when he came back. In the meantime, she would bath Adam and get him ready for bed, so that, when Alan returned, they would have some time to themselves.

"I don't expect to be all evening, but it just messed up our trip to Minnis Bay."

"There will be lots of other times," Zoe reminded him, and he gently kissed her lips before going out of the door. What an amazing woman she was!

He had rung Martha. She was in process of cooking her dinner, but had handed it over to her partner, Clive. He was also a PC, but Alan didn't know him that well. Martha was a good WPC, and also had all the necessary attributes for her other role as a family liaison officer. Since the shock realisation that a former suspect had been a psychopath, who had fooled everybody, including himself, Alan had realised that many people are not how they seem to others. When he had come to this area six months ago to solve the body on the beach murder at Herne Bay, Wendy Stuart had worked with him, but when he put in for a transfer, Wendy had opted to stay at Wimbledon. This was going to be his first case with Martha. She was only twenty-one, and due to marry Clive very shortly, but his first impression of her had been favourable; she was calm and organised, and had an air of confidence about her too. She did remind him a little of an earlier WPC partner, as she was tall with dark hair, but Martha had an uncomplicated nature, she was in a loving relationship, and her nature was stable.

When they reached the town of Westgate, his satnav was telling him to drive to the seafront. He had not visited this place before, and he was very impressed with it. He could see at a glance that the shopping centre was grander than that of Margate. There was an old fashioned cinema, which fascinated him, and when they reached the seafront he was impressed with the neatness of the area, no litter around, and as West Bay curved round it had a sandy beach, where locals could be seen exercising their dogs before it got dark. But he reminded himself impatiently, he was not here on a sightseeing tour, he was here to check out a death in mysterious circumstances.

He stopped outside the house, which looked very imposing, and then he noticed the drive which curved upwards. He drove slowly up; there were police cars and an ambulance outside the front door on the gravelled area.

"Wow, the troops are here already, sir," remarked Martha.

"Yes, we were not called first. Apparently it happened last night. Cause of death is not known yet, but we just need to visit the scene. It might not even be a crime," said Alan.

"It's certainly a nice house," said Martha admiringly, thinking of the modest flat she shared with Clive.

They noted the big oak front door. It had a notice on it requesting anyone who came to walk past the kitchen garden, then ring the bell on the back door. They went round, but when they arrived at the back door it was open, so they walked through the kitchen into the lounge after donning the shoes and equipment which were by the back door, making sure they didn't touch anything with any part of their bodies.

"Oh, there you are, Alan," said a man in full PPE. "We are just about to move the body, but you might as well take a look first."

"Thanks, Tom. This is my new partner, WPC Martha Fox, soon to be Brent."

Alan's eyes twinkled as he said that, and Martha smiled.

"You getting spliced?" asked Tom, genially.

"Yes," smiled Martha.

"Do you know Clive Brent?" asked Alan.

"Name sounds familiar," said Tom.

Their demeanour changed as soon as they took in the scene. This was Martha's first experience of viewing a dead body, and she felt sadness sweep over her when she saw the figure of a man sitting in an armchair with a telephone handset next to him. To all intents and purposes he looked peaceful, as if he was asleep. She had heard of Dr Ian Jones, and she knew he was only a young man. How on earth had he died?

"Was it a heart attack? He looks far too young," pointed out Alan. He felt great empathy for the man. You just never knew when your time was up, but this job did make him more aware.

"We'll let you know later, but no one else will be allowed in, just in case it does turn out to be a crime scene," said Tom.

Martha turned her attention to Tom. She knew she would have to get used to this, it was part of the job, but seeing a man who was obviously only in his forties, having passed away, was affecting her. Tom was tall and thin, with very penetrating eyes. She would imagine he didn't miss much.

"Right, who found him?" asked Alan.

"His brother David. He lives further down the road in a bungalow. He said Ian had invited him round for a drink. He is still in shock; said his brother had no health issues."

"OK. Well he will be the first person we interview, but I am going to wait until you let me know what the cause of death is."

"That will be tomorrow," said Tom.

"That's fine. Now we have homes to go to," said Alan briskly.

He guessed Martha was finding her first encounter with death quite an ordeal, as she had become very quiet. Alan still didn't find it easy, no matter how often he was faced with it, but his duty was to make sure that if there were any suspicious circumstances, they found the culprit, they owed that to the grieving families.

Once outside again with Martha, he spoke kindly to her. "I know that was unpleasant for you. I still don't find it easy. Best to go home to our families now, and leave it behind you until tomorrow."

Martha looked at him gratefully. Alan was such an understanding boss, and she knew she was lucky to be working with him. Everyone spoke highly of this man, who had real feelings, and a great dedication to his work. His reputation had preceded him before he even arrived at Canterbury Police Station, and she had been chosen to work with him, which made her feel proud. But right now she wanted to go home to Clive, and feel the warmth and comfort of his arms around her.

Alan was having similar thoughts. Seeing a man in the prime of his life, a well known and respected doctor, lying in that armchair dead, was distressing. He needed to be at home with Zoe and Adam. The security of his own family unit was so precious.

"Come on Martha, I'll run you home," he said firmly, touching her elbow and moving towards the door. Martha walked out to the car and got in next to him, and Alan drove back towards Canterbury dropping Martha off at her flat on the way, and then onto Birchington.

Chapter Three

"We found a small amount of a prescription drug inside him. Just enough to make him feel sleepy, enough to make him flop back in the chair."

"But not to kill him?" questioned Alan.

"No, whoever did this tried to cover up the fact that they had poisoned him."

Alan felt shock waves go right through him. The poor bastard must have been in agony! What sort of creature could do such a thing?

Tom explained. "They doped him, and when he was flopped in the chair, they may have forced him to drink poison. He was probably too sleepy to resist."

"What about the telephone which was next to him?"

"Looks like he picked it up. An unknown number rang about seven-thirty; we checked that. Whether he actually spoke, and who it was, we have no idea."

"I see." Alan was thoughtful. "If he was poisoned, then it was premeditated, not the spur of the moment, something like that needs planning."

"Yes, but they thought if they doped him up with Valium, we might think it was suicide, or an accidental overdose. Did they really think we wouldn't spot the poison?" said Tom darkly.

"What sort of poison?" asked Alan.

"Just ordinary household poison; weedkiller or even rat poison, can't be more specific than that."

"OK. Thanks Tom, we best get out there and interview anyone and everyone connected with him."

"Cheers, Alan," said Tom. "Must get on."

The next day Alan continued to think about what he had been told as he got dressed for work. Today they would interview all the family, and he had suggested to Martha that they do it in plain clothes. He was aware that when they turned up in uniform, some people became very nervous, so as they needed as much information as possible, they would dress casually. He opted for jeans today, with a check blue shirt, open at the neck, and Martha had also dressed in a denim skirt with a T-shirt, and on her feet she had brown sandals. Her dark hair was clipped back at the side with two slides, and she wore no make-up.

He had the address of the bungalow where Ian's brother David lived, so they decided to go there first. The door was opened by an ordinary looking man with brown hair. He bore a slight resemblance to photos Alan had seen of Ian.

"Good morning, sir. Are you David Jones?"

"Yes, please come in."

Alan and Martha entered the hall of the small bungalow. It had wooden floors throughout, and he led them into a lounge, which was modestly furnished with just a rug in the middle, a shabby sofa, and at the other end of the room was a table and four chairs. Following the opulence of Ian's home it was quite a shock. Alan guessed that David must be the poor relation.

After introducing himself and Martha, Alan offered his condolences. Whilst he was speaking, the door opened to admit a young man of about twenty, and David introduced him as Marty, Ian's son. Glancing closely at his pale face and red rimmed eyes, it was clear the death of his father had upset him greatly. He spoke falteringly.

"I can't believe he has gone, but how did he die?"

"We are investigating that right now. Did your father take prescription drugs?"

"Definitely not. Dad was as fit as a fiddle, he took pride in looking after himself. Why do you ask?"

"Traces of Valium were found inside him," said Alan, omitting to mention the poison.

"You are not suggesting he took his own life, surely?" said David.

"I am not suggesting anything, I am trying to get to the truth," said Alan, wondering why David had assumed that his brother would do that.

"My dad would never take his own life!" said Marty fiercely. His lip was trembling, and it was clear he was overcome with emotion.

"Of course not, please don't upset yourself," said Martha kindly. She guessed that Alan had not mentioned the poison for a reason, so she would not either. Her eyes took in Marty; he was a younger version of Ian, same dark hair, and obviously very close to his dad. She was noting down anything that might be useful, and she wondered if it would be right to mention the break-up of his parents marriage, or would it be like rubbing salt in the wound?

Alan was preparing to mention it. The subject could not be ignored, but David's next words meant he didn't have to.

"Don't forget your dad was upset after your mum left home. Maybe he was taking the medication to help him cope with it," he said, turning to Marty, who was having none of it.

"My dad would not have taken a drug like Valium. He always said he needed all his wits about him to do his job properly. He preferred natural methods of coping, like walking, swimming and playing golf when he had the time."

Alan could see the loyalty of Marty towards his father. The poor young man was hurting badly. He wondered how close Marty's relationship was with his uncle.

"I understand you found your brother, can you give us some more details about it?"

David had been expecting this. "Yes, let's all sit down. Marty, you too." The pacing up and down of his distressed nephew was making him feel decidedly nervous. Alan and Martha sat down on the sofa, and Martha set her phone to record the conversation. David pulled up two chairs from the table; one for Marty and one for himself.

"My brother invited me round for a drink. He just said after dinner, no specific time, so when I saw him come in. . ."

"What time was that?" interrupted Alan.

"Just after seven. I gave him about forty-five minutes to have a shower and eat. I came round the back, as I knew that on such a hot evening the kitchen door would be open. When I walked in the oven was still on, he hadn't eaten his dinner, and then I saw him laid out in the armchair. . ." his face creased with pain as he remembered. . . "I honestly thought he was so tired that he had fallen asleep, so I turned out the oven, and then went over to try and rouse him. But his eyes were not closed, he just stared at me, a glassy unnatural stare, and then I could see there was no sign of life."

There was a pregnant pause, and Alan gave him time to compose himself. Marty had tears in his eyes.

"Who did you ring first?"

"I rang Marty first, on his mobile, then I rang for an ambulance. When they arrived, they told me to ring the police. They said they couldn't move the body, and they would wait until the police arrived."

"How did you try to rouse your brother?"

"I tried to shake his shoulder, but his body was stiff, and then I saw his eyes, and I knew."

Alan addressed Marty, who was fidgeting in his chair, and twisting his fingers together.

"Did you try to go to the house first, Marty, before you came here?"

"Yes, but they said I could not come in as they had forensic people everywhere."

"He's going to stay with me for the time being," explained David, touching Marty's shoulder gently.

"It is normal procedure, but obviously you have both had a terrible shock. Martha is our family liaison officer, so if either of you need any support at this time, just tell us," said Alan gently.

"So, how could my father have been given Valium; was it in his food?" asked Marty, his face looked very puzzled.

"Well, all I can say at this stage is that traces of it were found in his whisky decanter, and also in the whisky glass we found right next to him."

Marty covered his face briefly, then he spoke angrily, "So somebody laced the whisky decanter. Somebody murdered my father! What kind of bastard could murder a man who spent his life trying to help others? If I ever find out who did it, they're a dead man!" and with that he strode from the room, into the kitchen, with tears streaming down his face.

"I am sorry about that. He always idolised his father. He doesn't mean that, it's his grief talking."

Alan nodded at Martha, and she went outside to the kitchen. It was her job to calm him, and she spoke in a low soothing voice to him whilst making everyone a cup of tea.

Alan waited to continue his questioning until Martha returned with a tray of tea, and an apologetic Marty, who tried to explain why he was so upset.

"It's OK, we understand how devastating all this is for you," said Alan. "Just a couple more questions. I understand Ian had a housekeeper, can you just tell me a bit about her?"

"Yes, Kate Bryant, she lives with her sister Lisa in the flats down the road. She's been the housekeeper for ten years or so. A very meek and mild person, who does her job and is always discreet."

"Yes, I know Kate. Even when my mother was at home, Kate used to do most of the cooking. She is a very quiet person, but also very dedicated to her job. She couldn't be more different to Lisa," added Marty.

"In what way?"

David broke in. "Lisa seems a bit unbalanced. She used to help Ian in his practice, but her behaviour was not right, and she clearly had an obsession for him which he found most embarrassing. He was able to remove her when he closed his own practice and joined the group practice."

Alan's ears pricked up at this, even more. Could this rejected woman have got her revenge by poisoning him?

"When did this happen?"

"Whilst I was still at home, about four years ago," interjected Marty.

"OK, well thank you both so much for helping us with our enquiries. We won't take up any more of your time."

28

When they got outside, Alan spoke his mind, "Well, they both seemed very upset. I am waiting on the final results before I tell them he was poisoned."

"Yes, I realised you didn't want to mention it."

"Good work, you are catching on fast," smiled Alan. "We best go and interview the sisters then. The flats are further down the road."

"Yes, sounds like they are completely contrasting characters."

"His wife and the boyfriend were told yesterday, but I want us to interview them ourselves so I can get an idea of what type of woman he was married to."

"Yes sir. It's interesting that Marty has gone to his uncle rather than his mother at this time."

"Well, it might not be significant. Don't forget his mother lives in a couple of rooms at Margate, and Marty might not feel comfortable around the boyfriend."

"Yes, you are right, sir. Since I joined the force, I get suspicious a lot more."

"That's all right, we are paid to be suspicious," said Alan, genially. "Before we do the next interview, we need a break. I spotted a nice little cafe called the Beano, just round Station road, and I could murder a bacon sandwich!"

Martha smiled, what was it with men and bacon sandwiches?

"OK boss. Let's go find it then."

Chapter Four

"Now promise me, Lisa, you won't get excited or give them any reason to be suspicious of you."

Kate looked anxiously over at Lisa, who was pacing up and down and clearly agitated.

"I know, I won't say much at all."

If it wasn't so serious, Kate could have almost found it funny to suggest that Lisa kept herself quiet. It had never been known before. Maybe this was why their relationship worked so well; they were complete opposites. Kate could keep anything to herself, but Lisa's character was such that she enjoyed revelling in making situations as dramatic as she could. Kate understood why that was; a mother who had been unable to show she cared, which had caused Lisa to grow up feeling unloved, apart from other issues.

"Let me do most of the talking. It is only an interview. I am still shocked at the news, and you must be!" she said, pointedly.

"That man turned my life inside out!" said Lisa with passion.

"No, you turned your life inside out because he didn't want you. It was you, Lisa, you were obsessed with him. You still are!"

Lisa's eyes flashed with anger, remembering she had been a woman scorned, and Kate moved to put her arms around her.

"You're OK with me, we have worked through it and you are much better now." Her voice sounded soothing, which was balm to Lisa's excitable nature.

"They haven't even said how he died," said Lisa.

"Not yet. I tried to go over there this morning, to clear up and wash the dishes, as I left him a meal in the oven, but they said I could not disturb anything. I wonder why that was?"

"They must think it's a crime scene!" pointed out Lisa.

Their conversation was interrupted by the entryphone. Kate picked it up, she was determined to stay calm and hoped that Lisa would too. When DCI Alan Clarke introduced himself, she clicked the button to allow them access, and then went to let them in the door of the apartment.

Alan had heard about these sisters, who were apparently very close and yet complete opposites by nature. The door was opened by a woman who was short, a little dumpy, and her mousy brown hair was drawn back quite severely from her face. There was something very insignificant about her. Except her eyes, they were big and they gleamed from behind her glasses. The frames were big, which enhanced them even more, and right now she looked just like a frightened rabbit.

"Good afternoon, I am Kate, and this is Lisa." She turned and pointed to another woman, who Alan guessed to be in her late thirties, and stood behind her. Alan's eyes took in the slim figure and long legs, as well as her long curly chestnut coloured hair which seemed to flow around her shoulders like a warm flame. Her eyes were like black coals, almost a little sinister, but he had to admit she was a very striking looking woman, in contrast to her mousy sister.

"Good afternoon, ladies, I am DCI Clarke, and this is my partner Martha Fox."

Lisa inclined her head towards them, she knew she must not put her foot in it, as there were too many secrets that must be kept, and saying nothing was safer. Kate ushered them both into the small lounge, and offered to make some tea. Martha was not bothered, as they had just had lunch, but she guessed Alan would not refuse.

"Thank you very much, one sugar and milk," he said, smiling.

Martha took out her notebook and got herself ready for the interview. It was amazing how Alan used his charm on anyone to get a cup of tea. Kate scurried off, she reminded Martha of a timid little mouse, ready to do anyone's bidding at any time. She obviously must have been the perfect housekeeper.

31

But Lisa couldn't be more different. Very striking looking, but her body language seemed to indicate anger inside herself that she was hoping to keep in check. Martha found analysing people fascinating, and in a case like this it was essential. It would be interesting, once the tea arrived, to see how both the sisters had taken the news of Ian Jones's death.

It wasn't long before Kate arrived back with a mug of tea for Alan, and she also held a small plate in her hand with a couple of chocolate biscuits on it. Martha declined one, as she wanted her wedding dress to fit her, so, to her amusement, Alan had them both.

"No point in wasting them," he said genially to Kate, whilst Lisa remained silent, her dark eyes fixed intently on them, which Martha found a little bit intimidating. This woman had hidden depths.

Alan took a sip of his tea, and then demolished the biscuits. He wanted to get on with this interview, as they also had Ian's estranged wife to see.

"First of all, thank you to you both for making time for us today. Especially you Lisa, I know you work as a nanny."

"I took the afternoon off, Abby has a doctor's appointment, and her mother came home to take her."

Privately Alan was thinking she didn't look much like a nanny. Her nature didn't seem particularly placid, or calm, there was a force inside her, he felt, waiting to be unleashed. But who was he to know? Maybe she was quite different when she was around young children. Her anger might be directed at them for probing into her private life, and they would certainly be doing that.

He turned towards Kate first. Just as yesterday, they were not going to mention the poison just yet; he wanted to see how they reacted to knowing Ian had Valium inside him. He spoke kindly to her, as she looked like she couldn't even say boo to a goose.

"Kate, I hope it's OK to use your Christian name?"

She nodded her affirmation.

"I understand you went to Dr Jones's house early yesterday morning, why?"

Kate looked uncomfortable. "I saw the police car and the ambulance the night before, so I knew something was wrong. But my job is to go to the house every day and do my work, so I went

32

as usual. They wouldn't let me go in, they said nothing could be touched. The first thing I do every day is load the dishwasher. I left the doctor a casserole that night, but evidently he never ate it."

"How do you know this?"

"His brother David rang me, and he explained his brother had been found dead."

"Was that after you had been to the house?"

"No, David rang me that night. The forensic scientists didn't tell me anything yesterday."

Alan walked over to the window. The doctor's house could be seen from the window. A car driving up the winding drive could easily be spotted from here.

"Did you see anyone go to the house after you came home that evening?"

"Yes, Dr Jones came home about seven. I did check because he was later than usual. Then David arrived about forty-five minutes later, and then, of course, the police and ambulance soon after."

At this moment Lisa interrupted her, unable to contain herself, or stay out of the limelight any longer.

"You haven't told the inspector about Pamela. She came sniffing around just after you came home."

"Oh, yes, before the doctor came home, about five o'clock."

"We know what she wanted!" snorted Lisa.

Alan turned his attention to her, clearly she wanted to be involved, and certainly she disliked Pamela Jones.

"What did she want, then?" he asked, pointedly.

"I reckon she was tired of living in Margate with her toy boy, and she wanted the good life back again!"

"Lisa, you don't know that!" said Kate, looking very worried. "It's more like she came back for some of her belongings."

She turned to Alan to explain. "The doctor hadn't got new locks fitted yet, and she still had her key. He was a very easy-going man."

Alan guessed he must have been, to allow his wife access to the house she had left to live with someone else. He decided to see what their reaction was to him suggesting the doctor might be taking Valium.

"Kate, you had access to many of the doctor's private things. Were you aware he was on Valium; if, indeed, he was?" he added.

Kate did not get a chance to reply, as Lisa interjected fiercely. "The doctor wasn't taking any medication, but Pamela was on Valium."

"She might not be now!" protested Kate, looking decidedly uncomfortable.

"And how do you know that?"

"I used to be his practice nurse, before he joined the group practice, and although she wasn't his patient, I used to handle her prescriptions, and get them for her."

Alan was finding all this very interesting, so he continued: "So Ian Jones didn't take Valium, but it was found in his system. I wonder how it got there."

Kate twisted her fingers awkwardly, looking very wretched. Alan guessed this interview was testing her loyalty to her boss. "Well, his marriage failed, as you know, so maybe he took some of his wife's left over medication. . ."

". . .He didn't commit suicide. More likely Pamela put the pills in something so she and her toy boy could take over the house."

Kate winced at her sister's angry voice.

Lisa was certainly hard work to interview; all that anger, it was probably left over from being a woman spurned by the doctor, decided Alan. He nodded at Martha. "Well, thank you so much, we won't take up any more of your time."

Martha stopped writing and put her notes away, and they both took their leave after thanking the sisters for their help. Alan was musing whilst he drove the car towards Margate.

"Well that Lisa is certainly a woman with a grievance. I wouldn't like to cross her!" he said, with feeling.

"It's her poor sister I feel sorry for. Kate was very embarrassed by her behaviour. She is such a meek and mild little soul; I think it's anything for a quiet life."

"Yes, but what Lisa says makes no sense. One minute she thinks Pamela came back to try and reconcile with Ian, the next she is accusing her of murdering him so she can bring her toy boy to the house and move in. I actually think she seems a bit unbalanced."

"Luckily we can now interview Pamela, and get her side of things."

34

By now they had reached Margate. They drove past the clock tower, and the satnav was telling them to turn right at the little roundabout.

"If you look to the right, you can see the inside of dreamland," explained Martha. "When Adam's a bit older he will love it!"

Alan stole a quick glance whilst he was navigating the car round the back streets, and he could see the rails of the big dipper rising and falling, with the big wheel standing proudly against the sky. Only a few people could be spotted in the grounds, as this was too early in the year for schools to be on holiday.

"It's really busy at the weekend," said Martha.

"Yes, did you live round here for long?" asked Alan, as they passed a row of shabby terraced Victorian houses.

"I didn't live here!" exclaimed Martha indignantly. "Margate isn't what it used to be, even with Dreamland, the Turner Gallery, and the beautiful sandy beach. Shops are empty, and the high street is so run-down."

"Well, it's a sign of the times. Covid has ruined many small businesses," said Alan, thinking he would still rather have the clean sea air in Margate, and a sandy beach where Adam could play, rather than the noise and pollution of London.

"I lived in Birchington, near Epple Bay, my parents moved here from the Bexley Heath area when I was a baby. I loved walking down to the clifftop and strolling on the beach; it's a sandy little bay. Obviously, with our flat being in Canterbury, it's much easier for us both to get to work, and we can manage with one car between us, but hopefully, later on, we can move back to Birchington."

Alan remembered driving along a seaside route, with the road curving round a couple of bays, and it had looked nice. He was still getting to know the area and he knew what Martha meant.

They had arrived at the address where Pamela now lived. It was a flat inside a Victorian terraced house, but the houses were shabby, and they looked grey and forbidding.

When they knocked on the door, it was soon opened by a woman Alan guessed must be the doctor's wife. She was tall and slim with dark hair, and she carried herself well. She only looked in her mid-thirties, but he had been told she was in her forties. The inside of the flat looked shabby; some old lino in the hall, peeling wallpaper, and a smell of mustiness. But, in contrast, Pamela was wearing white tailored slacks and a silk blue blouse. She looked very out of place in these surroundings.

Alan had already phoned to say they would be coming, so she let them in. Her face looked pale, and he guessed she was still in shock, so he briefly introduced themselves to her, before he saw the figure lurking by a door which led into a small room, which in turn led off from the kitchen. This also had the shabby lino, with a threadbare rug in the middle. He guessed the man to be about thirty, he had long hair in a pony tail, was unshaven, and his arms were covered in tattoos. He couldn't help wondering why Pamela had left her husband to come and live here.

"This is my partner, Stewart," said Pamela, inclining her head towards him. He simply grunted at them. So they sat on the shabby sofa, both declining a cup of tea, and Martha turned to making notes of the conversation.

Alan studied Pamela's face, he thought she looked nervous, and the expression on Stewart's face was guarded. He wondered what they were hiding. He addressed them, whilst watching their reactions.

"You were informed about the death of your estranged husband by our officers, I believe."

Pamela nodded. "It's still hard to take in, he was only forty-five." Alan thought he saw a flash of sympathy pass over her face, but Stewart appeared unmoved by this.

"Yes, and we have reason to believe there were suspicious circumstances," he said, noting that her face seemed to register surprise, although, of course, this could be an act.

"What sort of suspicious circumstances?"

The guarded suspicion on Stewart's face remained. He was definitely not going to show any sort of emotion. As with the other people he had questioned, Alan was not ready to mention the poison found in Ian's body.

"Ian had traces of Valium inside him."

Pamela paled visibly. "I didn't know he was taking Valium. When I was with him he never took any medication, and he took his health very seriously."

Alan knew he had to be tactful now. He glanced towards Martha, who looked up from her notes. She caught his eye, guessing that he now wanted her to take over.

"Pamela, are you on any medication?"

Stewart reacted to that; his expression now looked annoyed, and his eyes flashed. "What has that got to do with you lot?"

Alan cut in quickly: "Quite a lot, actually. If Pamela was on Valium, and she left any of her medication behind when she left the house, then it would have been around for Ian to take."

"Yes, I do take Valium, but I certainly did not leave any behind. Surely you are not suggesting that Ian took an overdose?"

Alan gave her a very steely look. It was funny how all the witnesses had jumped to the same conclusion.

"I am not suggesting anything. I am here to find out the truth."

Pamela did not meet his gaze head on, but she glanced towards Stewart who spoke for both of them.

"She said she didn't leave any tablets behind, so it's not to do with her!"

Alan ignored the hostility in his tone. This bloke was dog rough, and he clearly hadn't been to charm school. What was Pamela even doing with such a type?

"What were you both doing yesterday at seven o'clock?"

"We was 'ere, eatin' our supper; fish and chips," retorted Stewart, and Alan disliked him even more.

"Yes, I brought them in with me about six, from the fish and chip shop up the road," added Pamela.

At that moment a mobile rang, and Stewart took it out of his pocket and moved away from them to answer it. He joined them a couple of minutes later. Ignoring Alan and Martha, he told Pamela, "Gotta go out for a bit." She nodded at him, but after he had gone out it seemed like she was visibly relieved.

"Does Stewart know you went round to Ian's house early that evening?" asked Alan.

Pamela paled. "I suppose Lisa told you. She was in there, she has such an obsession about him."

"Why did you go round there?" persisted Alan, ignoring her words.

Neither Alan nor Martha were prepared for what happened next. Pamela crumpled into a chair, covering her face she started to sob. Martha sprang into action. Producing a clean tissue, she went over and handed it to her. She then put her hands on Pamela's shoulders gently whilst she cried herself out.

Alan always felt awkward when women cried, and he was glad Martha was there to support her. The suspicious part of his nature wondered if this was an act to draw attention away from Ian's death, but when Pamela spoke he could see in her eyes she was a desperate woman.

"Please help me, I made a huge mistake leaving Ian to live with Stewart. He has such a temper, he really scares me. I went back to wait for Ian to come in. I knew he probably wouldn't want me back, but I also knew he would help me."

She then proceeded to pull up the sleeves of her blouse, showing them both some very ugly bruises on her arms. Martha winced, the brute had certainly been vicious towards her.

"What makes him do this?" she asked gently.

"Oh, he's insanely jealous of Ian, always accusing me of wanting to go back. And now I can't."

"No, but you can leave him! No one needs to put up with that sort of violence!" said Alan firmly.

"Why didn't you wait for Ian, then?" asked Martha.

"When Lisa turned up, she also had a go at me, accusing me of using Ian for my own convenience. Ian was a kind man, who always made me feel safe. It's just that his job was his life. I didn't want to stay around with Lisa ranting at me, so I went and got some fish and chips because Stewart always expects his dinner the moment he comes in the door, and I am not a great cook."

Martha thought she sounded like a proper little 1950s housewife, and it was quite clear that Stewart was a bully. She couldn't help feeling sorry for Pamela, who had clearly bitten off more than she could chew.

"We can help you and offer you protection if you want to leave Stewart. In the meantime, just give me a picture of your life. Is Stewart at work during the day, and what about you?" asked Alan.

"Stewart is a gardener. After I met him, I got him the job of being our gardener. Ian never had the time. Yes, I have been working since I left Ian, I have a part time job in the newsagents, but Stewart kept telling me I needed to get a proper full time job."

"I see. Well I suggest you pack your belongings whilst he is not here, and we will find you a safe house for now. Martha will arrange it for you," said Alan.

Pamela wasted no time in going into another room to pack her belongings. Although they had not expected to walk into this, Martha proved to be very competent. Arrangements were made via her mobile phone, and an overnight room was booked for Pamela at a hotel in Westgate. Alan promised her that the next day a safe house would be found for her.

After they had taken her to the hotel and made sure she was safe, Alan drove towards the flat where Martha lived.

"That was a bit of a shock, wasn't it?" said Martha.

"It certainly was, but you coped very well."

Martha glowed with pride. So he thought she was doing OK, that was good.

"Stewart has to be a prime suspect," mused Alan. "Not only is he violent and dangerous, but he is also the gardener, and would have access to the shed. What's the betting we find weedkiller in there tomorrow."

"Wow, this makes Lady Chatterley's lover seem tame," added Martha, wondering if Stewart could be the culprit. Alan couldn't help smiling at the idea of the doctor's wife having an affair with the gardener, but it looked like Pamela had got herself in too deep with a violent man. He could now pass her over to the team who dealt with domestic violence, and concentrate on solving this murder. He didn't like to think of any man treating a woman like that, and he was glad that with Martha's help, they had got her out of that volatile situation. He knew that Pamela had obviously led a charmed life whilst she was with Ian. She had been spoiled, and had everything she could possibly want, but that didn't give Stewart the right to bully her.

"Are you planning on arresting him, guv?"

"Not yet, we need a team briefing, and then we will interview them all again, and this time we will say he was poisoned, and let's see what their reaction is to that."

"He may disappear when he knows that Pamela has gone. He won't want to be prosecuted for attacking her."

Alan was pleased to see she was working things out, and offering an opinion. Martha was a natural at the job. "We will go back to him soon, but first we will get him checked out and see if he has a record. If he does disappear, we can make an appeal for him to help us with our enquiries."

Martha had convinced herself, because he was rough and ready, and violent towards Pamela, that Stewart must be the murderer. Jealousy could have been his motive. But she knew Alan would want to check everyone in the family.

Alan guessed what she was thinking, so tried to explain to her.

"You see, Martha, in a murder case, when you interview the family, you find out things that were not obvious before. I agree he does seem a very likely suspect, but that doesn't mean we have to focus on him entirely. We must make sure that justice is done."

"Yes sir," agreed Martha. She knew that Alan had enjoyed success in past cases with his meticulous attitude, and she had a lot to learn, but he wasn't arrogant, and he respected her opinion. She felt pride inside that she was working alongside him, because she truly did admire him.

Chapter Five

By the time the team briefing took place, Alan had more information at his fingertips. Firstly, someone called Holly had texted Ian to say she was coming to visit him about eight that evening. He wondered if she was a girlfriend. And how could he find out more about her? Had she come? He still didn't know who had phoned the landline, which had been laying next to the body. The murderer had been cold and callous. To pour poison down someone's throat, and then watch them die in agony, wasn't done in the heat of the moment; it had been premeditated.

In Victorian times, it had been done by women who were anxious to rid themselves of an abusive or bullying husband, as they didn't have the physical strength to take him on. But they had disguised it in food. Would a man be bothered to kill in this way? Most men would use their physical strength, surely?

Ian's bank account had been checked. Apart from the usual household bills, he had made quite a few large payments to his brother David, who seemed to be in financial difficulties, a couple of payments to Holly Wheeler, which was helpful, as that would help them to trace her. A copy of Ian's Will was in the bureau in his study, it had been made three years ago, and it left the house to Pamela and Marty, and his assets were also to be divided between them both. It was ironic that they were trying to find a safe house for Pamela, and yet, with the death of Ian, she would be free to come and live in the house again, as surely Marty would not mind that.

Alan realised, as far as the assets and house were concerned, this gave Pamela a motive, and also Marty, but he felt Marty was in the clear because he was at the university when David had rung him. His principal had confirmed that, and he had given Marty permission to travel to Westgate to be with his family. Pamela and Stewart's alibis might not be true.

As far as the Bryant sisters were concerned, Lisa certainly had a grievance against the doctor as a woman scorned, and she seemed definitely a bit unbalanced. She had a habit of going to the house when she felt like it, and seeing Pamela had roused her jealousy. As for Kate, being a housekeeper gave her the best advantage, not only for putting Valium in his whisky decanter, but also for lacing his food with poison, although no traces of it had been found in the food. Could this mousy little woman, who seemed scared of her own shadow, be capable of pouring poison down his throat? Alan very much doubted that; what on earth would her motive be?

Having pointed out all the suspects and their possible motive, Alan's attention shifted to Constable James Martin, who had just entered the room waving some papers in his hand.

"Yes, Constable?" he said.

"Guv, it's Stewart Russell, he's got a criminal record," and he thrust the papers triumphantly in front of Alan.

Alan scanned them quickly. Stewart Russell had been convicted of petty theft back in 2008, which must have been his teenage years, but much more important than that, in 2015 he had been convicted of a serious assault in a night club. The man that he had attacked had been badly hurt and hospitalised. Russell had served two years, and been told by the judge at the time he needed to curb his temper.

"Thanks, James, you have done well," said Alan. He was not a bit surprised to read this. Pamela had shown them the evidence of his violent nature, and he was so glad they had acted quickly, and got her away from him. He was beginning to think that maybe Martha was right, and they should bring him in for questioning.

James was visibly pleased by the praise from his boss. He was a short man with a chubby face and brown hair. He had an earnest manner about him, and had, in fact, also checked out David Jones, but had found no record about him.

42

After the meeting had finished, Alan enquired if Pamela had been found a safe house.

"She is still at the hotel, sir, but I think she wants to move back to her former home when all the legalities have been worked out, and she doesn't want Stewart to be with her!" said Martha, darkly.

"So she knew Ian had left the house to her and Marty, then?"

"Oh yes, and she is hoping Marty will live with her again. Apparently Marty did not like Stewart one bit, and it caused a rift between them, but now she has broken away from Stewart, she thinks Marty will reconcile with her."

"I see, well you and I are going to interview Stewart again, here at the station. Can you arrange to have him brought in? We can return to the other possible suspects later."

Martha hid a smile. So the boss had conceded that Stewart needed to be brought in. He had been violent towards Pamela, and he also had a police record for violence. His motive might have been jealousy if he thought she might be leaving him and returning to Ian, but it could also be the fact that Pamela would inherit money and a share of the house.

"Yes, boss. I am on it."

Pamela had already texted Marty to tell him she had split up with Stewart. She realised just how much she had lost during the last year since she had been with Stewart. Losing the respect of her son had hurt, and she realised now that Stewart had been jealous of him. Stewart's possessiveness had stifled her.

When he had worked as a gardener at their home, flirting with him had been fun. She was a bored housewife. Seeing him working outside stripped off to the waist was exciting, and she had absolutely set her cap at him. She had only wanted an affair, but he had clearly become besotted about her, and when he spoke about them running away and starting a new life together, it had seemed so romantic. It was like an exciting roller coaster; once she got on, she couldn't get off, and she got caught up in something that she had believed would be a new life with a young virile lover, but, in fact, turned out to be just a fantasy.

Stewart had promised her the moon, but in reality, it was just a damp gloomy flat in Margate. She had even had to get herself a job, just so they had enough money to eat; and as time went on, all hope of having a better life died inside her. She was so frustrated that she had taken to self-harming. She had banged her arms repeatedly against the damp stone walls in the basement of the flat. She felt trapped, and she knew that Stewart would not let her go easily. He was obsessed with her. Her visit to Ian had been to try and go back home. She had realised she could not live without the good life she had enjoyed, but loopy Lisa, as she called her, had ruined that. It was too late to reconcile with Ian now, but at least she could go back to her home. She had no conscience about pretending to the police that Stewart had hurt her. Her lie had served a purpose because the police would make sure he didn't bother her again.

Stewart sat in the interview room with Alan and Martha. He had seen them earlier, and thought that was it, but then a police car had been sent round to bring him to the station. He was very unsure of himself, especially as he had realised, as soon as he got home yesterday and went into the bedroom, that Pamela had packed her clothes and left him. His first thought had been panic. He couldn't lose her. And last night he had been out and about to try and find her, without any luck, and then spent a sleepless night. Now, today, the police car had turned up.

He watched silently as Martha set the tape, and then DCI Clarke announced that, "For the benefit of the tape, this is an interview with Stewart Russell." He wondered how long this would take, as he wanted to try and find Pamela. He just couldn't imagine his life without her.

Alan's eyes met his. There was a steely determination in Alan's manner, as he wanted to take Russell by surprise; if only to question his alibi.

"Thank you for coming in, Mr Russell. Can you tell us again what you were doing between seven and eight o'clock on the 16th May?"

"Again? I got home at six, and Pamela came in soon after with fish and chips. We ate, and then I stayed in all evening. I was tired after gardening all day," he said defensively.

"Did you watch TV on the night that Ian Jones died?

"Yes, I had a beer. I was knackered."

"So what programme did you watch?"

"Oh, I don't know, I fell asleep."

"So, what about Pamela, was she watching with you?"

"She went to take a shower. When I woke up she came into the room and asked if I wanted a drink."

"So, in fact, although both you and Pamela said you were in all night together, you went to sleep, and you have no idea if Pamela stayed in or not."

Stewart became exasperated. Why were they asking him all these pointless questions? He wanted them out there looking for Pamela. His tone was impatient.

"She doesn't go out in the evening, and she certainly wouldn't have murdered Ian, so this line of questioning is a waste of time. She has left me, and I blame you lot, coming round and making us all feel as though we have done something wrong."

"Let me be the judge of that!" fired back Alan. He had only just got started; this bully didn't know what was coming to him! "You can blame who you like for Pamela leaving you, but if you are violent towards someone, it's not surprising if they leave you, is it?"

By now Stewart's impatience had changed to bewilderment.

"I have never been violent towards Pamela. She is everything to me."

Alan searched Stewart's face, but it showed no guilt. Was he a good actor? Alan had watched this uncouth man's eyes soften at the mention of her name; he was clearly besotted.

"Pamela asked us to find her a safe place away from you. She even showed us some very nasty bruising on her arms."

Suddenly the tough guy image was gone. Stewart looked vulnerable as he burst out.

"Surely she didn't say I did it. Pamela has mental health problems, she is on medication, and sometimes she self-harms."

Martha found herself feeling sorry for this man. Maybe he was telling the truth, and Pamela had manipulated them to help her get back into the house. They had wasted no time in whisking her away.

But whether Pamela was lying or not, she had clearly had enough of her time with Stewart.

Alan was feeling uncomfortable, wondering if they had acted too hastily. Which one of them was telling the truth? It was hard to know. He decided to change his line of questioning.

"I hear you are Ian Jones's gardener."

"Yes, that is my occupation. I am a gardener to several people."

It was amazing that even after Stewart had stolen his wife, Ian still employed him as a gardener, Alan could not understand that.

"So you stole his wife, and yet he was still happy for you to look after his garden," said Alan, sarcastically.

"I was in the middle of landscaping it. He wanted it finished," said Stewart, clearly feeling awkward.

Alan wasn't mincing his words. It seemed like Ian Jones, because of his busy working life, had been a pushover. And now the poor bugger was dead, and either of these two might have done it. After all, if Pamela was lying about Stewart harming her, then she could even be capable of murder, especially as her alibi was now unsafe. He looked Stewart straight in the face.

"My officers have found some weedkiller in the shed. Did you use it?"

Stewart did not look perturbed. "Yes, it's a big garden and I have been trying to keep the brambles and stinging nettles under control."

Alan spoke slowly and deliberately; he had to carefully watch Stewart's reaction.

"Ian's killer gave him some Valium to relax him and then, guess what, they poured weedkiller neat down his throat, and the poor bastard would have died in agony!"

Stewart went visibly pale, but he held Alan's intent gaze. "My God, how vile. But just because I used the weedkiller, you can't blame me. I might be a wife stealer, I ain't perfect, of course, but I ain't no murderer either!"

"You also have a police record for a violent attack," Alan reminded him.

Stewart could see this was looking bad for him, and he felt scared, he didn't want to go back inside. He had learned his lesson years ago, and he didn't want to repeat it.

"Yes, I was young, with an attitude and a temper, but I am not like that now. I can't believe that Pamela said I harmed her. Honest gov, I never would!"

Alan was silent for a moment. Years of practice had taught him not to make hasty judgements about anyone, especially the ones who seem to be most likely to have committed the crime. He had half believed it could be Stewart, after Pamela had said he was violent towards her, but now he wasn't sure. As much as he felt dislike towards the man, he had no right to judge him, because it looked like innocent looking Pamela may have fooled them. Of course, Stewart's fingerprints would be on the can of weedkiller, because he admitted to using it, but someone had used a cup or something to get enough of the toxin to pour down Ian's throat. He shuddered inside every time he thought about it. They would have to interview Pamela again, but surely she couldn't hate her husband that much to inflict such a death on him?

He glanced over at Martha, and repeated, "For the benefit of the tape, interview now terminated at 5pm." He paused while Martha switched it off.

"You may go now, Mr Russell, but we may want to question you again."

Martha escorted him out to the reception desk, where she explained to the duty constable that he was free to go. Stewart had been about to ask them to help him to try and find Pamela, but having realised that they had helped her get away from him, it was quite obvious that she didn't want to be found. He didn't need to feel jealous and inadequate in comparison to her rich, talented and handsome husband any more, but it was obvious she had found a way to go back to her rich lifestyle and former home, and she did not want him any more. Finally realising that he had now lost her forever made Ian's death pale into insignificance; it was like a dagger in his heart.

Chapter Six

When Alan reached home, Zoe was bathing Adam, and he went straight into the bathroom to see them both. Zoe was squatting down beside the bath, gently swishing water towards Adam, and Adam was chuckling, his chubby little face alight with happiness.

Alan bent and kissed her brow briefly, and Adam gurgled when he saw his father. This pleased Alan, and seeing his family after a gruelling day of questioning murder suspects was a welcome relief.

"Honey, you look all in. I can sort him out, you take a break."

Zoe smiled. She was tired. Today she had not been at work, but being at home with Adam had been very tiring. She spent a lot of the time running round after him. Now he was walking, he wanted to explore everything. He loved the garden, but this morning she had found him eating soil in the garden, so she couldn't really turn her back on him for a moment.

Adam had gone down for a nap after lunch, so she had heaved a sigh of relief, then prepared the vegetables for dinner this evening. Having done that, she decided to take a short nap on the sofa herself, but just as she had got comfortable he had woken, and when she looked at the clock, he had only slept for about thirty minutes. He just seemed to be able to keep going all day without much sleep.

"Yes, I am a bit knackered, but if you finish bathing and dressing him, I can put dinner on. We have shepherd's pie tonight."

"That sounds great!"

Zoe gave him a fluffy white towel for Adam, and went to cook the dinner. Alan was very good with his son. He had always been hands on ever since Adam was born, and no matter what sort of day it had been for him, he seemed pleased to put it behind him when he came home, and do normal everyday family things. He was incredibly proud of Adam, and most nights found him putting his son to bed, and reading baby books with big pictures in, which Adam loved. Zoe had always felt well supported, even though Alan's job was very demanding. She had always known that in emergency situations his work had to come first, but she had never resented that. Being a nurse, she had found the same, sometimes going into work when she had not planned to because a patient needed her support, or because they were short staffed or overrun with patients. She felt it was the right thing to do.

When they sat down to eat later, after Adam had gone to bed, Zoe asked Alan what his day had been like. She was not delving into private information, she knew that Alan was always limited in what he could say.

"It was OK, honey. Interviewing, you know, but we have only just started, a few more people to interview."

"How is Martha settling in? She must have her wedding on her mind as it's less than a month."

"She's doing good, and she has a calm manner about her, which is great." Alan's eyes twinkled as he replied to Zoe. "She doesn't mention the wedding. Which is just as well; you know us guys, we turn up, but we leave everything else to you ladies, who do a great job."

Zoe did remember. Her mother had been a great help to her, and even found a wedding planner. There had been some minor disagreements about who should be invited, and Alan had kept right out of it all. It had been a wonderful day, and had gone off very well. And now, after two years, she felt they had settled into a happy family life, and having Adam made it all complete. She counted herself a very lucky woman.

"I took Adam to the shops. And, guess what, we saw Helen in the Co-op with her friend Lisa, who apparently lives close to the house where the doctor was found dead."

Alan's ears pricked up immediately. He hadn't realised that those

49

two knew each other. Lisa seemed to be a bit volatile, and he was surprised that anyone would employ her as a nanny. But he knew from past experience that it was wrong to judge anyone, and it would be even more wrong to voice his opinion to Zoe, especially as she was a friend of their nanny.

"I didn't realise they were friends," he said, casually.

"Well, they met at a baby group. Abby and Adam are a similar age, so that is how they know each other. Helen says that people often don't understand Lisa, and that although she is quite a dramatic person when she speaks, there is another very caring side to her, and she really dotes on Abby. She is so patient and caring, and today she told me she would love to have her own child to bring up with her sister Kate. She said they could do a great job together."

Alan couldn't help wondering why there was no mention of a man in her life. Lisa was a striking looking woman, and she had certainly carried a torch for the doctor. Maybe she had felt he was the one, even though her feelings had not been reciprocated, so if she couldn't have Ian, then she didn't want anyone. But single women did now have their own children, either by using a sperm donor or a surrogate mother.

"Did she say how she would do that?" asked Alan.

Zoe was surprised that she had captured Alan's attention. He always had police work on his mind, and often replied yes and no when she was telling him things, and then later, when it was mentioned again, he claimed not to have heard what she said. But right now she had his undivided attention.

"Yes, she said she would like to adopt, because there are so many children needing a proper home."

This really did surprise Alan, as his impression of Lisa had been an angry and slightly unbalanced woman; but maybe adopting a child would be the making of her. It was a very unselfish act. When he returned to call on the sisters again, which he would do tomorrow, he would assess her again.

Lisa came home from work to find the police interviewing Kate again. She always felt nervous when the law was around. So many secrets that they might find out about her, and then, as far as they were concerned, it would be assumed that she had done the deed. She had already realised it would be a murder case. Ian would not have taken his own life, so someone had drugged him. As she put her key in the lock and opened the door, she heard the tail end of the conversation.

"I never took charge of Dr Jones's decanter. It was always full of whisky. When it got empty he washed it out himself and then added a new bottle to it. He always did like a whisky."

She saw Kate's eyes blinking rapidly from behind her glasses, and felt sorry for her. Obviously this police visit was upsetting her.

"Yes, I can vouch for that. It was a very expensive Waterford decanter. The doctor had inherited it from his mother, and he told both of us (because I used to help clear up sometimes after a dinner party) not to handle it; he said he would take care of it when it was empty."

Kate threw her a grateful smile, and Alan continued to explain whilst Martha was busy writing:

"Somebody put Valium into the decanter to make Ian Jones sleepy when he took a drink of whisky. But that was not the cause of death."

"What was it, then?" enquired Lisa, and both women gazed intently at him.

"Somebody poured neat weedkiller down his throat, causing him to die in agony!" said Alan dramatically, watching their reaction. Kate went very pale and put her hands over her face, and Lisa had a look of total shock, as though she found it hard to believe.

"Can you think of anyone who would be twisted enough to do that? They must have been angry, or had a lot of hate in their heart towards him."

"The doctor was a good man. He did not deserve that," said Kate. She uncovered her face, and Alan noted how pale she had gone.

"I loved that man, you know. He was kind to everyone. I hope you find them and lock them up for life!" said Lisa, and this time emotion took over, as tears rolled down her face. She was clearly still besotted with him, and had been moved to tears with the news of his violent death. As far as Alan could see, neither of these

51

women appeared guilty, only genuinely surprised by this revelation. Even Lisa was not displaying the wildness he had seen when he had interviewed them before.

"Oh, we will find them, make no mistake about that," he said grimly. "Thank you for your time, ladies, we will be off now."

Lisa showed them to the door, and her mind was working overtime. The DCI had said Ian was poisoned with weedkiller; it was unbelievable! "Ian had plenty of weedkiller in the shed, and his wife's boyfriend was the gardener," she said to Alan.

Alan ignored her insinuation. He had already been down that road himself.

"How do you know about the weedkiller?" he barked, staring intently at her.

"We both know about it. Stewart was trying to get rid of all the brambles and stinging nettles in the garden. And weeds were springing up everywhere. It was a great big can, and it stood on the bench on full display whenever anyone went into the shed," said Kate, blinking from behind her glasses with her owl-like eyes. "It was too heavy to lift."

"Yes, but it has a pouring lip. The culprit poured it into something they could hold up and tip down his throat," said Alan grimly. "I understand the shed was kept locked."

"The key hung on a hook in the kitchen," explained Kate.

"Ok, thanks," said Alan, and with Martha following him, he abruptly left the apartment.

Whilst he was driving, he spoke his thoughts aloud; "Well, they both seemed pretty shocked and upset. So did Stewart Russell. Did they all seem genuine to you?"

"Yes, sir. It's a horrific and brutal crime, it would shock anyone. I guess we must be looking for a psychopath who would do that."

"Yes, and tomorrow I have called a team briefing, as James Martin was also going to break it to Pamela, David and Marty to see their reactions. Let's face it, with the key on a hook in the kitchen, anyone could have got into the shed. Do we know who else, other than the Bryant sisters, Pamela and Marty had a key to the house?"

"David said there was a key left under the big brick outside the back door if anyone needed to get in."

"So pretty much anyone could get in when the house was empty, and use the shed key."

"Well, yes, if they knew it was the shed key," pointed out Martha. "It could be a key to anywhere, just hanging on a hook."

"You have a point there," mused Alan. "That narrows it down to family, or Stewart, or the Bryant sisters."

Alan was about to go into the room for the team briefing when the duty constable rang his mobile. "Good morning, sir, I have a young lady at the desk called Holly Wheeler, and she is asking to speak to someone. She seems very upset."

Alan stiffened. How great she had actually come to them before they had found her; this was good news. He guessed that now the press had got hold of the story, and with Westgate being full of people who would have been his patients, it would be generating a lot of interest.

"Show her in. Have we got some tissues, Martha?"

He always found sobbing women difficult to deal with. Sometimes it was genuine, but sometimes it was play-acting. Having a female assistant was useful. He was full of empathy for anyone in distress, but Martha's calming manner and natural warmth was comforting to anyone who was emotionally upset.

Martha put a box of tissues on the table, and the door opened to admit a young woman who looked to be in her early twenties. She had mid-brown hair and very dark eyes. Currently her eyes looked cloudy, as though she had been crying, and she already held a tissue in her hand suggesting she had just wiped them. He tried to make her feel at ease by smiling at her, but her lip trembled and her expression was very uncertain.

"Good morning, Miss Wheeler; may I call you Holly?"

"Yes," she gulped.

"What can we do for you?" he asked, pleasantly.

"It's my father, Dr Ian Jones. It's in all the newspapers he has been found dead in suspicious circumstances." Her voice broke, and she whispered, "He was only forty-five."

Alan and Martha exchanged incredulous looks. So this explained a lot.

"I was planning to visit him that evening, but then I got sent home from work because I felt sick and dizzy. I never got round to sending him another text, and then today I read all this about his death. If I had gone, he might be alive now!"

"You mustn't blame yourself, you could not help being ill. As painful as it is, we can't change fate," said Martha, sympathetically. She handed Holly another tissue, and Holly proceeded to wipe her eyes again.

"Are you Marty's sister, then?" asked Alan. This was intriguing.

"I am his half sister, I had only recently found my father, and I have not met Marty yet. My mother died last year, and before she passed away, she told me who my real father was. She never told Ian about me, and then married someone else."

Alan could imagine what a shock this would be to the family. It was funny how things came out after people died. Holly had not been named in the will, and if she had been at home ill then she was off the hook. But was there anyone to verify what she said?

"Can anyone confirm you stayed home that night?"

"Well, I live alone, but my company can confirm I was sent home, and my neighbour spoke to me when I arrived home. I told her I was going to bed, and my car stayed in the car park until the next day."

"OK, we obviously have to get that checked so we can eliminate you from our enquiries."

"I understand. Can I ask how my father died?"

Alan's tone was as gentle as he could make it. "I am afraid it was murder. Someone put Valium in your father's decanter. When he had a drink it made him very sleepy, so he flopped into the armchair. Then the killer took advantage of his inability to fight back, and they siphoned off some weedkiller and forced him to drink it neat."

"They did what!"

"Yes, I know it's a shock, and we have tried to keep as much from the press as we could until we were sure, but the post mortem has shown this to be the cause of your father's death; rather than a prescription medication overdose, which we believe was what the killer wanted us to think."

Martha managed to get someone to bring Holly a cup of tea, the girl seemed badly shocked. She then sent a message to say Alan would be a little bit delayed for the team briefing. They both realised that Holly coming to them like this was important, and it was another piece of the jigsaw fitting into place.

After she had taken a few sips of the tea, and seemed calmer, Alan continued questioning her.

"Was it just a social visit to see your father?"

Holly was feeling particularly vulnerable now that she had lost her father. Coming to Canterbury had been because it wasn't far from Westgate, and she wanted to have a place in his life. Ian had accepted her readily, and they had both felt a connection. And now he was gone. Last year her mother had also passed, and Holly was feeling really alone. The pregnancy was not going well; she had so much sickness and tiredness, she didn't feel she could cope. As a doctor, she knew her father would have been able to help her, but now he could not. Her first thought had been to have a termination, and she felt her father would have known best, but now she no longer had that support, and it all felt very scary. She had no qualms about being completely honest with this policeman, who seemed to have an empathetic attitude, and the lady PC was also very kind.

"I needed to talk to him. My boyfriend and I had split up, and I found myself pregnant and not feeling well. I am alone now, as my mother also died, as I previously explained, and the man who brought me up has never liked me. My sister is married with her own new life. My dad would have been supportive, I know."

Martha could see how low she was. Being pregnant and alone must be so hard, and then to find out your father had suffered the most horrific death. It might not be a police matter, but Holly certainly needed some advice. She put her arm round the shoulder of the girl, and smiled gently at her.

"Holly, we are not doctors, we solve crimes, but you must go and see one. There are people in the NHS who will give you support. How many weeks are you?"

"About ten weeks. But the sickness wipes me out, and the dizziness, and I don't want to lose my job."

"Of course you don't. But will you promise us you will see your doctor, because there are always options. Is there anyone who can go with you?"

"Well, my neighbour Julie knows I am having a hard time, but she has two children herself."

"Well ask her, and maybe when you feel a bit better, you could pay her back by doing some babysitting."

Holly visibly brightened. Something inside her mind was telling her that this baby had part of her father in its genes, and instead of having a termination maybe she should try and keep it. With her father gone, it put a completely different slant on things; life was precious. She would go and see Julie when she got home, and maybe the doctor could give her something safe to control the sickness.

"I want to be completely honest with you. I was going to ask my father to fund a termination. Having a baby on my own seemed impossible, but now you have told me about his death, I feel that baby would be my last link with him, and I should keep it."

Alan admired her honesty. What she had just said could make her a suspect, as if her father had refused to help her financially it would have been a reason to kill him, but a sixth sense told him that this young woman had spoken from her heart. Of course, they would still check everything out, but he really didn't think she was capable of killing her father.

"We can't advise you on that, but your doctor will. Let me come out to the desk with you. I am sure we have some leaflets on people who can help in a crisis," said Martha.

Alan waited in the room until she returned. "Poor girl. You did well there," he said.

Martha smiled. "Well, just because we enforce the law, doesn't mean we can't be kind to someone who needs support."

"Too true. We are human here, and the shock of knowing someone poisoned her father must have been tough. However, we still have to check her out, you know," said Alan, firmly. "Now let's get to the team briefing."

"Yes sir," said Martha, smiling to herself. Alan sounded so tough at times, but he was a pussycat really.

Chapter Seven

"This is the victim. Forty-five year old Dr Ian Jones, a very well respected GP, who has lived and practised in Westgate for over twenty years. Traces of Valium were found in his whisky decanter, and the empty glass was next to his body. He was given enough to make him very sleepy, but, whilst he was stretched out in his armchair, the killer came in with poison, in the form of weedkiller which had been siphoned off from a big can in the shed, and poured it down his throat. As yet we have not found the receptacle that was used, although every cup and container in the house has been tested." Alan paused, as gasps of surprise came from around him.

"Now, it could be a woman, as it would be much easier to kill him if he was dopey, and they wouldn't otherwise have the physical strength, but equally it could be a man, who did it like this becaue it was easier, or even to make us think a woman was involved."

James Martin put his hand up, and Alan nodded to him.

"Sir, we went back to his brother David, as you requested, and he seemed aghast. He seemed to think his brother might have committed suicide. But his son Marty is adamant his father wouldn't have done that, and was equally distressed at the manner of his death."

"Thanks, James. David lives further down the road," Alan pointed to the pinned photo on the board. "He is a compulsive gambler, and has lost his home and his wife because of it. Ian had previously bailed him out of debt, but if he refused to do so this time, David would have a very strong motive. David found his body, and contacted us."

Alan moved on, pointing to a photograph of Pamela. "Pamela Jones, estranged wife of Ian, living with her boyfriend, Stewart Russell, until a couple of days ago. Currently living in a hotel and most anxious to return to the family home. How did it go today with her, James?"

All eyes were on James, as he stood up and spoke in his earnest, but likeable, manner.

"Well sir, my impression of her was that she is self-centred, she seemed more concerned about getting back to her previous home than the fact that someone poisoned her husband."

"Hmm," said Alan. Both himself and Martha felt embarrassed to think that Pamela may have manipulated them. Who could they believe? Pamela and Stewart were both unreliable witnesses.

"Yes, I can believe that. I think Ian gave her everything she wanted, but again she is a definite suspect; his will favours her. She wants to get back in the house, but maybe didn't want to live with Ian again, and, from what I can gather, she is the only person to not be horrified at the nature of his death. Apart from that, her alibi is unsafe, as Stewart admitted he fell asleep that night, so she could have come back to the house and done the deed."

Next Alan pointed at the photo of Kate Bryant. Her glasses seemed to dominate her face, with her owl-like eyes blinking at the camera. "Kate Bryant, housekeeper and cleaner at Ian's home. A very timid lady. The meal she cooked was tested for Valium and poison, but there was none. She does not appear to have any motive, and her respect for Dr Jones was obvious."

Then he pointed at the photo next to Kate's. Lisa's looks were striking, and her eyes seemed to have unfathomable depths. Not only was she more interesting than Kate, but she was also a suspect.

"Lisa Bryant, sister of Kate. Two sides to her character. When I saw her she seemed an angry woman. Like her sister, the cause of death seemed to devastate her, but, of course, we know with any suspect, they will do anything to avoid arrest, so they are often very good at acting. She has always had an obsession about Dr Jones, but her feelings were not returned, and his wife was keen to return to him, so her motive could be jealousy. The other side to her character is that she loves children, would love to adopt one, as she feels together, with Kate, they could give a child a loving and happy home."

Everyone stared at him, so he added, "She is a nanny, she cares for a year old little girl, and apparently she is very good at her job. But I will say I detected a certain barrier when we interviewed her. I feel she is hiding something. Did you notice it, Martha?"

"I noticed she was angry sir, but I also noticed it affected Kate a lot. She was embarrassed and tried to calm Lisa down."

"Well, I just think Kate is old school, even though time has moved on. Kate may well remember when she was a child, and held respect for her mother and others in her family, which doesn't exist now. But she clearly dotes on her younger sister, and is protective of her."

"Yes sir, I could see that, too," admitted Martha.

Alan's mind was on Holly. As yet they did not have a photo of her, but she could not be excluded. Looking at it with an unbiased view, because he had been touched by her obvious distress but did not want to be fooled again, as they had been with Pamela, he felt she must be mentioned.

"Before we study this list of suspects, and discuss our thoughts, there is one more person to mention. A young lady called Holly Wheeler, who apparently found out recently, when her mother died, that Ian Jones was her father. She was the result of a relationship he had when at university, but her mother never told him. Holly traced him, and as yet his son Marty does not know, so we have to be discreet. Whether Pamela or the Bryant sisters know remains to be seen. Holly must have thought all her Christmases had come at once when she discovered her true father was a wealthy man. And recently finding herself pregnant and alone, she says she had planned to go and see him that evening to ask for financial help."

Alan stopped at that point, feeling Martha bristling a little beside him. He couldn't bring himself to mention a termination, as Holly had said quite clearly that she was now having second thoughts.

He smiled at Martha. "Although we both found her to be an honest and caring young woman, who was equally devastated by Ian's death, she had a motive, so we have to check out her alibi that she was at home because she was feeling ill, and interview the neighbour who she said saw her."

"I am on it, sir!" said James, enthusiastically.

Stewart could not remember ever having a mother. He knew he must have, but all his life he had either been in care or with various foster parents. He had grown up with an attitude, becoming hard because he had never felt loved and he realised he did want to survive, so would have to make his own way in life.

He started off as a gardener's labourer for Thanet Council. Bert, the gardener he worked with, took pity on the young lad who appeared to be such a loner. Stewart had not been to school very much, and Bert could see something of himself fifteen years previously. He had also been in care, but then later adopted by a couple who had been supportive, and it had been the making of him. He was now married with a baby son and a happy life. He felt Stewart deserved a chance.

He found Stewart to be a quick learner, and a good worker, with a sharp memory. He remembered the names of many plants and shrubs, and definitely had green fingers. So with much encouragement from Bert, Stewart became a gardener, and eventually set up his own business. Bert had been his one friend in life, and he never forgot this; it was someone who had faith in him.

He stayed in Margate, living in a ground floor flat near to the sea front. To him it was just a base, somewhere to crash at the end of a busy day. He enjoyed his work. Being a gardener was a peaceful job for a loner like himself, and in the summer, he would treat himself to a pint of beer when he finished. He had a few customers in Westgate, and when he had finished work, he would sit outside 'The Swan at Westgate' overlooking the sandy beach and reflect on his day.

At the age of thirty-six, he had not had many girlfriends. Most women found him abrupt, but the truth was he didn't have much self-confidence, his earlier life had left him with unresolved issues. Then there had been a woman he had liked at a night club in 2015, but he hadn't realised she had a boyfriend, and that had ended up in

60

a fight. He shouldn't have lost his temper with the arrogant boyfriend, and he never would again, because he felt when he went to prison he had let Bert down, so since then he had gone straight.

He had met Pamela at The Swan. She had been a typical bored housewife, but way out of his league. She had told him her husband was looking for a gardener, and right from the moment he saw her, he had fallen deeply in love with her. She said she was lonely, and neglected, and he had no defence against her. The affair was passionate, and although to her he was a welcome diversion, for him she was the love of his life.

He had begged Pamela to leave Ian and come and live with him. He was sure with her beside him he could conquer the world. But living with Pamela made him realise more about her. Pamela was selfish and manipulative, and she seemed to be able to get anyone to do anything for her. Even her own husband bore her no malice for leaving him. But for Stewart she was a complex woman to understand. When the glamour of running away had worn off, he sensed she was tiring of him, and although he wanted to give her a better future, it could not be achieved in five minutes, and Pamela didn't want to wait. He felt doom was coming, even before the death of Ian. He was not enough for her, he had aimed too high, and he became obsessive about letting her out of his sight.

Now that she had gone, although his heart felt broken, there was a sense of relief that now what he had been dreading had happened. With the doctor now dead in suspicious circumstances, and Pamela manipulating the police to help her escape from him, he had decided, for his own peace of mind, that he would move on. He wanted to be as far away from police as possible, so no matter what his heart was saying to him, his head was telling him just to let her go. He did not intend to return to the Westgate house as a gardener any more. He was never short of clients, so it was definitely time to move on.

David felt that Ian would have wanted him to take care of Pamela now that he was no longer around. He had always envied Ian. He had been born with the looks, the brains, and then made himself a lot of money. So, of course, he had been a fine catch for Pamela.

Right now Pamela had done the right thing and left her scruffy gardener boyfriend, but it would not be long before she was back in the family home. David might only be living in a modest rented bungalow, but it was very close to the family home, so instead of being in a hotel, he could offer her sanctuary with him until such time as she could move back into the house. Marty had stayed for a night when he got the news about his father's death, but was now back at university until the funeral could take place.

David wasn't sure who was taking care of all that; he presumed the executors. He knew why Ian had not asked him because he couldn't be trusted with money; he might just gamble it away. His brother had loved him, anyway, but he knew he had been right, money and him were soon parted. There were two reasons to invite Pamela to stay with him: One was because she was family, and it was the right thing to do, the other was because when she moved back in the house, and inherited the money, she might just remember that he had helped her in her hour of need. Maybe she might help him pay the arrears on his rent.

Pamela was pleased to hear from David. It wasn't that she had been close to him; she had always known about his gambling, and how Ian had many times bailed him out of trouble. It was simply that she was already fed up with being in a hotel. She didn't have any of her personal belongings with her, she didn't know anyone here, and the idea that she could go and stay just down the road from her previous home was certainly appealing.

"David, that sounds a good idea. I have been put here with police protection, but surely I will be safe with my own family."

"Protection from what?" asked David, bemused.

"Well, you know I have left Stewart, and he won't have taken the news well. I showed the police some marks on my arms, and they helped me to leave him."

"Pamela, has he been attacking you? You are well rid, but maybe we need a police presence here, just in case he decides to turn up."

David was shocked, but he had never understood why Pamela had left the wonderful life his brother had provided her with to go

62

and live with a gardener. He had never met Stewart, nor had he wanted to, as he had a natural loyalty to Ian. Thank goodness she had seen sense and left the brute.

"Leave it with me. I will explain to them, and maybe I can get protection," said Pamela, glibly. She had guessed that Stewart probably would stay as far away from Westgate as he could. Since she had been told about Ian's poisoning, and the fact that it was weedkiller, no doubt Stewart would be scared stiff he would be put in the frame. Westgate would probably be the safest place for her right now.

Chapter Eight

"Have you heard the latest, sir? Pamela Jones is going to stay in the bungalow with her brother-in-law. She's no longer poor little beaten up girlfriend, and she doesn't want police protection. She says there is no way Stewart Russell would come near the place."

Alan considered Martha's words. Gone was the frightened abused woman, and in her place was someone who wanted to get back inside the house she had left, now that her husband was not around. It was clear how selfish and manipulative she was. Would she stop at nothing, including poisoning him, a man she had once loved and was the father of her son?

"Well, it could be a joint crime, you know. He discovered the body, he says, but he could have administered the poison. We only have his word on that. He is broke, so maybe he wants to move back in there with her. They might even be having an affair," he said, thoughtfully.

"So you think she left Stewart for David. Could be, I suppose, or she might just be using him until she gets back into the house. He will expect her to settle his debts. If it's a joint crime, they will both have something on each other, and she will be stuck with him whether she likes it or not," said Martha.

"I think we should go and see her again, at the bungalow. Her alibi isn't safe anyway."

"No, it isn't. Stewart fell asleep, so he has no idea what she was up to. We could also see the Bryant sisters again. Lisa always maintains she doesn't go near the house any more, but she was there earlier in the day when Pamela turned up."

"That's right. According to Lisa, Pamela was trying to get back with Ian. Maybe he said no, she saw the threat of a divorce looming and no money, so she decided to act quickly," said Alan.

"Shall I get us some coffee, sir, then we can get going?"

"Yes, sounds good," said Alan. He was trying to decide who he thought could be the most guilty. Both Stewart Russell and Pamela had a strong motive, but so did David Jones. Then Lisa Bryant was a very complicated woman to understand, and also had a motive. After all, hell hath no fury like a woman scorned. When Martha returned with the coffee, she also had a packet of biscuits with her. She was already learning how to keep Alan happy, although she ignored the smell of chocolate when he opened them. She was determined that there would be no more fittings of her wedding dress, and she wanted to stay a size ten.

On the way over to Westgate, Alan asked her if she had any ideas about who might have committed the murder.

"I have been thinking about it, sir. It looks like Ian Jones had the looks, the brains and the money, yet David had nothing except a bad gambling habit. We need to find out if he invited Pamela to stay with him, or whether she manipulated him. She has left Stewart, so she is now using David until she gets back into the family home. I think they may be an item, or else she is manipulating him, but importantly, I think he may have murdered his brother, as we only have his word that he found him like that."

"Yes, well we can't prove that either way," Alan reminded her.

They had arrived at the bungalow now. It was further down the road, past West Bay itself on a curve of the road, but still within walking distance of Ian's home. David answered the door to them, and as they entered the small lounge area, Pamela was sitting on a sofa that had seen better days. She looked out of place with her silk blouse and white tailored slacks. Her face was heavily made up, which made her cheeks look very pale.

"Good afternoon, Inspector. As you can see, David has kindly offered me sanctuary. It's what his brother would have wanted."

"Sanctuary from what?" asked Alan. He was fed up with her

theatrical attitude. "I understand you have a habit of self-harming. Are you sure Stewart Russell inflicted those bruises on you?"

Pamela went even whiter; she had not expected Stewart to reveal her secret.

"Well you saw what sort of life he gave me," she said defensively, looking at David for support.

David couldn't help remembering the way she had always managed to get everything that she wanted. Ian had indulged her every whim, and it sometimes had irritated him that she had that power over his brother. She had told him the same story about Stewart. Maybe the bloke hadn't hit her; after all, Pamela always liked a good drama.

"Can we move on from this. Now that Pamela is back with her family, it no longer matters, surely."

He didn't know why he was defending her. Maybe it was because he felt uncomfortable with the law around.

"We can't move away from anything until the person who murdered your brother is found!" said Alan, pointedly.

"We both want that to happen, of course, but the sort of job he had; sometimes people feel they have a grievance," said David.

Alan looked at Martha, who was busily taking notes. "What do you mean by that? Your brother was very well respected around here. People speak very highly of him."

David felt a rush of colour come to his cheeks, and he could see they had noticed. He had struggled for all of his life with feelings of jealousy towards Ian. He had loved him, but he could never compete, and Ian had always been the favourite of their parents.

"Well, doctors do their best to help people and prolong their lives, but sometimes a patient dies and then a grieving relative comes looking for retribution."

"Do you know of anyone who felt that way?" asked Alan, realising he did actually have a point.

"No, it was just a thought," muttered David.

"Inspector, were any of the doors forced open?" asked Pamela.

"No, the killer was known to your husband; no forced entry," said Alan, looking her straight in the face. She held his glance, but he

66

noticed the words did not seem to bother her. She was a cold woman.

"Ian would not have invited a stranger in. Once he got home, he felt his time was his own. I was married to him for over twenty years, and if anyone knocked he used to ask me to get rid of them."

"Well, he didn't have you to answer the door that night," commented Alan, trying hard to keep sarcasm out of his voice.

"Well, you know I was there earlier. Maybe it wouldn't have happened if I had stayed, or maybe we would both have been killed." Her eyes widened dramatically, and Alan marvelled how she managed to make every conversation end up being about herself.

"When we interviewed Stewart at the station, he told us that after he had eaten the fish and chips you had brought in for him, he was so tired he fell asleep in the chair."

"Yes, he did, and was snoring very loudly. He even drowned the TV."

"What time did he wake up again?"

Pamela knew what he was getting at. Stewart had no idea where she was whilst he was fast asleep with his mouth wide open. She had looked at him in disgust, and wondered why she had ever left Ian for him. This man was not a romantic lover any more, he was a boring old fart, but she dare not admit she had taken her car and gone out.

"I went upstairs and took a shower, then I got ready for bed. I suppose by the time I came down it must have been at least eight o'clock, maybe even a bit later."

"Can you remember what was on the TV?"

"No, I switched it off because he wasn't watching it."

Pamela had wanted to say they had watched the TV together, but she wasn't sure what Stewart might have told the police, and she didn't want to be exposed as a liar. If she remembered correctly, David had rung her at about eight-thirty to tell her of his brother's death. Luckily he had rung her mobile, so had assumed she was home.

"We only have your word for it, that you stayed in, Mrs Jones," said Alan. She didn't look guilty. Her face gave nothing away, so reluctantly, because he could not prove otherwise, he would have to accept what she said. But they could always check with Stewart what time he had woken up if he could remember.

"Well, thank you both for helping us with our enquiries," Alan said curtly. He nodded at Martha, it was time to go. Pamela saw them out. It was almost like the bungalow belonged to her. David had left them to it.

Alan drove the car along the road, parking outside the block of flats. He noted that both the cars were in their allocated spaces, which meant both of the sisters were home. "Right, now it's these two," he said.

"Yes," said Martha.

Kate let them in. She was wearing an apron, and there was an inviting aroma coming from the kitchen. "Oh, have we disturbed your dinner?" asked Martha.

"No," said Kate calmly, "I have been baking cakes."

"Sounds good to me," said Alan cheekily, and was rewarded with a smile. He noted that on the rare occasions that she didn't look worried, Kate's smile transformed her face. Although she had a look of a hard working fifties housewife about her, when she smiled she had white and even teeth, and attractive eyes.

Kate bustled off to make tea, promising him a cup cake, and they both went into the lounge area where Lisa was using a computer. She had spotted their car arriving, and felt uneasy. Why were they coming back again? She didn't like it. Police had a habit of snooping through files, and the last thing she wanted was for them to delve into her past.

Alan smiled at her. "Good afternoon, Lisa. I remember, when you were interviewed the other day, you said you rarely went into the doctor's house any more, yet you were there when Pamela made a visit. Was there a special reason why you were there?"

Lisa could feel that anger enveloping her, brought on by fear, but she tried to curb it. Kate had said she mustn't get angry when they interviewed her, because it would only rouse their suspicions. For once in her life, she did as she had been told. After all, it was for her own good. She opened her mouth to speak, but was beaten by Kate coming in carrying a tray of tea and cakes.

"I can answer that, Inspector. Lisa went in because I had left my mobile in there. I was cooking dinner, and she was free, so she offered."

"Yes, I found it on the table. She was there poking her nose in," said Lisa, disdainfully, making it clear that there was no love lost between them.

"And she told you she had come to pick up some more clothes?" asked Martha.

"Yes, but she wasn't, because she had already taken them all," said Lisa, triumphantly.

"You know what's in all the wardrobes, then?"

"Yes, Lisa helped me with a spring clean after Pamela left," said Kate.

Alan noted again how protective Kate was of her sister. It was almost as though she felt she had to speak for her. He wondered why? He was pretty sure that Lisa had probably snooped around the place quite a bit, and Kate was making it sound better. Lisa certainly was a strange character.

He sipped his tea, and ate the cake. Martha had drunk her tea now too. He wondered why he got the impression every time he came here that Lisa was hiding something, and Kate was protecting her. He could sense her unease.

"Are you any nearer to finding the person who killed the good doctor?" asked Kate, sounding anxious.

"We are following a number of lines of enquiry," said Alan.

"I do hope you get him soon," commented Kate.

"We don't actually know if it's a man or a woman."

"Well, there is no point looking here. Try his brother, or his wife, or even Stewart," said Lisa, pointedly, and Alan watched Kate flash her a look of disapproval. It was clear to him that Lisa was acting in a guilty manner, and even her sister looked worried. He made a mental note to get them both checked out at the station, to see if either of them had a suspicious past.

Alan put his teacup down. "That was very nice, thank you," he smiled, and Kate returned his smile, her owl-like eyes softening behind her glasses.

"Before we go, can you remind me ladies, how long have you lived in Westgate?"

He was quick to notice the look that passed between them. Was it panic? He wasn't sure. Kate spoke quickly for them both.

"I moved here ten years ago, just after my mother died."

"I see, where did you live before?

"Faversham. Lisa moved into the flat with me shortly afterwards."

Martha turned towards Lisa. Was it fear she could see in her eyes? She addressed her directly so that Kate could not answer for her.

"Where did you live before you moved here, Lisa?"

Lisa's heart was pounding so loudly she felt like her insides would explode. The bloody police, they never stopped snooping or digging into your private life, but she knew she could not afford to blow this; it was crucial!

"Well, I have always been a bit of a free spirit, and for three years I was travelling around the world, but before that I also lived with mother in Faversham."

Alan smiled. "That is fine, ladies. Now we are going to leave you in peace."

After Kate had shown them out, Lisa let rip. "Now they are going to check all that, and guess what, it will put me in the frame!" She flung herself down dramatically, and Kate was quick to put her arms around her and soothe her.

"You don't know that. My side of it is true. I nursed mother until she died, and they can't prove you didn't go travelling. The inspector didn't seem that interested after we explained."

"You know I didn't kill him, he was my icon."

"Yes, I know he was to you, but you must realise he wasn't to everyone, otherwise he would still be here now."

"People kill for many reasons; greed, jealousy, spite. It's the killer who was tainted, not Ian," said Lisa, defensively.

Kate could see that Lisa was still enamoured by him, even in death. He was her hero, so there was no point in falling out about it. It was best to change the subject.

"If you stay calm when you see them, it's the best way, and I think the inspector was busy enjoying my tea and cakes. We might not see them again. After all, Ian's own family all had a motive to kill him, so the police will be dissecting their relationships."

70

"Yes, well I did steer them more towards Stewart Russell. He was the gardener, and had use of the poison."

"Yes, you did say all that. You put the idea there, I heard you!"

Kate smiled gently at her. "So stop worrying, your secret will always be safe with me." She watched Lisa jump up impulsively, and put her arms around her. It was that secret that bound them together forever, they both knew it.

"Thanks to you I have a new life and another chance. You know how grateful I am," said Lisa, with tears in her eyes.

"Yes, I do. Now let's have some supper and open a bottle of wine. We both need to unwind," said Kate with feeling.

Chapter Nine

"I am so sorry to let you down, Zoe. It's a bad dose of flu, and the last thing I want is to give it to Adam."

"You are not letting me down, tuck yourself into bed and have a good rest," said Zoe kindly. Helen was such a good nanny, and she adored Adam, so she knew she would not be taking time off without good reason. Zoe was finding being back at work was very tiring. Initially she had enjoyed going back to her new job, but after a month a weariness had crept over her, so a few days off might do her good.

Alan had already left for work. When he was involved in a murder case he was always up and out early, so he didn't know about Helen calling in sick. Zoe was doing a stint in Casualty, it was quite challenging, particularly on a Saturday night, when it was not uncommon for local youths who had drunk too much, to be fighting over girls, or trying to prove themselves in many ways, to be brought in with various injuries and plenty of lip.

Like the other staff in Casualty, Zoe allowed it to roll off her. Having a sense of humour helped, and she ruefully hoped that one day Adam would not behave like that. Both Zoe and Alan took their parental duties very seriously, and although their son was still very young, they had both vowed they would try not to spoil him, and would try to bring him up with a sense of how to behave properly.

Zoe dialled the hospital, then clicked the number of the extension she needed. Kelly answered it, and Zoe explained why she could not come in today. Kelly was a mother of three, all at school and old enough to be left at home if they should be ill, but she had been there for fifteen years, and could still remember the 'good old days' when it had been a struggle to balance working life and home life because nobody was sympathetic to her problems.

"We have a new student nurse coming in today. I can ask Angela to keep an eye on her and help her until you come back."

"Oh Kelly, you are a superstar. I just don't have anyone to leave Adam with today, but my mother lives in Whitstable, and she may be able to help out tomorrow. I will let you know."

"OK, that is fine. Hear from you later."

Zoe clicked off her mobile, and then wondered if she was being selfish asking her mother to have Adam. She was well aware of how hard her parents worked. They had turned their home into a bed and breakfast, and it was going well. If her mother came over to look after Adam, that would mean her father would have to manage the breakfasts alone; but as both of her parents adored their grandson, they would be hard pressed to say no.

This coming weekend was her turn to work on Saturday evening. She only did one in four, and because with Alan's job she could never be sure if he would be called out for an emergency, her parents had agreed to be on standby should that occasion arise. So far they had been lucky, his call-outs tended to be during the week.

There was a timetable pinned up in the kitchen with days marked when Adam went to various baby groups. Today was the baby gym session. Not much gym was done, but it was a reason for mums and nannies to meet up and compare notes. The babies were all under two years old, and they just rolled about on the mats gurgling with fun, whilst the adults sat drinking tea or coffee. They were too young to play properly with one another. Some were more adventurous than others, whilst the cautious ones sat watching with wide-eyed innocence.

Helen had suggested this class for Adam, and had reported back that he loved it. He was always in the thick of things, a naturally friendly and inquisitive little boy who wanted to try everything, and made every effort to climb on anything. Zoe was pleased that she would be there herself today to see him. It was from 11 o'clock until 12,

d

which was perfect, as, after that, she could bring him home for his lunch and then a nap. The hall was just up in the town at Birchington, where the library was, so she didn't even need to take the car, she could just walk round there.

Adam came toddling up to her, and fixed his big eyes on her, then started chuckling. She felt her heart glow with happiness and pride. He was such a happy and healthy baby; they truly had been blessed. "Come on, buster, let's get you dressed. Mummy is taking you to baby gym. Poor Helen can't come in today." She had no idea how much of that he had understood, but she knew she would enjoy her day spent with him.

Lisa arrived at work a bit early, so she sat in the car and checked her 'phone. She was disappointed to receive the text from Helen saying she wasn't well and would not be at baby gym with Adam today. It was particularly nice that Abby and Adam both seemed comfortable with each other; there was no hair pulling or biting, or any of the behaviour that might suggest they did not get on.

When it was time to start, she pulled into the drive and got out of the car. She loved Abby, she was like a little ray of sunshine, and always a smiley baby. Caring for her gave her happiness and pain in equal measure. It was no wonder that sometimes, when off duty, her emotions got the better of her. It would never heal, that ache inside her. This is why, as each day passed, she wondered if adopting a baby and caring for it might just erase some of the misery that was always there, deep inside her. Staying with Kate shielded her quite a bit, so if they were going to adopt, she knew that Kate would have to fill all the forms in. Authorities were not averse to single mothers these days, as long as the child was loved and cared for; and it certainly would be. She might even have to move out for a little while, so they couldn't check up on her. But it would be worth it.

Abby toddled over to her with a shriek of joy, and Lisa lifted her up, feeling the warm little body against her. If only Lily had been like that. Why had she cried so much? She had been healthy and happy, but Lisa had felt inadequate, and Ryan had not understood. For all of her life, Lisa had put her heart into every relationship, and

Ryan was the father of her beautiful baby, and the two of them had been her world.

It may have been fifteen years ago, but she could still feel the tears in her eyes at the painful memories. This was why she was so grateful to Kate for helping her to rebuild her life. Without Kate there to lean on, she wasn't sure if she could have held herself together. With a mother who had never really cared about anything other than clothes, make-up and men, who judged her without asking what had happened, Kate had been the only one who had not judged, who had listened to her.

She sat down with Abby in her arms, and the baby's mother, Sally Mason, came bustling along the hall. She was smartly dressed, as was in keeping with her job as a lawyer. "Good morning, Lisa. Abby knew it was you. I have left a note on the table, and I should be home by six."

"It's fine," murmured Lisa, and Sally was gone in a cloud of perfume. Her navy suit and white blouse were immaculate, her blonde hair elegantly styled on top of her head, and her navy stilettos clicked on the wooden floor as she left the house.

Lisa made herself a coffee, and sat down. Abby sat on the floor with her toys. Lisa watched her whilst she drank it. She was such a placid little girl, and a joy to take care of. It was almost like she had given birth to her. She felt like her own child, and instead of feeling glad when the day was over, she felt like she didn't want to leave her. She knew that Sally was very career minded, and didn't have much energy left at the end of the day to give Abby attention, and her father Don was a barrister, so he also had a demanding job. In her mind, people like that did not deserve children, but she did. Her maternal instinct was so strong.

She read through the note, which reminded her that Abby had baby gym at 11am; not that she needed reminding. She wasn't looking forward to going without Helen to talk to. Some of the other nannies were a bit cliquey, and Lisa didn't do cliquey. She was not popular, but Helen seemed to accept her, even though she knew she was a bit outspoken and erratic at times. Well, maybe she would just sit on her own today.

Lisa wondered why Sally had dressed Abby in a pink frilly dress today. Honestly, she just didn't have a clue! Lisa had told her so many times just to leave her in her pyjamas, and she would dress her. She found some leggings and a T-shirt, then coaxed the lively little girl to hold her arms up so she could take off the dress. Like all babies at that age, she didn't want to stay still and be dressed, but Lisa remained calm and organised, and soon Abby was wearing more suitable clothes for rolling around on the floor.

When she reached the hall, she saw the groups of chatting nannies going in. Nobody acknowledged her, she told herself she didn't care, she was only here for Abby! Abby had no such hang-ups about the other babies, she sat chuckling in the midst of them, and Lisa pulled her chair nearer so she could watch her.

"Hello Lisa, this must be Abby. I am glad you are here, as I don't know anybody."

Zoe smiled in a friendly way, and Lisa noticed her very white teeth and blonde curls that she pushed hurriedly back from her face. She was a beautiful woman, but then her husband was a very handsome man; he wasn't Lisa's type, no one in the force would be, but she could appreciate the fact that they made a beautiful couple.

"Hello Zoe. I am glad you brought Adam. Abby and Adam get on really well together."

"I expect you know that poor Helen has the 'flu. But I didn't want Adam to miss baby gym, so I have taken today off to bring him."

The two babies were now sitting next to each other, and Adam touched Abby's arm.

"Oh, look at that," said Zoe, wonderingly. When she was at work she was missing all this. Their interaction was really sweet, as Abby touched Adam's chubby little leg.

"She won't do that in about fifteen years time," said Lisa laughing. And Zoe smiled, the innocence of the babies, who had yet to experience life properly, was touching.

The next hour passed pleasantly and quickly. Zoe and Lisa found themselves chatting quite naturally. Being with Abby showed a different side to Lisa. She was patient, calm and caring, and Zoe was impressed with her professional attitude.

As they said goodbye, Lisa asked Zoe if she knew how long Helen would be off work.

"Well, with 'flu, it lasts a few days at least, so I am not expecting her back this week."

"And the hospital have given you the whole week off?"

Zoe grimaced. "Kelly the staff nurse has been very understanding, but I am hoping my mother can help out. When I get home I am going to contact her. She lives in Whitstable."

"Well, if she can't, I don't mind looking after Adam. As you can see, Abby and Adam get on great together."

"Oh, would you? That is so kind!" Zoe didn't hesitate. She had formed her own opinion of Lisa; she clearly loved babies, and they would be safe in her care. "I will ask mum first, but if she is too busy, I would be so grateful, and naturally I will pay you."

"I wasn't even thinking about the money, just how much fun Adam and Abby will have together," smiled Lisa, and Zoe's heart warmed towards her. Lisa clearly did love all babies.

David was finding having Pamela around very tiresome. He had to put on a good show now that Ian had gone. She would soon be moving back into the house, together with Marty, so he had to keep in with both of them. Hopefully they would take pity on their relation who had fallen on bad times, as he liked to think of it.

He had hoped that Ian might have left him something in his will. Just a few thousand would have helped, but no, he had shared it with his estranged wife and son. He had been a fool to leave anything to Pamela after she had left him so callously for the gardener, but then Ian had never stopped loving her, and she had taken advantage of that.

All she thought about was clothes, shoes and money. Her one saving grace was that at the moment she had a part-time job and was buying some food for them both, but she had said that as soon as she got her inheritance she would give up working, as she didn't need to.

David had lost his job because of his gambling. He had taken time off to go and place bets, and frequently took time off when his horse lost because he felt depressed and couldn't face going to work. He had become unreliable, his wife had left him after suffering years of mental torture knowing he was gambling away everything they had. It had been a steady job in an engineering firm with a regular wage, and a pension when the time came, but through his compulsive gambling he had lost everything, including everyone's respect. Only his long suffering brother had stood by him, and he couldn't be sure that Pamela and Marty would do the same. It had been a sad day for him when Ian died, and he was really not sure what the future held for him. He didn't think he could face looking for another job at his age, he didn't want to face rejection, and he had no money left to gamble with. His only hope was that Pamela would remember that he had given her sanctuary when she needed it, and she had lived rent free with him. But with her sort of attitude, which was walking over everyone to get what she wanted, he doubted it. Of course, there was Marty, he had his father's fair and honest attitude, so maybe he was the one to work on. After all, he came home to stay in the holidays. David knew he would just have to be patient for now.

Chapter Ten

"I checked out the Bryant sisters, guv. Kate Bryant was born in Leeds, lived up north for many years, but as was to be expected, she has no police record. Her mother moved to Faversham twelve years ago, then Kate moved to be with her and lived with her for two years until her death. She then moved to the apartment at West Bay. But as for Lisa, I can't find any records of her birth. Something doesn't seem right here, so I thought maybe I should take a trip to Faversham to see if I can find anything out from a neighbour?"

Alan stiffened. "No birth record of Lisa, now that is strange. She said she went travelling, but there must be a birth record, unless she changed her name. But then, why would she do that?"

"Well, if she has, then we can't trace her unless we challenge her about it, sir, can we?"

"James, I think it's a good idea for you to go to Faversham and see what you can find out, and then check back with me."

"Yes sir, I am on it."

Alan clicked his mobile off. James was a reliable man, and he would take one of the new WPCs with him. They took down the notes of any conversations, and generally made themselves useful. It was always good practice to interview people in pairs, as one person on their own might not remember everything, and they could also support one another.

Martha's boyfriend Clive had picked her up tonight. They were going out for dinner and to the theatre, so she needed to get home quickly to get changed. Alan looked at his watch, it was just gone five o'clock, so he decided to go home now. Whereas Martha seemed to think that Ian's brother David was the culprit, Alan was veering more towards Lisa, who he knew was hiding something. She was volatile, and a little strange, and he needed to know more about her. But as Kate's sister, surely she must have the name Bryant? It was all such a puzzle.

As he drove from Canterbury to Birchington it was the time of day when the traffic was queuing, so he drove along the A28, passing through Westgate Towers. After negotiating a couple of busy roundabouts, he got stuck in a line of traffic whilst the railway barrier came down at Sturry. He had to sit and wait patiently for about ten minutes, but all the while it was all going round in his head. Somebody had brutally poisoned the good doctor. Could Lisa have assumed that name because she had a guilty past? And, if so, maybe she wasn't even Kate's sister. So many questions without answers, and it was up to him to find those answers.

A horn behind him beeped, and he came out of his reverie to see the gates were open and the traffic moving. He drove over the crossing, and then headed along the main road towards Thanet. Once he had left Canterbury behind, the traffic was moving much quicker, and he couldn't wait to reach home and see Zoe and Adam, his little family unit that meant so much to him.

As he drove onto the garden estate and reached the bungalow, he noticed that Zoe's car was there. She must have come home early today, as she had said she was working until six. Helen must have already gone home. It was still only five-thirty.

Adam was in his high chair, he had a bowl of fish fingers and chips, which he was eating with his fingers. His peas as yet remained untouched, although Zoe had scooped a few onto a spoon and was holding them hopefully up to him. She smiled as Alan came through the door.

"Oh, just in time, our son is going great guns with his fish fingers, not so with his peas."

He kissed her cheek lightly. Zoe always smelt so good, and his son rewarded him with a cheesy grin, which immediately revealed the contents of his mouth.

"OK honey, I'll take over."

"Thanks, my love. I will put the kettle on."

Alan pretended to make his hands like a train, with the spoon chugging towards Adam's mouth, and managed to get the peas into his open mouth. He watched his son's puzzled expression as he worked out whether he did like peas. They were followed by a chip which had tomato ketchup, which he did like. So Alan continued the process of getting him to enjoy his dinner. Since Adam had come along, and he had taken an active part in caring for him, he had learned to slow down. Patience was a virtue he had not possessed before he had become a father, but it hadn't taken him long to find out that it took ages to get a child dressed and ready to go out. Eating a meal lasted a long time too, and as for taking them on a walk, there were distractions everywhere, puddles to splash in, walls to climb on, and any manner of things that he took for granted, but were fascinating and distracting to a young child. He hoped that the patience he now had not only made him a better person, but also a kinder father, because it had all been such a learning curve.

Later, when Adam was in bed, and they sat down together, he was able to speak to Zoe properly. "I was surprised to see you home before six tonight; how come you finished your shift early?"

"I didn't, Helen is ill and she did not come in, so Kelly said I could take the day off. Did you not get my texts?"

Alan took out his phone, and then saw the unread texts from Zoe. "Sorry honey, the usual busy day, you know. So you've been home with Adam all day, then."

"Yes, and it was lovely. We went to baby gym, and I ended up chatting with Lisa. She really is very nice when you get to know her, and she absolutely adores the babies."

Shock and horror flooded through Alan at the mention of Lisa's name. Lisa was a dubious character, who was currently under investigation because there was no trace of her ever being born. She was a woman of secrets, and he didn't want her anywhere near Zoe or Adam!

"It's best if you don't speak to her, you know, honey. It's too close to home. She is a witness in my murder case."

Zoe always thought the best of people, and she knew that Lisa had a volatile side to her character, but she had also seen how gentle and caring she had been with Abby. Usually she listened to Alan, but right now she felt he was judging Lisa when he should not be. Just because she lived a few doors away from the murder scene, that surely didn't mean that Zoe couldn't speak to her?

"Well, you never said before. She even offered to look after Adam if my mother couldn't do it tomorrow."

There was a note of defiance in her tone. She had not needed to say that, especially as her mother had agreed to come over the next day to take care of Adam. Maybe he didn't mean it, but Alan was making her feel like a schoolgirl being disciplined by a headmaster. Her words had truly hit home, as his face looked like thunder.

Alan loved his wife with all his heart, and they very rarely argued, but her stubbornness scared him, because all he wanted to do was to protect his family. Ever since Zoe had been abducted by a psychopath before they had married, he had been so grateful that her life had been spared. Being a policeman was a dangerous job, and sometimes it rebounded on the family. There was no way Lisa could look after their son, and Zoe must realise this.

"Zoe, this is serious. Lisa can never look after Adam. I would rather stay home myself if you had to go to work. Promise me you won't do that."

"OK, I won't go against you, but she is not exactly Dr Crippen." Her tone was sulky, which wasn't like her, and for the rest of the evening there was an atmosphere between them. Alan hated being like this, but he would do whatever it took to keep Zoe and Adam safe.

The next morning, James and his WPC Natalie were standing outside the row of terraced houses in Victoria Road. They were all so close together, it would be hard not to know what their neighbours were doing. Kate and her mother had lived at number forty-four, but it wouldn't be any good asking the current owners about them. They needed to find someone who had lived in the road for many years. On the corner of the road there was a general store, so James suggested that they used it to get some sandwiches for lunch, and hopefully some local information.

Natalie agreed with him. This was her first trip out doing an interview, so she was nervous, but anxious to please. They crossed the road and entered the shop, which was a bit like an Aladdin's cave. It had food, household items, anything that someone might need quickly, and it was stocked from floor to ceiling, with only just about enough room to walk up to the counter without knocking something over. James saw a notice behind the counter which said. 'ONLY TWO SCHOOL CHILDREN AT A TIME'. He doubted there would be enough room for any more!

A bell had rung when they opened the door, and an Asian man appeared from behind a curtain at the rear of the shop. Natalie was busy choosing sandwiches for them both from a fridge, leaving James to open the conversation.

"Good morning. It's OK, nobody is in trouble."

The man had spotted their uniform, and looked pale, but James had tried to sound reassuring.

"Good morning, sir. How can I help you?"

Natalie had chosen some sandwiches and crisps, which she brought to the counter smiling. James paid for them, and then replied to the man, who was studying them intently, his dark eyes looking straight at them.

"How long have you been running this shop?"

"It's over fifteen years, sir," he said proudly.

"Can you remember back to twelve years ago? Do you remember who lived at number forty-four."

The man paused to think. James judged him to be in his middle fifties, so then he would have been early forties.

"Oh yes, you mean Rebecca Bryant. A very nice lady. She worked up in London, always looked very smart. I think she was a buyer for a fashion outlet, so she always took pride in her own appearance."

"Did she have any family, do you know?"

"Yes, a daughter called Kate. She used to live up north, but her mother's health was deteriorating, so she ended up moving in and caring for her. After a couple of years Rebecca died, and Kate moved away. I haven't seen her since."

"Do you know what illness she had?"

"Well I never actually asked, it may have been her heart. She stopped coming in the shop. Kate used to pick up what was needed. Kate was a very quiet person, never had much to say for herself. Unlike her mother, who had always been a very friendly lady."

"Do you know if there were any other brothers or sisters?"

"Not to my knowledge, sir. Rebecca told me one day she would have liked more children, but Kate's father had left them when she was very young, and she never felt the need to marry again."

James and Natalie exchanged glances. "Well, thank you very much, Mr. . ?"

"Aaran Gupta, sir."

"Would you be prepared to sign a statement if we need you to, later?"

"I would, sir, but can you tell me what it's all about?"

"We have ongoing enquiries about the murder of Dr Ian Jones, and we just needed you to confirm what you have done about Rebecca Bryant and her daughter Kate."

With that James and Natalie left the shop. James didn't want to say anything more than that to the shopkeeper, but he couldn't wait to share the news with Alan. Kate's past checked out just as she had said, but there didn't appear to be a sister. So who was Lisa, and what was her connection with Kate?

Alan felt bad about jumping on Zoe the way he had last night. Not being able to discuss a case made it harder, but a sixth sense told him that Lisa was trouble and he didn't want her anywhere near Zoe and Adam. He had broken out in a sweat when he realised that she had offered to look after Adam. What a lucky escape, but in making it clear to Zoe how he felt, he had upset her. Usually when they went to bed she cuddled into his back, but last night she had turned the other way to avoid bodily contact with him. He knew he had hurt her.

Breakfast this morning had been a hurried affair as usual, and then her mother had turned up to look after Adam, so nothing much had been said. However, when he was leaving for work, he put his arms around Zoe, and she responded to him by hugging him back.

He hoped that meant he was forgiven, and maybe, in due course, she would understand why he had been so pedantic.

When he got the phone call from James, he was not that surprised. There was definitely something suspicious about Lisa, and why would Kate be protecting her if she wasn't her sister? What sort of hold did she have over Lisa?

"You have done well, James. We now have no alternative but to search the home of the Bryants. That might give us some clue as to who Lisa really is."

"Yes, sir. Would you like me to make the arrangements?"

"Good man. I am now going to grab a bit of lunch, and later this afternoon we will have a team briefing."

Martha took that as her cue. She went to buy sandwiches and coffee, as apparently Alan had left his behind this morning, and he would not want to address the team on an empty stomach.

Whilst she was gone, Alan rang the florist and asked them to make up a bunch of all Zoe's favourite flowers. They already knew what that was, as Alan often used their services.

"I will pick them up on my way home. You are open until six aren't you?"

"Oh definitely, we will be open for you, Inspector. What message do you want, or do your prefer to write it yourself?"

"Yes thanks, I will write it," smiled Alan at the other end of the phone. He knew he was simply going to write I LOVE YOU!

Chapter Eleven

James didn't want to wait until the next morning to visit the Bryants. It was highly likely that the women would be at work. It was now four-thirty, but maybe at least one of them might be home. He rounded up a couple more of the team, and instructed them to search the place properly.

Kate's car was parked in her usual space, but there was no sign of Lisa, which is what he had hoped for. He knew she was likely to create a scene if she knew that her room, and indeed the whole apartment, was being turned over.

Kate opened the door to them, but as soon as she spotted how many of them there were, she went pale. James tried to explain calmly to her. "Good afternoon, Miss Bryant, we have a warrant to search these premises."

"Why, we have not done anything wrong?"

"Then you have nothing to fear. This is an ongoing enquiry into the death of Ian Jones."

Kate felt helpless. There were policemen darting about everywhere, with drawers and cupboards being pulled open, and she actually felt really invaded, as though the apartment didn't belong to them any more. She had nothing to hide, and if they checked on her, there was nothing to fear. But her heart lurched with fear when they entered the room where Lisa kept all her clothes and possessions. Lisa wasn't the tidiest of people, and she tended to hoard things she should have got rid of years ago.

She just hoped and prayed they would not find anything incriminating, because if they interviewed Lisa, chances are she would pour it all out. Kate had worked hard to build up this safe family unit for both of them, and would be devastated if it was all ripped apart by meddling policemen.

Whilst James was in Lisa's room, he checked the drawers carefully, and there was nothing other than clothes, underwear and T-shirts in them. In the wardrobe hung clothes, a nurse's uniform from previous times, and shoes. There was a jewellery box on a shelf at the top of the wardrobe, with a piece of paper folded up behind it. He slid it out. It was quite a few years old, and the folds were weak and almost ready to tear.

He glanced at it quickly. It was a newspaper cutting some fifteen years old, and the heading made his blood run cold:

MOTHER CONVICTED FOR SHAKING HER BABY TO DEATH

He didn't stop to read any more. He could hear footsteps in the hall, so he put the cutting in a plastic bag and dropped it into a holdall. He was just in time, as Kate appeared at the door, her owl-like eyes blinking in confusion. "I really don't like you searching my sister's room when she isn't here, you know, even though you have a warrant."

"I know how you feel, but we are done here now, so we won't take up any more of your time."

He smiled at her, trying to look calm, but inside his heart was hammering with shock about those headlines. It was obvious that it was not going to be pleasant reading. His only thought now was to contact his boss and share these latest revelations with him.

Alan had finished his team briefing. It was after five, and he wanted to pick up the flowers and go home to Zoe and Adam. Martha had gone home, so he got in his car and drove to the florist to pick up the flowers. They had done him proud, with a beautiful colourful display, which he knew Zoe would love. Just as he got into the car his mobile rang, and he was very tempted to ignore it; after all, tomorrow was another day.

But in the end he couldn't, he saw the name flash up and it was James.

"Yes, James, what can I do for you?"

A breathless voice came over the line, the words spilling out quickly, as though he had no control over them. "I have a newspaper clipping, sir. I only read the headlines, it said MOTHER CONVICTED FOR SHAKING HER BABY TO DEATH.

"Where did you find it?"

"Behind a jewellery box in the top of a wardrobe in Lisa's room."

"Why did you only read the headlines, then?"

"It's falling apart, sir. I put it into a plastic bag as I didn't want to damage it."

"Good man, where are you now?"

"Stuck in a traffic jam on the way to the station. I thought you ought to see it now. It is very important."

"OK James, I will head back there, then we will sit in my office and read it."

Ruth had been more than happy to come and spend a day looking after her precious grandson Adam. Because she helped her husband Gerald run their own bed and breakfast business in Whitstable, it didn't leave a lot of spare time, so they usually only got to babysit on an occasional evening when Alan and Zoe went out, and Adam was in bed asleep.

But today Gerald had said, as they only had one guest, he was happy to cook breakfast and generally hold the fort. Ruth was really looking forward to having Adam all to herself for one precious day, and she was determined they would have fun together.

The furthest she had been into Thanet had been Birchington, but she had heard that West Bay was a very sandy beach, and she thought it would be fun to take Adam there with a bucket and spade and build sandcastles. Although she would not admit it to herself, there was another reason that she had gone there. She knew that a local doctor had been murdered there, the newspapers were full of it, and curiosity to see what the area was like could not be ignored.

It was a lovely sunny day, so after Zoe had gone off to work, she got Adam ready to go out. She had already mentioned they might have a trip to the beach, and Zoe thought it was a great idea. So after putting Adam into his baby seat, she lifted him into the car, and drove along towards Epple Bay. The coast road wound round towards Westgate, with a golf course on the other side of the road.

She was enjoying the panoramic views around her, and eventually she arrived at West Bay. The tide was out, and there was a broad expanse of sand, so she spread out a blanket and put Adam on it. But he was more interested in tipping water out of his bucket than making sandcastles. Then he spotted other people, and always a sociable little boy, he toddled over to say hello, so she found herself spending most of the time trying to bring him back. But the comments that he was such a bonny boy resonated with her. Ruth was a very proud grandmother.

She had brought a picnic lunch, painstakingly prepared with Adam's health in mind. Sticks of celery and raw carrot, teamed with slices of cheese and cocktail sausages. She also had a tangerine and slices of apple. He ate them sitting on the blanket, and then lustily drank from his baby cup. Ruth had made herself a ham sandwich, which she ate, breaking off pieces of ham to share with him. She had brought a flask of coffee for herself, and after drinking that, she noticed that the tide was coming in, and people were leaving the beach, so she quickly changed Adam's nappy, and folded up the blanket. It was time to go.

She put him in his buggy, and pushed it up the slope. There was a grassy area at the top with seats and a panoramic view of the bay. On the far side there were rows of beach huts, which dated back to past times. Ruth walked along the path, noting that there were blocks of flats and Victorian houses set back from the road. In one of these the doctor's body had been found. It all looked so peaceful and had such a holiday atmosphere, that it almost seemed impossible that a murder had taken place in this area.

Even further along the road were bungalows, but she decided not to walk any further as Adam had now dozed off. She turned the buggy round, and retraced her way back to the car. Adam remained asleep when she transferred him into his baby seat, so she decided to explore even further. She continued to drive along the coast road until she reached a crossroads. Over the other side was Station Road, so she drove along it, rounding the bend at the end, and then came across a row of local shops.

She stopped outside a charity shop, noticing that there were free spaces if she stayed for up to an hour. That suited her nicely, so she got the buggy out and transferred Adam back into it. He started to wake up, and she spoke gently to him. "It's OK Adam, granny wants to look round the shops," and he rewarded her with a smile.

Ruth worked her way along the parade, starting first with the charity shop. Then she popped in the Co-op, where Adam was being duly admired by a friendly elderly lady. She bought him some white chocolate buttons. Hopefully he wouldn't get in too much mess with them.

When she went round the corner at the end of the road, she saw the Carlton Cinema, a very elegant Edwardian building, which was still very much in use. She had read about it, and knew it dated back to 1910, and it certainly gave her a wave of nostalgia, as she remembered when she was a young girl going to Saturday morning pictures. She made a mental note to bring Gerald here. She knew he would really enjoy reminiscing about the sixties and seventies.

Glancing at her phone she saw it was now four o'clock, so she should think about heading back. After transferring Adam back into his car seat, she drove over the railway line, and out to the main road which led back to Birchington. It was busy now because pupils from a local school had just come out, and mothers in cars were parked everywhere, intending to pick them up and drive them home.

She drove along the main road towards Birchington. She was feeling a bit tired now, so when she got to the bungalow, she would sit down for a bit. Once inside she put the kettle on for tea, and put Adam down onto the carpet to play with his toys.

But before she made her tea, she changed Adam's nappy, then gave him a drink and a biscuit. It was now four-thirty, and Alan was expected home just after five. But whilst she was drinking her tea, a message came through on her mobile.

SO SORRY RUTH. GOT HELD UP, BUT ZOE SHOULD
BE IN AT SIX. ALAN.

She sent Gerald a text to say she would be a bit later. Adam was getting a little bit fussy now, but it was to be expected at this time of day. Zoe had said it was OK for him to watch CBeebies, so she put him in his high chair, and put it on to distract him.

In the fridge was some minced meat in sauce with pasta, so she heated it up for him. Eating had never been a problem for Adam, although he managed to get quite a bit of the savoury sauce round his mouth. When he had finished eating it with her help, she gave him a yoghurt, and then a drink of water.

She guessed that Zoe would feel very tired when she got in from work, so she decided she would make sure Adam was all ready for bed when his mother arrived. She fought against her own feelings of weariness, and went into the bathroom to run his bath. Then she undressed him and put him in. She enjoyed watching him splashing about, but she decided against washing his hair. Zoe had said he didn't like getting water in his eyes.

Adam stayed in the bath until the water was getting cold, and then she managed to coax him out, and wrapped him in a warm fluffy towel. But, to her surprise, he didn't want to sit still whilst she dried him, instead he got off her lap, running round and laughing, so she had to chase him to get him to keep still and be dried. Eventually, when he was all ready for bed, she put him back in his high chair, and turned up the TV volume. He could now watch CBeebies again, and she flopped wearily on the sofa.

Zoe's car rolled into the drive. It was ten minutes past six. Alan had texted Zoe first to say he was held up, and she had replied to tell him he must let Ruth know. She felt bad that her mother, who had been so kind to come over, now had to wait until she got in. But she didn't blame Alan, not at all, his job was demanding, she had always known that, and she wouldn't have married him if she could not accept that.

Kelly had been great, and after dinner was served in the ward, at five-thirty, she had said they could manage, and just this once Zoe could go. She could have hugged her, because even negotiating the traffic would take a while, but she should be home by six.

When she came in, such a peaceful scene greeted her. Adam was watching TV in his high chair, but her mother looked exhausted, a whole day looking after Adam was exhausting, she knew that.

"Oh mum, you have bathed him for me, and got him ready for bed. I didn't expect that. You do look tired."

"Well, he is a little live wire, but I have loved spending the day with him. I expect you are glad you are not at work tomorrow. What about Saturday?"

"I have swapped it, I shall do next week instead."

"Maybe Helen will be back on Monday?"

"Yes, hopefully. But I refuse to worry about it."

"If you are stuck, perhaps you can let me know on Sunday."

Zoe looked at her mother, and smiled gratefully. She had never seen her look so tired, and she made a vow to herself that even if she had to take the day off herself, she was not going to ask her mother again so soon. She would find another way, but she would not go against Alan and ask Lisa. She had moved on from their conversation about Lisa. Alan was right, she couldn't leave Adam with someone she only knew briefly. Their son's safety must come first.

Ruth rose from the sofa. Zoe had by now taken Adam from his high chair and was holding him, and then Ruth kissed his cheek. But Adam was not in a cuddly mood, he wanted to get down. He wriggled free, and Ruth laughed.

"Bye little buster, we did have fun, didn't we?"

"Did you let dad know you were held up?" said Zoe, worriedly.

"Of course, he is watching the slow cooker, as we have a beef stew when I get in."

"Thanks again, mum, now go home and rest."

Zoe stood at the door with Adam, encouraging him to wave as Ruth got in her car. She stayed there until her mother's car had pulled out onto the road, then after giving a final wave she went inside.

Chapter Twelve

"Lisa, please tell me there was nothing in your room for the police to find. They have been here snooping!"

Lisa was playing with Abby on the floor at Abby's home, but fear shot through her at Kate's words. She had always been terrified that the police would find out about her past. She had burned the passport, and now had one in her assumed name, but she had kept that newspaper cutting, simply because there was a photo of her holding Lily. She had loved her little girl so much, it was all she had left of her.

"I hid the newspaper cutting behind my jewellery box. You know I had to keep that," her voice was pleading for Kate to understand, and she did. Kate's heart went out to her, but there was fear inside her too. When she had entered the bedroom, she remembered seeing the jewellery box on Lisa's dressing table, just where the policeman was standing.

"Are you sure you didn't leave it on your dressing table?"

"No, I don't move it ever, it hasn't got much inside it. I keep my earrings on the dressing table."

Kate gulped with fear. It was all going to be exposed, and they had worked so hard to keep it a secret. And now Lisa was in severe danger!

"Oh, my God, they have it then. Lisa you have to get out of here!"

Lisa felt like her world was falling apart. She had never

recovered emotionally from the loss of her beautiful Lily, nor the time spent having treatment inside a secure unit. Nobody had believed her when she said she was innocent, and Ryan, who had been the love of her life, had known the truth, but allowed her to take the blame. For the last ten years she had built herself a new life with encouragement and help from Kate, but now all of her past flashed before her eyes and she had no idea how to deal with it.

"Where can I go?"

"Our holiday home. Nobody else knows it, you can lie low there for a while. Don't come home, you must move fast!"

"I will. Right now!"

Lisa clicked her phone off, and looked at Abby quietly playing on the floor. She loved this little girl as if she was her own. She could not just disappear and leave her on her alone, but neither could she bear to be locked up again as if she was mad. All commonsense had temporarily deserted her; she didn't even have time to think this through.

She grabbed enough things to tide her over for Abby. As far as she was concerned, all she could do was tuck her hair into a hat she had in the car, and put on some dark glasses. She would dye her hair as soon as she could, but Kate had injected such a sense of urgency into her voice. It was time to go!

Alan carefully smoothed out the newspaper cutting. As James had said, the folds were weak, but it was very important to read it. His worst fears were realised when he read the headlines. Lisa was a child murderer. He felt stunned, especially when he realised she might have cared for Adam if he hadn't put his foot down. The thought of his son ever being in danger was abhorrent.

The photo was definitely Lisa. Younger but unmistakable, she was holding the baby she had murdered. It made him feel sick inside. What sort of madness had caused her to do this? He read the report carefully. It was dated 14th June 2007.

"23 year old Sheila Black was convicted of shaking her 6 month old baby Lily to death because she would not stop crying. The baby's

94

father Ryan Lee told the court how he heard Lily crying, then suddenly she became silent, so he came into the room to find his girlfriend Sheila holding her. When he checked, Lily was dead. He called the emergency services, and Sheila simply sat there staring into space and refusing to speak to anyone. She had been suffering from postnatal depression. Miss Black will be detained in a secure unit pending further investigations into her mental health."

"Wow boss, how on earth has she managed to get a job working with babies? It's insane!"

"My god, it is. We have to look into this! After changing her name she's been let loose to continue her evil deeds!"

"Well, in fairness, boss, she was obviously mentally ill; must have been to kill her own child. She may have had treatment and medication for it."

"She may have, but she should never work with children again!" said Alan vehemently. The anger in his voice was because he realised how close it had been with Lisa offering to look after Adam. He wasn't going to tell James that; it had been a bit too close to home.

"We need to bring her into custody. She's a mad woman, and there's a good reason to think she might have killed Dr Jones. I wouldn't put anything past her," he said darkly.

"What, now sir?" James was startled. They didn't have any evidence. Her past deeds didn't prove she'd killed the doctor, but he could see his boss was determined .

"Right now," said Alan firmly. All he could think was that he wanted to make sure that no one would suffer at the hands of this mad woman. It was his duty to keep everyone safe. Right now all they could do was question her. He felt the need to have Martha with him. A woman might understand more, because all he could feel was anger. He recognised he was biased, and that wasn't good. Perhaps he shouldn't go flying round there right now, maybe tomorrow he could take Martha with him. Maybe he should sleep on it. They could pick her up tomorrow and bring her in for questioning. He felt that tomorrow he would be in a clearer frame of mind. He realised he had to keep himself from being emotionally involved, it clouded his judgement.

"On second thoughts, James, let's sleep on it. Maybe tomorrow you can see if we have a file for Sheila Black. I intend to bring her in for questioning."

"OK, sir." James felt a little confused.

"Let's get off now. We both have homes to go to."

James felt relieved, it had been a long day.

"By the way, many thanks, you did well today."

"It's fine, sir. See you tomorrow, then."

Alan waited until James had left the room, and then he sent Zoe a text: 'LEAVING WORK NOW, HONEY. BACK HOME SOON.XXX'

Her reply made him smile: 'ADAM IS STILL UP, WAITING TO SEE YOU. I AM COOKING SAUSAGE AND MASH. DRIVE SAFELY. XXX'

By the time he arrived home, Adam looked very sleepy, so he spent a few precious minutes cuddling him before transferring him into his cot. He sat quietly by the cot. The smell of sausages and onions assaulted his senses, and when he was satisfied that Adam was fast asleep he left the room. He had left the flowers for Zoe in the car, so he went out to get them.

When he gave them to her, she smiled. "What have you done?" she said, jokingly.

Alan became serious, drawing her into his arms he said huskily. "I know I am not a romantic person, but you and Adam are both my world, and I could not manage without you both. All I ever wanted to do was to keep you both safe."

"I know, and I didn't mean to go against you. You were right about leaving Adam with other people. If it's not our family, or a professional like a childminder or nursery, we just shouldn't do it."

Alan hugged her tightly to him before he spoke. "You know how top secret my work is, and I don't usually share much with you, but this time I have to!"

"Go on," said Zoe, quietly. This must be really important. She never usually asked Alan anything. When cases were solved, the newspapers were full of information, but he obviously had something worrying him.

"We have uncovered evidence that Lisa Bryant is an assumed

96

name. Sheila Black is her real name, and fifteen years ago she was convicted for shaking her baby daughter to death."

There was a silence whilst Zoe digested his words. She was amazed that Lisa, who really seemed to love the baby Abby in her care, had done such a terrible thing. But at the same time she felt fear run through her at the thought of what might have happened if Lisa had looked after Adam.

"Oh, my God, Alan, I had no idea about her. She seems devoted to Abby. All I can think is some sort of mental illness caused her to do that."

"Yes, this is what we think, and tomorrow we are going to bring her in for questioning again, because that same mental illness may have caused her to kill Dr Jones."

"It's so awful. How long did she serve for doing it?"

"I won't know any of that until tomorrow. I have set James onto checking it, and because we were both so shocked, I have delayed bringing her in. She was suffering from postnatal depression at the time, so assuming she has gone on to kill the doctor may not be fair, and we were obviously swayed by our emotions. Naturally you won't share any of this. When she is brought in, it will be in the newspapers."

"Of course. Do you know, I can't help feeling very sorry for her. I had a bit of postnatal depression after Adam. It made me feel inadequate as a mother. It can affect people in different ways."

"Yes, but it didn't make you want to kill him!" said Alan, darkly. "There is a difference."

"Well I just hope she got the help she needed. But don't worry, I shall never leave Adam in her care, and I will instruct Helen not to as well when she comes back."

Alan was glad that was over. He had dreaded telling her, but he knew it would go no further. He had made a vow that he would always keep Zoe and Adam safe. Being in the police force made him realise that although most people were law abiding, there were always a few who were not. To have someone so close to his family with such a horrific past had shocked him to the core. But now they were both aware of it, Adam was safe. In view of Zoe's comments, he had decided that when they questioned Lisa, as he thought of her,

e

tomorrow, he would make sure Martha played an active part. He would exercise empathy and not judge Lisa for what she had done in the past. Zoe might well be right, she might have her illness under control, otherwise why would she be living back in society?

Later, when they were in bed, Zoe curled into his back as usual. All the tension had gone from their relationship. No matter what drama tomorrow held for him, tonight he felt peaceful. With that thought in his mind, he drifted off to sleep.

It hadn't taken Lisa long to realise what a perilous position she was in. Firstly, she should not have taken Abby with her, but in the moment, she had not been able to think clearly. Panic had seized her senses. She had always had a duty to keep Abby safe, so there was no way she could have left that house without her. But she soon realised it would not be many hours before the whole of the country would be aware that she had taken Abby, and police would be searching everywhere.

The holiday cottage was set on farmland, well off the beaten track amongst the Essex countryside. The farmhouse had once belonged to Kate's uncle, who had left it to her mother in his will. But it had been too expensive to restore it, and it had become a crumbling ruin. However, the cottage, which had once belonged to the grounds manager in more affluent days, had been looked after and maintained, so it had been used as a quiet retreat and holiday home.

It took Lisa two hours to get there, and then she stopped off at a local shop to get some food and other provisions. She put Abby into the trolley, and walked around quickly, choosing what she needed. She hoped the big dark glasses were enough to hide her features, but every time someone looked at her she froze inside. How long could she get away with this?

By the time she reached the cottage, it was three o'clock. Sally didn't get home from work until six o'clock, so nothing would be suspected until then. She busied herself getting the cottage warm inside, and making up a bed for herself. She didn't have a cot for Abby and there was no way she could go out and buy one, so she would have to make up a little bed for her with cushions. She could lie next to her in the bed. But Lisa wasn't sure about that, she might turn over and suffocate her. Fear ravaged through her at the thought of it.

Abby was restless and fussy, which wasn't like her; it must be the change of routine. So she ran her a warm bath, and she was soon sitting in it playing with a couple of empty yoghurt pots that Lisa had found.

Later, when she had given Abby her bottle, the little girl had fallen asleep next to her on the sofa from sheer exhaustion. Suddenly a text came through on her mobile. It had remained silent all day, and she stiffened with fear when she saw it was Sally.

'HI LISA, WAS WONDERING IF YOU COULD HELP US OUT. DON AND I HAVE TO GO TO A VERY IMPORTANT DINNER IN TOWN TONIGHT. I KNOW IT'S SHORT NOTICE, BUT WOULD YOU BE UP FOR STAYING THE NIGHT?'

This was nothing new from Sally. Lisa had many times dropped everything to stay over with Abby because her parents had such a hectic life, and she had never minded. On this particular evening it was a blessing, as it meant that Abby's disappearance would not be known about until the morning. So she texted back:

'IT'S FINE, SALLY. GO OUT AND ENJOY YOURSELVES, ABBY AND I ARE FINE.'

Then another text came through from Kate, asking if she had arrived safely. Lisa took a chance and rang Kate. She explained that Sally and Don were out for the night, so nobody would know until the morning that Abby was missing.

Kate could not believe her ears. She had not realised that Lisa would take Abby too. With her past record, it was going to cause the police and Abby's parents a lot of worry.

"Lisa, you shouldn't have taken Abby, it will be so much harder for you to lay low. You should have brought her to me."

"I had no choice. No way would I have just gone off and abandoned her, and leaving her with you would have made you an accessory."

Kate realised that it wouldn't take long for the police to find Lisa and bring her in. They would assume, because of her past, that her intentions had been to harm Abby. She felt desperation flowing through her; things always looked bad for Lisa, but Kate knew they were all wrong about her. It wouldn't be long before she was back in police custody, and knowing how badly she had been affected emotionally in the past, Kate wasn't even sure Lisa would be able to cope with it all. She must think of a way to help her out of this tangled mess.

Chapter Thirteen

"Good morning, Kate. Is Lisa here?"

"No, I am afraid she is not."

Kate's owl-like eyes blinked from behind her glasses. They had come for Lisa, and now she had to protect her as best she could.

Alan was trying to understand her expression. She didn't look worried. She had sort of retreated inside herself, almost as though she had no idea of what was going on, but then maybe she didn't.

"Where is she, at work?"

Kate had lain awake all night worrying and wondering how she could best help Lisa, and she had decided that being honest was the only way. She would have to tell them about Lisa's sad past. She could only assume they wanted to take her to the station and question her about her past. The police were very good at making assumptions and, whenever there was a murder, they always wanted to find someone to blame. It was their duty to the public, but not at the expense of Lisa, who had suffered more than enough in the past.

"Can you tell me why you want to see her?"

Alan was getting tired of this stalling. It was almost as if Kate lived in another world. But because he was now very keen to bring Lisa in, he kept his tone polite, hiding the irritation that he felt.

"We want to question her at the station, so I would appreciate if you would tell us where she is."

Kate fixed her eyes on him, and blinked. "Inspector, would you both come in," inclining her head to include Martha. "I will make some tea as I need to explain to you about Lisa."

"No, we don't want tea, this is not a social call!" said Alan, firmly. He did not want to waste any more time, he was now regretting not bringing Lisa in the previous evening after James had found the newspaper cutting.

"I have something to tell you, but not on the doorstep."

Her tone sounded urgent, so Alan nodded to Martha, and they entered the apartment, but stood in the hall.

Kate took a deep breath. It rested with her to try and save Lisa from the situation she was now in. "I presume that when our apartment was searched you found the newspaper cutting behind Lisa's jewellery box?"

Alan hadn't expected her to be so blunt. But it would save time.

"Yes, and after checking further, it appears that Lisa was in a secure unit for five years, receiving treatment for a mental condition which was believed to be the reason which caused the death of her baby daughter."

Kate totally ignored Alan's words and launched into her story.

"I grew up with Lisa, we went to school together and were best friends. We lived up North for a while, but then came to Kent years later. Lisa became involved with Ryan Lee. I could see he was a charmer, and I didn't trust him. Lisa was suffering from postnatal depression after Lily was born, but he did nothing to help her."

She paused and Alan wondered where all this was leading.

"The night it all happened, Lisa told me, and I believe her, that Lily was fretful and she thought she was teething. She had been soothing Lily for hours, then Ryan said why didn't she go up and have a shower, and he would rock Lily off to sleep. As Lisa was coming out of the shower she heard Lily. She was crying really loudly, then she heard Ryan shout, and then silence. When she came into the room, Ryan had disappeared, and when she picked up Lily, she could see she was dead. The shock robbed her of her speech. She just sat holding her, and was still holding her when Ryan came in and called the police. He was such a glib storyteller, both to her and in court, that he was believed, and she got convicted."

"But you have no proof that she didn't kill Lily?"

"I don't need proof, I know Lisa. I wrote to her when she was in the secure unit, and when she came out I suggested she move in with me. My mother had recently died, so she came to Westgate. She had already been given a new identity, but I changed her surname to Bryant, as I hoped it would protect her."

Alan could see that Kate was devoted to Lisa; it was almost as though she was in love with her. Maybe she was, but were they a couple? He wasn't sure about that. They both had their own bedrooms, and judging by Lisa's infatuation for the doctor, she clearly liked men. None of this was helping to find where Lisa was, though. He tried to make his voice sound kind, even though he could feel his patience waning, he just wanted to track down Lisa.

"Kate, this is a very sad story, and I understand that you feel Lisa was innocent of the crime, but we cannot waste any more time. We need to bring her in for questioning."

Kate's owl-like eyes filled with tears, and she hoped she was putting on a good show. "But that is just it. Lisa got wind that you had found her newspaper cutting, she panicked, and she ran off with Abby because she had no one to leave her with." She wrung her hands together in agitation. "Now you will all think Abby is in danger, but I promise you she is not!"

Alan was startled by her words. Not only were they investigating a murder, but now a prime suspect, who had already been convicted of killing her own child, had run off with another baby! Could this investigation get any more stressful?

"Kate, just tell us where she is."

Just at that moment Kate's mobile pinged, and she scanned it to read the message.

"Oh no, we have to save her!" she said, in desperation.

Lisa had been given time to try and work out what to do, now that Sally and Don were out for the night. They would not be home until six o'clock the next day, so had no idea she had taken Abby and run off. But her mind was disturbed when she realised just what she had done. All the nightmares she had suffered when Lily had died came back to haunt her. She had tried to ward it off by taking her medication, but sleep was impossible, and as the night wore on, her fears heightened, and a feeling of hopelessness swept through her. She had tried so hard, with the help of Kate, to lead a normal life, but it hadn't worked. She could not face being locked up again, so there was only one alternative; to end all this misery she had to leave this world, she had to take her own life. Now she had decided to do this, she felt much calmer.

Where she was going, no one could touch her. God knew she had not killed Lily, and she was not a bad person. But first she must make sure that Abby didn't suffer in any way. Dear little Abby. She was sleeping peacefully beside her, but the only person she could ask to help was Kate. Kate would come to the cottage and take care of Abby, and when her car drove up outside, and she knew for sure she was coming in, then she would do it.

"Save her from what?" asked Alan.

"She's going to take her own life. She's had enough!" said Kate in desperation. "She doesn't think anyone will believe her!"

Martha was finding this very hard. Being about to get married and have children of her own, the thought of losing a baby, and being convicted of killing her, was harrowing. Lisa may well have had a mental illness that caused her to behave like that, but if there was the slightest chance that she had not done it, it was up to them to check it out. This development had diverted them slightly from the murder enquiry, but her heart told her she must tell Alan what she was thinking.

"We have to stop her, sir, and we also have to find Ryan Lee, and check him out."

Alan looked at her admiringly. He was thinking the same. It was unthinkable that Lisa may have been wrongly convicted. Being a father himself, he felt great empathy towards Lisa. But they had to find her first.

Kate knew for sure that Lisa would not do anything until she had arrived. Lisa would not leave Abby, but fear and panic rushed through her when she realised she only had to take an overdose of her medication.

"We have to move fast. I know where she is, and I can take you straight to her, but the journey may take a couple of hours."

"Right, give me the address and postcode. We are going to need backup," said Alan, briskly. Finally they were getting somewhere.

Martha made the necessary contacts on her mobile whilst they were travelling to Essex. James and a backup group were going to meet them there. Caution had been urged, as Lisa was in a suicidal state of mind, so they would all regroup outside the cottage and decide the best way forward.

Alan resisted the urge to exceed the speed limit. Kate had texted back and told Lisa she was on her way, and not to do anything silly. However, Lisa's state of mind was such that she felt she could not take any more, and death was her only way out.

Nobody spoke in the car. The atmosphere was tense, and Alan felt relief flood through him when the satnav brought them right outside the cottage garden. Backup had not arrived yet, so Kate suggested that she walk into the grounds alone to see if she could reason with Lisa. She knew that seeing a strange car, which she might even recognise as Alan's, would only stress Lisa even more.

Lisa was sitting with Abby in her arms when she saw Kate come in the gate. Immediately she knew that something was wrong, otherwise she would have driven her car in. She texted her to find out why.

'KATE, WHERE IS YOU CAR?'

Kate responded: 'I WAS GIVEN A LIFT, AND WE ARE HERE TO HELP YOU, LISA. WHERE IS ABBY?

Lisa's mind whirled. Why would anyone give Kate a lift? Why had she even told anyone? How would anyone help her, except by locking her up again? If she had any thoughts about not going through with committing suicide, they had all gone now, and even as she looked out of the window, she could see a group of armed policemen walking towards the cottage.

Kate also saw the backup men advancing behind her, and she knew she had failed, and Lisa would panic now. "Get back!" she screamed at them. But it made no difference, they slowly advanced towards the door of the cottage, passing her, and then she was being told to go back to the safety of the car.

She ran back to the car, and implored Alan to do something. He was now standing at the gate.

"You must let them do their job," he told her.

"But they might shoot her, and there is Abby inside!"

Martha quickly sent a message reminding the backup group about Abby. She hadn't expected this to happen, and she knew if she was in Lisa's place, she would find the sight of these armed men advancing on her terrifying.

"Isn't there another way, sir?" she asked Alan.

Alan turned towards Kate. "Is there a back way in?"

"Yes, over by the hedges." She pointed towards a group of overgrown hedges.

"You keep her talking on the mobile, and I will try to reach her. Martha, tell backup what I am doing."

Martha and Kate watched him slink away, and then Kate's phone pinged again.

'ABBY IS IN HER BUGGY IN THE FRONT ROOM. TAKE CARE OF HER!'

Kate was about to reply, then everything went dead. The phone was now switched off, and she knew why. Just then a voice boomed over a loudspeaker.

"Come out with your hands up. We are armed, resistance is futile. Do not harm the baby."

Kate froze with fear. How could any of them save Lisa now?

Chapter Fourteen

Alan ducked behind the bushes, making his way to the rear of the cottage. If the back door was locked, he was sunk, it was made of solid oak. He pushed at it, but it didn't budge. He had to think quickly. The operation had gone wrong. The backup officers should have met him at the car instead of going straight in. Obviously they had frightened the life out of Lisa, and he would take that up with them later. In the meantime he needed to go in and possibly calm her down.

He ran at the door and tried to budge it with his shoulder, groaning with pain at the impact, as it was not going to move. The kitchen window was tiny, but the window frame was weak, he reckoned he could break that open. He found a piece of rock and threw it at the glass, which shattered immediately, then he wrenched at the wooden frame, and the rotting wood splintered and broke in his hands. But it was still too small to get his lanky figure through.

Alan heard a movement beside him; it was Kate. "Let me come too," she panted, "she might listen to me."

He was about to remonstrate with her for following him into danger, but then he looked at her small frame, Kate was not very tall, but how agile was she? With a bit of help, she might be able to get in the window.

"Right, now you are here, you might as well make yourself useful. You have to try and climb in," he said, gruffly.

*　　*　　*　　*

Inside the cottage, Lisa had made up her mind. Hearing from Kate had made her wish she could just go back home and pick her life up again. But she knew she had messed everything up by running away and bringing Abby with her. She did not in any way blame Kate. She had always tried to protect her. Although only two years older, Kate had cared about her more than her own mother ever had, and if this was what having a sister was all about, even though she was no blood relation, Kate certainly deserved that title. Lisa just accepted that her own life wasn't meant to be a happy one, so it was best to end it now.

Lisa had switched her phone off so she could no longer hear Kate's voice. Abby was strapped safely into her buggy. Lisa had thought about just taking an overdose of her pills, and hopefully she would slip peacefully away, becoming released from all this stress and fear. But she knew that Kate would never just let her go, and they would take her to hospital, then pump her stomach out, and then when she had recovered, she would be locked up again.

There was a very sharp knife in the kitchen drawer, but she wasn't sure if she had the courage to stab herself, and although this had once been a gamekeeper's cottage, there were no guns or rifles here. The only choice she had left was to open the door at the bottom of the very steep stairs, climb up, and then jump out of the bedroom window. The thought of this scared her; it was quite a way down, and maybe she wouldn't die immediately but be in dreadful pain.

Her fears escalated when she heard the glass breaking in the kitchen. They were coming to get her, so she had to move quickly. She opened the door at the bottom of the stairs, and climbed to the top, she had to do it now!

Kate struggled to get through the window. Alan had helped to push her through, but it was very tight. Now she was poised on the windowsill. She had no choice but to tumble head first onto the hard and unforgiving quarry tiled floor. Her hands took most of the fall, and they were hurting, but she ignored the pain. With blood dripping from her fingers, she straightened up and went to draw back the bolt on the back door.

She could now hear Abby in the room beyond, chanting, "Bubbub, mumum," in her baby language. At least she wasn't upset. She called out to Lisa, telling her she was here, and not to worry, but when she heard Lisa's footsteps going up the stairs, she knew what Lisa had in mind.

"She's going to jump!" she screamed at Alan. "We have to stop her!"

Alan crashed the door open at the bottom of the stairs, just in time to see Lisa at the top. He tried to keep his voice calm; he didn't want her death on his conscience.

"Lisa, please don't run away. We only want to help you."

Lisa wanted to believe him, but he was a policeman; as if they were going to help her. They had sent armed police to shoot her, and maybe she should have let them do it. She ignored him and ran into the bedroom. The bedroom here had old fashioned French windows, with a balcony which overlooked the beautiful countryside. All she had to do was climb onto the iron railing at the top, and then in seconds it would all be over and she would be at peace.

With Alan and Kate now gone, Martha took the opportunity to enter through the gates. The armed police officers stayed poised, their guns were loaded and ready, but she noticed they were all looking upwards. Her eyes travelled up and, to her horror, she saw Lisa, poised on an iron railing outside the bedroom window. She knew Alan and Kate would try and stop her from jumping, but would they succeed?

In the midst of all this, she remembered that there was a travelling rug on the back seat of Alan's car. Would it be enough to break Lisa's fall? She spoke quickly to James.

"I'm bringing a rug from the car. It's just a small one, in case she falls."

"Good idea, and someone needs to go in and rescue the baby," said James.

Martha sped off, and was soon back with the rug. Abby had now been brought out of the house in her buggy, and James told Martha to take her to the safety of the car. He then got four other officers to position the rug below the balcony, just in case Lisa tried to jump.

Meanwhile, Alan and Kate had reached the bedroom, only to find Lisa poised on the balcony, her face was ravaged with fear, and it was enough to make Kate break down.

"Lisa, please don't jump, I love you! If you come with us, we can help you."

"How can you help me? No one can, just let me go," pleaded Lisa.

Her words touched Alan. There was something sincere about her, and she really seemed to be speaking from her heart. He spoke slowly and soothingly, moving very slightly towards her.

"Lisa, if you didn't kill your baby, then there has been a huge miscarriage of justice. I promise you that if you come with us we will make it a priority to track down Ryan Lee, and maybe he will admit his guilt."

"You must be joking, he was only too happy for me to take the blame. I always knew he had a temper, but never thought he would lose it with his own baby daughter!" Lisa said bitterly, and her body racked with sobs.

Without even thinking about it, Kate rushed forward to comfort Lisa. She couldn't bear to see Lisa so distraught, and Lisa moved on the narrow parapet, then overbalanced, and with a scream she was gone. Alan went white, and then he heard shouts. He didn't want to look, but when he did he saw the outstretched blanket. Lisa's body hit it, but then bounced out onto the grass. She lay there, not moving, with blood trickling from her head.

Sally was busy in court, and when she had finished, she noticed that she had a voice mail. She had been planning to go home a bit earlier today, after being out all night. She had missed Abby, although she knew she was in very good hands. She sat in her office to listen to her message.

It was from Canterbury police station, asking her to ring them as soon as possible, and apparently they had left it during the morning. Her phone was always switched off when she was in court.

She was totally bemused as to what it could be about, so she rang and explained that she had been without her phone for most of the day. The duty sergeant had been told not to make her duly alarmed, so he chose his words carefully.

"Mrs Mason, we don't wish to alarm you, but do you employ a nanny named Lisa Bryant?"

"Yes, of course. Why? Is Lisa OK? What has happened?"

"Unfortunately Lisa went missing yesterday afternoon, and has taken your daughter Abby with her."

"Well, that is a bit odd. Doesn't anyone know where she has gone?"

Sergeant Potter was surprised that she didn't appear to be upset, but he had been expressly told not to mention anything about Lisa's past because not only would it cause Abby's family much distress, but also it was going to be reinvestigated.

"We do know now that she is at a cottage in Essex. Abby is fine, and DCI Clarke and his WPC are there right now, and will soon be bringing Abby back."

"But what about Lisa, has she had an upset with her sister? This is not like her at all."

"I am afraid that is all I can tell you, madam, but rest assured Abby is safe and well."

"I am going to get on a train and come home right now," said Sally. It had not occurred to her that Abby might not be safe; she had seen how loving and gentle Lisa was to her, and the little girl loved her very much. But she felt concern for Lisa. She had been a good nanny, and something must have caused her to run away. She had to send Don a message because he was at a meeting. She just told him she was going home to see Abby, the rest could be explained later when she had found out properly just what was going on.

Kate had to be physically restrained from touching Lisa whilst they waited for the ambulance. She was distraught with grief, wailing "No, No, No!" over and over again. Martha wasn't there to comfort her, she was in the car with Abby, so Alan did his best to support her, wrapping his arms around her shaking body.

He was so relieved when the paramedics arrived. They had found a very faint pulse, and got her into the ambulance to get her to

111

hospital as quickly as possible. One of them noticed that Kate's hands were covered in blood, and asked her what had happened. Kate had been so wrapped up in Lisa, she had forgotten her own injuries, so they decided to take her in as well. Kate was glad, as she wanted to be as close to Lisa as possible, and she prayed with all her heart that Lisa's life would be spared.

Alan was used to many distressing and frightening situations; it was part of his job. He had dealt with violent men with knives and guns in the past, and managed to survive, but this harrowing story, and the thought that Lisa may have been convicted for a crime she didn't do, had affected him more than physical violence. Maybe it was because he was a father, but the situation had tugged at his heartstrings.

He returned to the car. Martha was sitting in the back holding Abby, who was now fast asleep.

"We need a car seat for Abby," he said. "We need to take her home now."

"It's in Lisa's car. I saw it, but it may be locked."

"No problem," said Alan, triumphantly. After breaking into the cottage, he was sure he could get in the car. "I will just check the key is not in the cottage."

He returned to the cottage. The backup police were dispersing now, so he told them they could go as everything was in hand. He found the car keys on a little table by the door, meaning he didn't have to break into the vehicle. From the car he picked up the bag with Abby's nappies and wipes in, and took them to the car with the baby seat.

As he was driving back he remarked to Martha.

"You know, I've dealt with some evil characters in my time, I've even been attacked, but today has affected me far more, to see that desperate woman wanting to end her life. Something deep inside me makes me think she is telling the truth."

"I am glad you said that, sir, because I think it too. We have to find out for sure."

"Yes," mused Alan, "but I think I will have to pass it on. I have to solve the murder. I didn't expect the investigation to take a twist like this."

"Nor me," admitted Martha. "Who will you pass it on to?"

"I was thinking of James, he is hard working and diligent."

"Do you think that Lisa will survive?" asked Martha, anxiously.

"I sincerely hope so. They don't tell you much, but we will keep in touch. The blue light was flashing when they left."

"They were definitely doing their best, and now we must wait and hope," said Martha.

Chapter Fifteen

Pamela was very anxious to get Ian's funeral over and done with. The cause of death had been confirmed, and his body had now been moved to a chapel of rest, although so far the police had not charged anyone. She had thought that once the funeral was over, Ian's will would be read, and she could then move back into the house, but the solicitor had told her it might take several months. She was sick to death of slumming it at David's bungalow. She wanted her old life back, and this time she would not be tied to a man who was married to his job rather than her. Marty was coming back from University for a holiday, so they could sort out the details together.

Luckily her wise husband had taken out an insurance which would cover the cost of his funeral, which had been good thinking on his part, as neither herself nor David had any money to spare. The thought of staying in the bungalow for several months did not appeal to her, as it seemed David had taken out a loan to pay his back rent, but then she could hardly criticise him, as money and Pamela were soon parted.

She had promised him that she would give him some rent money once she got the inheritance. She didn't want to, but she couldn't afford to rent anywhere whilst she was waiting, and David was also going to let Marty stay there, so she probably would have to part with a few thousand pounds when the time came.

The funeral was going to be very well attended. Her husband had been very well loved by local people, he had been dedicated to his job, and went above and beyond what was expected of him, so had saved lives that might otherwise have been lost. He was also very well respected by other professional people, and known to members of parliament. Luckily the executors of his will, which were the solicitors who held it, had agreed that funds could be released from his insurance to foot the bill.

Pamela would have liked to have held the gathering of people who had attended the funeral at the house, but as it didn't yet belong to her legally, it was decided that Ian's body would be taken from the chapel of rest in a coach with white horses, and it would pass along Station Road, so that local traders as well as the public, could come out and pay their respects. Everyone would then gather after the service at St Augustine's, a very grand building full of character up on the main road. It would be easily big enough to host everyone, although this did not include the general public, because that was impossible. Local churches would all be giving thanks for his life and his work, as Ian Jones was a man that would never be replaced, and not easily forgotten.

Pamela was looking forward to playing hostess and being the centre of attention, seemingly having forgotten that she had left Ian and in time probably would have become his ex-wife. She had used her already stretched credit card to buy a new black dress. She looked very glamorous in it, and she knew it, and she had told herself, for Ian's sake, she must look her best.

Marty arrived home a few days before the funeral, and was keen to help his mother with the arrangements. Ian had been a classical music fan, so he reminded her that they must choose suitable music. Pamela though that a bit stuffy, but allowed Marty to have his say. After the rift between them when she had left Ian, she now wanted to make sure they became close again.

"Have they allowed you access to sort through Dad's clothes and stuff?" he asked.

David suddenly remembered that the police had given him a carrier bag containing the clothes that Ian had been wearing on the night he had died. All tests on them had now been completed.

"That reminds me, the police dropped off a bag containing your dad's clothes earlier today."

"What are we supposed to do with them?" said Pamela. She wasn't fussed about sorting them out, then they would probably need cleaning. "Perhaps we could donate them to charity."

"I'll take care of them," said Marty. Although he loved his mother, her attitude at times got under his skin. Those clothes were the last thing his father had worn, and right now he was not ready to give them to a charity. His dad had always dressed smartly, and he felt he wanted to see and touch those clothes as they were the last link with his father, but his mum would not understand that because she was insensitive.

"They are in the cupboard in the hall," explained David. He was glad that Marty wanted the clothes, as he had not been sure what to do with them.

Marty went out into the hall, and took the carrier bag out of the cupboard. It felt sacred to him, so he shut himself in his bedroom to examine the contents. Pamela had by now gone to have a shower, so was clearly not interested, and David had settled himself in front of the TV.

His dad had been wearing light cotton trousers and an open necked shirt, and he had obviously changed out of his suit when he came home. Also in the carrier was another small bag, and inside it was his dad's wallet. Inside it there were various cards. His bank account had been frozen, so they could just be cut up and put in the bin. There was just £20 in there, but that was not surprising, as like everyone else, his dad had changed to paying by card for everything.

As he shuffled through the cards, he noticed a photograph between them. It was of a young woman, probably in her early twenties. There was something familiar about he; it was almost as if he already knew her, which felt strange. On the back was written: LOVE HOLLY.XX

His mind whirled when he saw that. Surely his dad had not had a secret girlfriend. She looked young enough to be his daughter. But why shouldn't he? After his mum had so cruelly left him, he had been a free agent.

Under the inscription was a mobile phone number, and he felt like ringing it. Obviously she must have read about his father's death in the newspapers, and if his dad had carried a signed photo of her around with him he must have cared about her, so she should be invited to the funeral. Naturally his mum would not like it, but it wasn't all about her, it was about his dad.

Her voice came over the line. "Hi, it's Holly."

Marty drew a deep breath. He was sticking his neck out he knew, but his curiosity had now got the better of him. "Hi Holly, you don't know me, I am Marty, son of Ian Jones."

There was a definite pause while Holly digested his words. She had not expected to hear from her dad's family. He had spoken about telling Marty, but it was to be in time because it would be a shock. He had not mentioned his estranged wife Pamela at all, but Holly guessed that Pamela would not be interested in hearing about a child that had been conceived before Ian had even met her, and then grown up without even knowing he was her father.

Her heart was beating fast when she realised she was talking to her own brother. He sounded nice too, and her heart glowed.

"Hi Marty, I was so very sorry to hear about your dad. He was a good man, and did not deserve that."

"Yes, that is true. I wonder, Holly, could we meet for a coffee or something?"

"Yes, of course."

"Where is good for you? I don't even know where you live."

"I have a flat in Canterbury. You are welcome to come to mine for coffee if you like."

"Splendid. If that is OK then, I can be there in about half an hour."

"If you are coming by car you can pull around the back." She then gave him the address and postcode.

"Many thanks."

Marty grabbed his car keys, then called out that he would be out for a couple of hours. David barely raised his head from the TV. Marty was twenty, not a child now, and could come and go as he pleased. His mother was still in the shower, and when she came out she would probably spend the rest of the evening in her own room. She had her own TV, and was not into the sort of movies David liked to watch.

Marty drove past St Nicholas at Wade, then picked up the road that passed by Grove Ferry, eventually arriving at the level crossing at Sturry. He had to wait there for about ten minutes, and he was tapping his fingers impatiently. Holly's flat was in the heart of Canterbury, just where the roads were very narrow, and not far from the Cathedral. When he arrived, he pulled round the back and found a parking space, and then pressed the buzzer.

Holly was nervous about meeting Marty. She was not sure what his reaction would be, but the thought of having a brother spurred her on. She loved her sister, but had always known the man she had believed was her father until recently, had very little time for her. She had agonised about it for years, wondering why he didn't like her, so when her mother had explained who her real father was, it all made sense.

She wasn't sure she could handle another rejection, but when she opened the door to him, she knew right away it would be all right. Marty smiled at her, and it lit up the whole of his face. He was like a younger version of his father. Very handsome, without appearing to be vain, with kind eyes. She could immediately feel a connection with him.

"Do come in," she said hospitably, leading him into a cosy living room. He could see the flat was very small, but it felt homely. He could see why his dad had liked her. She was charming, with beautiful expressive eyes, and she shyly returned his smile.

"I hope you don't mind me coming to see you," he said.

"Not at all. Would you like tea or coffee?" she asked, smiling.

Holly wasn't bothered about a drink herself. She had just met her brother, first impressions were important, and she liked him. But she wasn't sure he had realised. She could no longer keep it to herself.

"Marty, I have always wanted a brother, but I had no idea you would come looking for me."

As he looked at her, it all made sense. The closeness he felt already, her likeness to him, same colour hair and eyes, and the age gap between her and his father. Of course, she was his sister, maybe a few years older.

"My sister?" he said, wonderingly.

"Did you not realise?"

"I should have done," he admitted, feeling a bit embarrassed. "I found a photo of you in my dad's wallet, with your phone number, and I am afraid curiosity got the better of me."

Holly then went on to explain how her mother had told her about Ian just before she died, and her determination to find him. She also explained how she had felt rejected by the man she had believed to be her father, and Marty's heart went out to her. Not only had she lost her mother in tragic circumstances just last year, but after discovering her true father, she had lost him too. It made him all the more determined that Holly should be at the funeral to say goodbye to her father if she wished.

After she had finished explaining, he gave her a hug. "Holly, what a bad year it's been for you. Would it make you feel better to come to dad's funeral and say goodbye to him?"

Holly was taken aback. She had not for one moment expected to be asked. She explained to Marty that Ian had wanted to tell him about her, just before he died, but he had not mentioned telling Pamela.

"I would love to come, but I do not want to upset your mother. It might come as a huge shock to her, although he knew mummy before he ever met her," she explained.

"Don't worry about my mother. I will explain it to her," said Marty, firmly.

"Well, if you are sure."

"Yes, I am sure, and you can come round and meet her before the funeral so you are not complete strangers."

Holly felt a glow of happiness pass through her. Losing her dad after finding him had devastated her, and now she was carrying his grandchild. She was not ready to tell Marty that yet, she didn't want to sound like a charity case, but she felt honoured that she would be allowed to go to the funeral. She recognised in Marty the same kind and caring nature that his dad had possessed.

"You have just made my day!" she said, smiling. "And now I am going to put the kettle on."

Chapter Sixteen

"She's not coming to the funeral, it will make us a laughing stock!"
This was exactly the reaction Marty had expected from his mother.
Pamela would never want another female stealing her thunder. In
the past Marty would not have argued, his nature was always non
confrontational, but since his father had died, he had changed. He
had become his own person, and he wasn't going to let his mother
always call the tune. He couldn't help wondering if his dad had been
less compliant with his mother, maybe she would have respected
him more and not left him. Who knew?

"No one will laugh, and we don't have to say she is my sister. Not
that it's anyone else's business, but she is part of the family and
deserves the chance to say goodbye to dad."

"You can't suddenly produce her from out of the blue and expect
no one to take any notice," said Pamela, firmly.

But Marty was even firmer. Please or offend, he was going to
speak his mind.

"Mother, don't be such a hypocrite, you ran off with the gardener,
everyone knew, and Dad must have felt embarrassed. Now you are
acting as if you were still with Dad. Holly is going to sit down the
front with us, and she is coming to the meal afterwards, too. Dad
knew her mother before he ever met you, and Holly was the result.
She is simply his daughter from a previous relationship who has
come to celebrate her father's life. Now get used to it!"

Pamela looked at him in horror. David kept absolutely silent, he wasn't going to be bogged down by this. Marty had always been such an easy-going boy, what had happened? But Pamela did love him, and she wanted to heal the rift that leaving Ian had caused. Marty had totally refused to meet Stewart, but she was glad now, as Stewart was history.

She wasn't used to having anyone stand up to her. Pamela always seemed to get her own way. Ian had been easy to manipulate, but Marty wasn't growing up to be as easy-going. Part of her didn't want to back down, but she couldn't help admiring him for staying strong. Maybe it wouldn't be a huge drama if the girl came. She had always wished that Marty would have a sister, but it had never happened.

"Well, I need to meet her first," she said reluctantly.

"Yes, she can pop round tomorrow," said Marty, touching her shoulder gently. "It will be OK, Mother. I will make sure."

He had the same charm that had first attracted her to his father. He looked so like him, and it brought memories back of when they had been happy. When Marty smiled it reached his eyes. Her son was a genuine caring young man. She felt proud of him.

Now having succeeded he felt relief flood through him. He had expected his mother to flounce out of the room and sulk, and he had been a bit cruel in mentioning her affair with Stewart, but it had reminded her that she was not in a position to judge anyone else. The wise thing now would be to change the subject.

"Have you made a list of all the guests. I guess the church will be full."

"I have, and it's a long one. We have four people wanting to speak about him, and a couple of MPs who want to come as well as everyone else."

"Sandra and the children want to come," said David, anxiously, knowing it would be a difficult day for him.

"Of course they do, it's for Dad," said Marty proudly.

"Do you think I should ask Kate, the housekeeper?" said Pamela, sounding disdainful.

Marty hid a smile. His mother with her council house roots didn't want the housekeeper to come; it was quite amusing. "I definitely think we should invite Kate, once we both move into the house we will need her again, and she has always been a good housekeeper."

f

"I suppose so. At least we don't have to put up with loopy Lisa."

"That is not very kind. By all accounts she is lucky to be alive," said Marty.

"Yes, but nobody knows what happened."

"Kate told me. Apparently Lisa was hit by a car. She suffered head trauma, which affected her ability to walk and talk. She had been in hospital for a month, then she was moved to the rehabilitation centre at the cottage hospital in Whitstable. She is doing well now, remembering who she is, and why she is there, with lots of physio to help her recover and get back to normal."

"I didn't realise she was that bad, but it's good she is getting better," said Pamela, suitably chastened. But she still couldn't help feeling relieved that Lisa wouldn't be able to come. She had always been such a drama queen.

Alan now had Natalie working with him whilst newly married Martha was on her honeymoon. Natalie was kept very busy, as it had been decided that when Alan needed her for interviews, she would accompany him, but when he was working in his office, she could partner James. Alan had explained that he had to carry on investigating the murder, but James was going to find out as much as he could about Ryan Lee.

It hadn't taken James long to discover that Ryan Lee had been convicted for armed robbery in 2010. He had been released from prison in 2018. His current address was in Margate, and this was a surprise, that he was living so close to Westgate. Presumably Lisa did not know that. He showed the photo of him to Natalie. His age was now thirty-eight, he had jet black hair and very penetrating blue eyes; the sort of person that left an impression on you.

When Natalie saw it, she couldn't help noticing how handsome he was. No wonder Lisa had fallen hook, line and sinker for him. He was Irish, so she imagined he was probably full of the blarney. A plan was forming in her mind, but as she was a junior WPC, having not been in the force for long, she was not sure how James would react to it, or even whether Alan would allow it to happen.

"We need to go and interview him at Margate. We have to try and help Lisa, but I don't see how we can get him to admit he killed Lily in a fit of temper," said James, thoughtfully.

"Maybe there is another way," said Natalie, mysteriously. "Will you hear me out?"

Alan was still in two minds about whether Lisa was guilty or not of murdering Ian Jones. In his heart he really wanted her to be innocent both of the doctor's murder and her baby Lily. It was now over a month since she had fallen out of the window, and for a while she had not been expected to recover.

But she had, and now she was getting help to walk and talk again, and doctors were optimistic that she would make a full recovery. But the sad part of this was that when she was OK again, she would be moved to a psychiatric unit, and he had been told quite frankly by Kate, that it was the thought of being locked up again that had made her want to end her life.

He had relied on James to find out more about Ryan Lee. If they could somehow get proof that he had killed his own baby in a fit of temper, Lisa might just think her life was worth living again. The courts had not succeeded in convicting him, and certainly if he was interviewed there was no way he was going to admit it. Alan felt revulsion towards the man.

Alan was not surprised to hear that Lee had been convicted of armed robbery and served time. It was a shame that had happened after Lily died, because the court might not have been so ready to believe him over his daughter's death. It was surprising that he now lived at Margate, so close to Westgate.

His mobile rang, and he picked it up quickly. It was just after nine o'clock, and he had planned to read through all the notes again about the suspects, to see if anything in particular stood out for him.

"Sir, we have just taken a call from the QEQM. An elderly lady was found dead in her armchair, her body was taken to the hospital, and it looks like she was poisoned."

"Who found her?"

"Her daughter; she dialled 999. It was first assumed she had died of old age, as she was ninety, but now the hospital suspect foul play."

123

"OK, do you know if the daughter is at the hospital?"

"Yes, I believe so, sir. She is very shocked about it all."

"OK, I am on my way."

When he arrived at the hospital, Alan was immediately shown into the relatives' room, where a nurse was doing her best to comfort a lady who was possibly in her mid sixties. She was slim and slight, with grey hair cut short, and had obviously had a huge shock, as fear and worry lined her face.

"Good morning, Inspector. This is Karen Wilcox, her mother Eva Scott has passed away, and naturally Karen is in shock," the nurse said gently, her arm still supporting the lady.

The lady looked so fragile, and Alan felt so sorry for her. Discovering a death was always unpleasant. She wiped her eyes. "She was fine yesterday. We had a cup of tea together, and then I went home about five o'clock. Was it a heart attack?"

It was obvious that Karen had not been told as yet, and Alan wanted to find out more about it. If the nurse knew, she wasn't saying.

"May I call you Karen?" she nodded. "I am so sorry for your loss. Don't worry, we intend to find out the cause of your mother's death. Did she have any health problems?"

"She was ninety, you know, but she still lived in her bungalow independently. Didn't need carers. She used to come shopping with me. She wasn't on any medication, just used to say her limbs were a bit stiff sometimes when she got up in the morning."

"I can imagine it was a huge shock for you. Would you like us to arrange for someone to give you a lift home?" he asked kindly. Surely Karen had not driven in?

"I will be OK. I have rung my husband, and he is coming to collect me, but thank you anyway, Inspector."

Karen, in the midst of her grief, noticed the kindness in his tone. She felt comforted by his words, and she had a feeling of trust in him; his attitude was empathetic.

"As soon as I know the cause of death I will pay you a visit. Can you give me your home address?" he asked gently, wondering how he could break that sort of news to her. Nobody of any age, especially at ninety, should have to die in such a horrific way. Whoever was doing this was just so sick!

124

Karen produced a business card. She was a physiotherapist, and he noted that her address was also in Westgate.

"You live near to your mother, then?"

"Yes, two roads away. Mother's bungalow is along the street just past the block of flats. It's the same street that Dr Jones lived in."

"I see, thank you very much."

After he had been directed to the morgue, Alan was greeted by Tom.

"Glad you are here. This poor little lady was poisoned, just like the good doctor!"

"Poor little soul. Ninety years old, what a way to die. We will catch the bastard!" said Alan vehemently, wondering what sort of creature could be behind this.

"It's exactly a repeat of what happened to Dr Jones. Given Valium first to make her sleepy, then the poison poured down her throat."

"OK, that is what I needed to know," said Alan.

As he drove back from the hospital, when the shock had worn off, he felt even more determined to bring this evil person to justice. Whoever it was had now committed two vile murders.

But one thing was obvious, Lisa was innocent, probably of both murders, as she was presently in hospital. So if she wasn't a murderer, maybe she hadn't killed her baby, and her instability was caused because she was a grieving mother, and also a wronged one. He vowed to get justice for her.

Chapter Seventeen

"Do I look OK?

Pamela glanced nervously at Marty. She had competition in the form of a twenty-something girl. She already disliked the thought of playing second fiddle to her, but Marty had been adamant, and she didn't want to lose her son's respect. For his sake only, she would be polite to Holly; she was Marty's sister, and her stepdaughter.

"Mother, you look fine, you always do. I think when you meet Holly you will realise how nice she is."

Pamela smoothed an imaginary crease from her silk pleated skirt, and Marty hid a smile. His mother would never change. Everything she wore was expensive, she didn't do casual clothes. Even if she was out in the kitchen preparing a meal or washing up, which was not very often, she could still be relied on to be wearing silk blouses and tailor made clothes. She didn't buy anything off the peg.

Today she had a pale blue silk skirt with knife pleats, and a crisp white blouse with frills round the sleeves and neck. Her nails were painted scarlet to match her lipstick, and she also had eye make-up on. She sat nervously on the couch, twisting the folds of her skirt. She jumped when the doorbell went. "It's OK, Mother, I will get it," said Marty. He was sure that Holly was feeling just as nervous as his mother was about the meeting.

Holly stood on the doorstep. At four months pregnant she had now managed to overcome her morning sickness and dizziness. She had been to the hospital and had her scan, and been assured that all was well. It had taken all her courage to tell her boss at work she was pregnant, but as her stomach was now becoming rounder, it seemed best to speak about it now. He had been OK about it. She had never discussed her private life with him, so no doubt he thought she had a boyfriend, and she wanted to keep that part of her life private.

She did intend to tell Marty, but not today, not in front of his mother. She didn't expect or want anything from him, but emotional support would help her from feeling totally alone, if he was prepared to give it to her. She had dressed in a loose smock type dress that hid her expanding waist, unlike modern pregnant women, who tended to wear tight tops and proudly show off their bump. Maybe in time she could do that, but right now, because she so wanted to go to the funeral, discretion was the better part of valour.

Marty opened the door with a wide smile on his face, and she was fleetingly reminded of his father, who she had found to be the kindest man she had ever met. Marty kissed her cheek gently.

"Great to see you, Holly. Come and meet mother."

"Hi Marty," she said, and then she felt her throat close up with fear when she saw Pamela behind him. She found herself tongue-tied as she looked at her. She was very beautiful, her skin looked young, and she was wearing beautiful clothes. Holly felt completely out of her depth.

Pamela had made up her mind that she would not like Holly. Her husband's daughter by an ex-girlfriend, probably young and beautiful, would try to steal her thunder. Oh no, she would hate her! But when she looked at Holly, she could see her resemblance to Marty. The girl was clearly shy, she was not full of herself as Pamela had expected, and there was a gracefulness about her that Pamela liked, and honesty and kindness shone out of her just as it had with Ian. Although she didn't like to admit it to herself, there was nothing about Holly she could dislike. There was also uncertainty in Holly's eyes, as if she was wondering if she would be accepted as Marty's sister. And, for once in her life, it wasn't all about Pamela. Something about this girl had touched her heart, and she could see why Marty had already formed a bond with her. Pamela smiled graciously.

"Hello Holly, Marty has told me all about you. Do come in and sit down."

Holly felt as if she was in a daze. Everyone was being so kind to her, she had not had much of that lately, and it felt wonderful. She sat down on the sofa next to Pamela, and before she knew it she was admiring Pamela's outfit, and they were talking about fashion. Having seen they were getting on well, Marty went into the kitchen to put the kettle on. David was out there on his laptop, and he was in a good mood, as he had just booked himself a job interview for the next day, so Marty asked him to come in and meet Holly.

Up until now, David had kept out of the discussion about Holly attending the funeral. He knew that it was not what Pamela wanted, and whilst she was staying with him, David wanted a quiet life. But to his amazement, Marty had stood up to his mother, and insisted she meet the girl, and seeing as she was his niece, David was curious to meet her too.

He shut his laptop down, smiling. "Yes, of course." When he entered the lounge he could see the two women in earnest conversation, which surprised him. He always got the impression that Pamela didn't much like other women, as she preferred to be the one in the limelight.

"There you are, David. This is your niece Holly, she's going to join us at the funeral," said Pamela hospitably. He was momentarily taken aback. Had his sister-in-law had a brain transplant? She had certainly changed her tune.

"Welcome Holly, that is good news to hear. You ladies keep chatting and I will go and help Marty with the tea. We are modern men in this house," he said, winking. Holly laughed, she felt so welcome, and even friendly vibes seemed to be coming from Pamela. Had she finally found some family of her own?

By the end of her time there, Holly felt much more confident. It had not been the ordeal she had been expecting. What a nice family they seemed. Her yearning for a family was so strong now, after losing her own mother, and then finding Ian, her real father, only to lose him too. Now a new baby was growing inside her, and it was part of this family. She wondered how they would feel about it.

When they started to make arrangements for the funeral, which

128

was two days away, Marty told her she would be walking with himself and his mother into the church, and, to her surprise, Pamela confirmed it. So by the time she went home, everything had been finalised. She felt she belonged to this family, and it was a new feeling for her.

Marty was delighted at just how charming his mother had been. He knew she had it in her, as she had always been a loving mother to him, so he gave her a hug of appreciation. "Thanks for that, Mother, you have been a star!"

Pamela liked his approval, and deep down inside she liked the idea of him having a sister. She had always wanted a daughter too, a little girl to dress in pretty clothes, and at the age she was now, to go shopping with, to share mother and daughter lunches out, trips to the spa and hairdressers. And she didn't feel threatened in any way by Holly. She could sense the girl's vulnerability, and found it endearing. Pamela's position would remain unchallenged, so, as far as she was concerned, Holly was now one of the family.

Kate smiled at the nurse who opened the door to her. "Good afternoon, I have come to see Lisa. How is she?"

"About the same," smiled the nurse, leading her towards Lisa's bedroom. "She didn't want to come into the lounge."

The bedroom doors were always kept open during the day, and Kate spotted Lisa. She was slumped in her armchair, and there was a complete attitude of defeat. Kate was praying that the news she had would lift her spirits, and give back some meaning to Lisa's life. She slid inside, putting her arms round Lisa's shoulders to gently hug her.

"Hello, Lisa, I am going to pull up the other chair."

"Would you like some tea and cakes?" said the nurse, kindly. She was a tiny woman, very slight in build, but empathetic in her manner.

"That sounds lovely!" said Kate warmly, lowering herself into the chair next to Lisa.

After the nurse had gone, Kate spoke to Lisa. "Lisa, I have something really important to tell you."

"What?" asked Lisa. She was past caring about anything. She knew she had lost weight, and she didn't really care. They had got her walking again at the cottage hospital, and now she was here, not totally locked up, but at the same time with no freedom to be able to go home again.

"There has been another murder, and the circumstances are the same, so you are off the hook, as they know you couldn't have done it."

Lisa felt a glimmer of hope inside her, but then she shrugged her shoulders. "But they still think I am a child murderer," she said, bitterly.

"I don't think they do!" exclaimed Kate. "They have found out that Ryan has been in prison for armed robbery, and that he has a temper, and the inspector told me they were going to leave no stone unturned in trying to prove your innocence. So you must be patient, as it might not be too long before you can come home."

Lisa felt hope flooding through her. She couldn't help wondering how they would get Ryan to confess, but the knowledge that they believed her was heartening. The nurse appeared again briefly with a tea tray with cakes and biscuits.

"Now get some of these cakes down you," ordered Kate, smiling. "I want to see some more flesh on your bones."

James wanted to know more about Ryan Lee. Now he was out of prison, was he keeping his nose clean? His flat at Margate had been under surveillance, and he seemed to lead a pretty boring life. He didn't have a job, and there was a young woman living with him, probably about thirty, always dressed in jeans or track suits, with her hair in a ponytail. She went out daily in an overall, and appeared to be some sort of home help. Ryan liked his beer, and could be spotted about three times a week sitting on a stool at Sheldon's, the local pub.

Maybe he shouldn't have done, but James disliked the look of Ryan intensely. The bloke was clearly popular with women. He had dark hair and very arresting eyes; nothing seemed to escape him. He came from Ireland, had a very strong Irish accent, and he chatted them all up. His domestic goddess never came with him, but maybe she would cramp his style. He had an eye for every woman that came into the bar, so clearly he wouldn't be able to keep it in his trousers if any of them were willing to allow him to seduce them.

He explained all this to Natalie in much politer terms. Martha was now back at work, the honeymoon was over, so Natalie was working with him again as his partner. Alan and Martha were trying to leave no stone unturned in finding the killer, and there was pressure even more now that there had been another victim.

"Well, as sorry as I am about the murder of Eva, it does mean that Lisa didn't do it, as she was in hospital. So chances are she didn't murder the doctor either, and that also means she is simply a grieving mother, who deserves us to get justice for her!" said Natalie, firmly.

James looked over at her, determination written all over her face. Natalie may have only been in the force for a while, but she was keen and definitely her own woman. She was friendly with Martha, who also felt strongly about how Lisa had suffered, and they were keen to support someone of their own sex who they felt had been greatly misunderstood.

"Yes, you are right," said James. "It's knowing how to do it."

Natalie sprang out of her chair, her face alight with animation.

"Ryan Lee has a weakness for women. Get him drunk, and he might spill the beans."

"It's not that easy, people like him will smell I am a policeman from a mile off."

"I meant a honey trap. He won't know that I am!"

James stared at her. Natalie looked younger than her twenty years; more like a teenager. She was a beautiful girl. Her red gold hair was long and straight, it flowed around her shoulders, and she sported a full fringe which framed her tawny and expressive eyes. She was tall and very slim with beautiful shapely legs, and when she was out of her police uniform, she was a stunner. James felt like an older brother, and he wanted to keep her safe.

"No Natalie, he is a dangerous man. I can't have you risking your safety."

"It's the only way, you know it. Sir is relying on us to find out if Ryan killed baby Lily."

Her last words resonated with James. He had promised Alan he would do his utmost, and so far all they had achieved was finding out that Ryan Lee was a lazy unemployed bum, who was more than likely living off benefits with a girlfriend who was keeping him.

"You can sit in the pub and chat to him. You are not to leave it, or go off anywhere with him. See if you can find out his girlfriend's name, then I can check her out. Anyone living with him isn't going to be a Florence Nightingale. I will be sitting over the other side, keeping an eye on you both."

Natalie smiled happily. This was going to be fun. Taking down a man who had got away with murder, literally, and righting a wrong for Lisa, who had suffered for over fifteen years. Oh yes, she was going to enjoy this.

Alan felt like he was starting the investigation all over again. With another murder in very similar circumstances, and clearly not committed by Lisa, much to his relief, he had to re-examine the evidence. Somebody either in the Jones family, or close enough to know them, had laced the whisky decanter with Valium, and when the doctor was drowsy, forced him to drink neat weedkiller. Surely these could only be the actions of a psychopath. Now, with the death of Eva, who would stand to gain from it? The only person to gain from the death of Eva was her daughter, but she had no connection with the Jones family whatsoever.

Forensic experts, when checking the murder scene, had found traces of Valium in a teacup. Clearly a cup of tea had been made either by Eva, or by the murderer. This would indicate surely that she knew the person who killed her. She might even have let them in.

Alan returned to Karen's home, accompanied by Martha. He now had to tell her the grim manner of her mother's death. Karen lived in a detached house, just a short walk from her mother's bungalow. As they opened the gate, he took in the spaciousness of the plot, the well tended garden, and beyond the hedge he could see the top part of an inside swimming pool.

"Wow, very nice," was Martha's response.

Karen opened the door and showed them into a small room with a computer in, and bookcases dominated all the walls. Beyond that was a hall with a luxurious fitted carpet and stairs leading up to another floor. The wallpaper was elegant, blinds were positioned at every window, and there was an air of opulence throughout. Clearly Karen did not need her mother's home or money to improve her life, she was surrounded by beauty and elegance.

"Good afternoon, Detective Inspector, can I get you both a cup of tea or coffee?" Karen smiled at Martha to include her, and she returned her smile.

"This is Martha, my partner," said Alan. "Don't worry about the tea, we are fine."

This surprised Martha. Alan was always ready for a cuppa, but she guessed he was feeling nervous about explaining how her elderly mother Eva had died. They both sat down on the sofa, and Karen perched herself on a nearby chair, looking expectantly at Alan.

Alan cleared his throat. "I am afraid your mother did not die from a heart attack, she was poisoned."

Karen stared wonderingly at him whilst she tried to digest his words. Then she burst out angrily.

"It's not possible; a dear sweet little lady of ninety. Everyone loved her. Who would want to poison my mother?"

"I agree," said Alan wearily. Sometimes this job really got inside his head. Who could be that sick? "Whoever did this had to be mentally sick, and we have to work out why they would choose your mother. It wasn't robbery, as nothing was stolen."

"Mummy didn't just open the door to anyone, you know!" said Karen, fiercely fighting back tears.

"I am sure she didn't," said Martha soothingly. "Apart from yourself, does anyone else have a door key and access to your mother's bungalow?"

"Only Tiffany."

"Who is Tiffany?"

"Mummy's cleaner. She comes to clean every Friday. I think her surname is Preston."

"So she would be due to come tomorrow then?" said Alan thoughtfully.

Suddenly Karen gave a gasp, and put her hands over her mouth, wailing, "Oh no, oh no," and rocking herself backwards and forwards.

"Whatever is the matter?" asked Martha, eyeing her with unease.

"It's my fault Mummy's dead. Last week Tiffany stole a £20 note from her purse, it was pathetic, and I was so angry. Mummy said to let her keep it if she was that poor, but I wasn't having any of it. I went round to the place where she lived in Margate, and told her never to come back, and not to expect a reference. Obviously it must have been her. With Mummy dying so suddenly, I had forgotten."

"OK, just give me her address in Margate, and we will pay her a visit," said Alan grimly.

Chapter Eighteen

Pamela was very pleased at how well the funeral had gone off. The coach and horses had been a really elegant send off for Ian, and many people had lined the high street when it passed through to pay their respects. The sun had shone, so her hair and make-up had remained intact, and she felt she had been a good hostess afterwards when everyone had gathered together for the sit-down meal.

It was almost as if she and Ian had never been parted. Everyone treated her as if they were still together. Pamela had realised that Holly might feel awkward, but with Marty as well to help, they both made sure she felt included as part of the family, sitting together in the church, and again at the sit-down meal.

Pamela didn't really understand herself at all. Having always been a selfish woman, the fact that Holly brought out a protective instinct inside her made no sense. Maybe she felt that Holly was the daughter she had never had, but she was grateful now that Marty had brought them together. She was ready to do mother and daughter things with her, and after being away from her home for a year, she realised just how important family ties were.

Soon after the funeral, Holly had told her about her pregnancy, and already Pamela felt excited. She was expecting a daughter, which meant another female in the family. Pamela was looking forward to showing her new step-granddaughter off, especially when people would tell her she looked far too young to be a grandmother. As well as all this excitement, the solicitor said Ian's will was going to be read, which meant that soon Pamela and Marty would be able to move back into the house. Pamela had told Holly, as it was such a big house, if she wanted to move in until such time as she could get back on her feet and return to work, she would be welcome.

Marty was delighted to see how much good knowing Holly had brought out in his mother. She had become far less selfish, so his stand had been worth it. It had actually not only made his mother realise he wasn't a push-over, but she respected him as an adult, which made their bonds of love even tighter. Pamela was changing into a much nicer person. The only sad thing about it was, he wished she had done it for his father, but it was too late for that. And his dad would never see his grandchild.

Natalie had put on a dress this evening, which was unusual. When off duty, she usually wore casual clothes like shorts and T-shirts, or jeans in the winter. Hanging in her wardrobe was a honey-coloured sheath dress. It was tight, showing the contours of her body, with a slit up the side to reveal her shapely legs. It also had a low neckline. She had bought it to wear to a Christmas party last year, but then found out the other girls were going casual, mostly in trousers. She was at an age where she didn't want to stand out as being different from the others, or considered odd, so it had remained in her wardrobe, and she had gone in jeans and a shirt blouse. But tonight she thought she might have a use for the dress. After all, she had to make an impact to encourage Ryan Lee to notice her.

Her red-gold hair was shimmering, and her make-up had been carefully applied.

James felt full of misgivings when he saw her. She was only a kid, just twenty, and dressed like that she was offering Lee her goodies on a plate. The man was a womaniser, but if he got wind of what Natalie was doing, he could turn nasty. James wasn't sure that Alan would approve of this method of exposing Lee, but Natalie was adamant, and he knew that if he tried to stop her, it was likely she would do it on her own anyway. At least with him around to keep an eye on her, she would be safer.

He entered the room after her and sat at the back of the bar. The barman brought the pint of beer over that he had ordered. Whilst up there, he was aware that she was perched on a stool, but he made sure not to look her way at all. He had no idea if anyone in this bar was connected with Lee, so he had to pretend he didn't know Natalie.

Natalie was sipping a glass of wine, and as the cool liquid slipped down her throat, it made her feel good. She wasn't in a relationship with anyone right now, so she didn't have to make any explanations. She hadn't told her parents because she knew they wouldn't like it, but, at twenty, she felt she knew her own mind. Knowing how Lisa must have suffered, firstly by being blamed for her baby's death, then being locked away in a secure unit, when what she should have had was bereavement counselling, was what was driving her on. She wanted justice for Lisa. There was no room in her mind for the possibility that Lisa was guilty of shaking Lily to death, and Natalie was convinced that if she could get Ryan Lee to talk, he would admit it.

The door opened several times, men stopping for a quick pint on their way home from work, and because she was a female sitting on her own, she attracted a lot of looks, some even smiled and tried to make conversation with her. But none of them were Ryan Lee. She sat there for nearly an hour, but it seemed that he wasn't coming into the bar tonight.

She ordered another glass of wine, and by the time she had finished it she was feeling quite light-headed. As she decided to go, the barman said sympathetically, "Have you been stood up, love? He's not worth it!"

Natalie tossed her head. She was annoyed because it was an evening wasted, and she would have to return again. "Nobody stands me up!" she said haughtily, sliding down from the bar stool, and trying to pull her dress over her exposed leg.

James saw it all, but he knew he couldn't come over and help her. He hoped when she got outside she would text him, then he could see she got home safely. He watched helplessly, as she made rather unsteady progress towards the door. And just as she got there, it opened, and she practically fell into the arms of Ryan Lee, who was entering the pub.

*   *   *   *

137

Alan had put in an appearance at the funeral of Ian Jones. Pamela had expressed a wish for him to come, so together with Martha they had been at the church. There had been a large gathering, Dr Jones had been such a part of the community, and beside that, some influential people in high places had known him, so one of the speakers, who highlighted his work of serving his community, had been a prominent MP. Alan and Martha had not gone to St Augustine's afterwards, as they felt that should only be family and close friends.

The thing that Alan was most surprised about was the close relationship between Pamela and her stepdaughter Holly. He would have expected Pamela to snub her and also reject her, but no, she had made her part of the family. And because a policeman always has a suspicious mind, he wondered if they were both involved in the doctor's death, but then reasoned with himself, why would Pamela join forces with her at all? She stood to inherit half of everything, with Marty getting the other half. Believe it or not, it would appear that including Holly as part of the family had been a kind gesture, so he had now revised his opinion of Pamela. She did have some good in her, after all.

When he spoke to Marty it made more sense. He told him how he had insisted on his mother being charitable towards Holly because he wanted her to come to the funeral. It seemed Holly herself had won Pamela over with her unassuming and sweet nature. It was hard to find any fault with the girl. She was polite, and just so grateful to be liked. But then he remembered she had had a difficult time before she had found Ian, so now that she was being shown kindness and respect, it must have meant such a lot to her.

Of course, none of this was helping him find the murderer. With another person now poisoned, living in the same street, it made him feel the culprit must be close by. What was he missing? He couldn't actually think of any possible suspects for the murder of Eva. No burglary had been committed, and it just made no sense at all. Was the cleaner, Tiffany, who had stolen £20, capable of murdering Eva?

"Martha, the Bryants have lived in Westgate for over ten years now, so maybe we should go and see how much Kate knows about Eva. She might even be able to fill us in about Tiffany."

"I think that is a good idea, sir. We can't ask Lisa really, she has enough on her plate right now."

"We might have to include her as well. By all accounts Kate said she is quite depressed, but I know James is doing his best to bring down Lee. As soon as he is exposed for the liar he is, then Lisa can come back home and we can make sure she gets support. That poor woman needs bereavement counselling. She has been carrying such a heavy burden for the past fifteen years; what a tragedy!"

They both got in the car, driving in silence towards Westgate. Alan was busy with his thoughts. He had the Margate address of Tiffany Preston, but he wondered how well the Bryants knew her, if at all. Another thing that bothered him was whether Kate had told Lisa that Ryan Lee was living in the area. This man had been the love of her life, and he had totally destroyed her life too, so she probably would never want to bump into him again. Lisa had a right to know.

Kate let them into the apartment, her owl-like eyes blinking rapidly. She was such a quiet soul that Alan wondered how she was coping with all this, he always got the impression she was homely and just wanted a quiet life.

"How is Lisa?" Alan asked politely.

"She was better today after I told her that you believe her about Lily and we are going to try and expose Ryan, but when I first arrived she was depressed. She has lost weight and has been off her food."

"Oh no, she must eat and stay strong!" said Martha, emphatically.

"When we get him, and we will, she will need to be very strong if she has to see him in court."

"I know, I told her that."

"Did you tell her that Lee is living in Margate?" asked Alan.

Kate seemed irritated by the question. She wrinkled up her face in distaste. "Not yet, and you mustn't either if you go to see her. She needs time."

"I know you said he was the love of her life, so she won't want to be bumping into him."

"The trouble with Lisa is she's not a good judge of character. If she hadn't met him, then there wouldn't have been a baby," said

139

Kate darkly. Alan could see she didn't like talking about Lee, so he changed the subject.

"Did you know Eva at all? Apparently she had lived around here for quite a few years."

"Oh yes, Eva was a sweet old lady, everyone knew her. I have been ironing her sheets for a few years now. She liked to sleep in all cotton, and they were heavy for her to lift and fold. But she did everything else herself; ironed all her clothes. She was a remarkable ninety year old. I still can't comprehend why anyone would kill her."

"Did you know her cleaner, Tiffany?"

"Only to speak to in passing. Sometimes she was there when I took the sheets round."

"Last question. Did you have a key to Eva's house?"

"No, she used to let me in. I usually took her sheets round at about five o'clock. Tiffany used to change her bed for her before she went home."

Alan nodded at Kate. "Thank you, that is all we need for now, and rest assured we are doing all we can for Lisa. We know she needs to come home."

Kate gave a shy little smile. "Thank you, Inspector, if I can get her home, I can help her to get better."

Chapter Nineteen

Ryan Lee was thirty-eight years old, he had very dark hair and penetrating blue eyes. His hair was thick and curly, and when it flopped over his brow, it gave him an air of innocence, and it fooled everyone, especially women, who were drawn to his enigmatic personality and handsome looks. But behind this facade was a man with a quick temper. His Irish accent and gushing praise hid a man who deceived everyone. He was a glib storyteller, knowing how to sound totally sincere, and he fooled many people.

He had only a vague recollection of his mother, as he was about three years old when social workers broke into the flat and rescued him before it burnt down. His mother had left him to go out drinking, but she had not put her cigarette out properly before she went. So Ryan was taken into care, and did his rounds of temporary foster homes. He learned to use his wits and distort the truth to survive in life. He became hard and unfeeling, and he made no attempt to control his temper, which could be terrifying to an onlooker.

When he met Sheila, he had tried to get his act together, as he thought he did love her. But he was haunted by thoughts of his own inadequacies, which he hid very well most of the time. She was a beautiful vivacious girl, a free spirit, and he was worried he couldn't tame her or hold onto her. When she became pregnant he was happy, and a protective and then a loving side to him was exposed. But after baby Lily was born, he became obsessed by the idea that she wasn't his child. There were frequent arguments, and Lily seemed to pick up on the uneasy atmosphere.

She cried a lot, and Sheila had changed; she was depressed. It was all too much for him. So, one evening, when the baby just wouldn't stop, he sent Sheila upstairs for a shower, and something inside him snapped. He picked the baby up and shook her violently until she stopped crying, and then he went outside for a smoke; his nerves were in pieces. When he came back in, Sheila just sat there, saying nothing, rocking her dead baby.

He wasn't proud of what he had done. He hadn't meant to kill the baby, even if it wasn't his, but he certainly wasn't going to go to prison for it. Sheila was struck dumb, and not able to defend herself in any way. He convinced himself she had gone barmy anyway, so she wouldn't even realise she was being locked up. In his head it was only right that she should get the blame so he could keep himself out of prison.

He had done pretty well over the years, up until the armed robbery, and then he had to do a stint. He didn't really think about Sheila any more, it was all in the past. With his looks and charisma he could easily attract women, and there had been a lot; he didn't count how many. He was in and out of jobs. Working hard was not for him, and he moved around a lot, finally coming to Margate. He worked for the council for a while. His smart appearance got him into a clerical job, mainly because the office manager was female and liked the idea of having him around, even though he had "lost his references".

But eventually she had seen the light, and sacked him when he was caught having sex in the stock room with the office junior. The girl concerned had thought he was 'the one', and informed him she was pregnant, which had made him want to disappear. Luckily for him, she decided to have a termination, and her parents decided to move away so she could have a fresh start, which saved him the bother of having to up sticks and go again.

He was currently on job seeker's allowance, which he thought was a funny name for it, as he wasn't doing much seeking. He had picked up with Tiffany at a pub one day, and now she had moved in. He was happy with the arrangement, as she worked as a house cleaner, so she bought all the food, and even gave him a bit of money for himself. His rent was paid by benefits, and so this is how he went through life; after all, it was survival of the fittest.

Tonight she had come in exhausted as usual, so she was no fun. He told her he was going to pop out for a swift half, and she had given him fifty pounds, which she had just earned that afternoon by cleaning a house from top to bottom. Like most women before her, Tiffany was besotted with him and could hardly believe he was her boyfriend, so anything she could do to bring a smile to his face made her day. She believed that when he went to the pub he just met a mate for a drink, and it never crossed her mind that he would ever be unfaithful to her, so she sent him off with a hug and a kiss, and then went to have a relaxing bath before bed.

To his great surprise, as he opened the pub door, a young girl, who looked a bit unsteady on her feet, practically fell into his arms. For a fleeting moment, when he saw her, his memory took him back to a time when he had first met Sheila. The girl had a striking similarity; the colour of her hair, her figure, and the way her face lit up when she laughed. He quickly squashed that memory down. This girl was young, maybe just a teenager, but even slightly drunk as she was, didn't hide the fact that she had a vivacious personality.

"So I have just met my knight in shining armour," she giggled, as he held her upright. He was enjoying the feel of her body in his arms, so there was no rush to let go.

"Oh begorrah, 'tis an angel I have in my arms," he said jokingly.

Natalie giggled. Her first encounter with him was not meant to be like this, but at least she had made contact with him. Because she felt slightly drunk, she knew it would not work tonight. Her idea had been to get him drunk and talking, because she would need all her wits about her.

"I am not used to drinking. I am going home. I was waiting for a friend, and she didn't show," she said as way of an explanation, gently extricating herself from his arms.

"Ryan Lee at your service, madam. Can I walk you home?"

"No thanks. My brother is on his way."

"May I know the name of this beautiful angel before she departs," he said, smiling and making a mock bow. And as she

143

looked at him, she could see why Lisa had been smitten, but it was all fake, he was a bastard!

"Yes, Jane Seymour, now I have to go."

She was worried that James might have followed her out. She had to get rid of Ryan immediately, so she walked quickly away, then turned and gave him a friendly wave.

"Will I see you again?" he asked, and she could feel the intensity of his eyes boring into her.

"Maybe," she said, and was relieved to see him turn and go into the pub.

Within a couple of minutes James was beside her, making sure she could walk properly back to his car, which was parked unobtrusively in a side road.

"Well, now you have made his acquaintance, but next time soft drinks only, he can get drunk but not you. And don't forget if he says anything juicy, record it on your phone."

"Yes James, I know. Can you take me home now," she said.

"Right, so now we are off to Margate. If you remember, Karen said Tiffany cleaned her mother's house on Fridays, so she might not have another job to take its place yet."

"OK sir, address and postcode please," said Martha, bringing out her phone.

"St Anne's Drive," read Alan after consulting the piece of paper that Karen had written it on.

Martha shuffled her file of papers; that address sounded familiar. Then she brought out a print-off of Ryan Lee, and she stiffened with surprise. "Did you realise, sir, they live in the same road, um flat, number 6, I correct myself. Tiffany lives with Ryan Lee. She is his girlfriend!"

Alan was thoughtful, as nothing much shocked him any more. "Mmm, so that puts him in the frame for the murder of Eva. And we know he has a temper, so maybe he did it?"

"Well they both obviously have a connection with Eva, but would he have even known Dr Jones?" pointed out Martha. Alan couldn't help thinking that if he was callous enough to let his sick girlfriend take the blame for the death of their baby, then he would easily be capable of murder, but he couldn't think what the motive would be.

They had by now arrived at St Anne's Drive. There were Victorian and Edwardian terraced houses, now converted into flats. They found flat number six, and Alan pressed the button. A male voice with an Irish accent came over the line. "Yes, who is it?"

"It's police. We would like to have a word with Tiffany Preston."

Ryan stiffened, no way did he want the law hanging around here. "She is not here. She is at work, and doesn't get home until after five o'clock."

"Right, I am DCI Alan Clarke. Who am I speaking to?"

There was a distinct pause whilst Ryan decided whether he should say his name. But sometimes lying made things worse, and Tiffany would probably have mentioned his name anyway. He decided on this occasion, honesty was the best policy.

"I am her partner Ryan."

"And your surname?"

Bloody police, they were so persistent, but he couldn't believe they had come round because of that twenty quid. They must have many more serious cases to solve.

"Lee, it's Ryan Lee."

"Can you spare us just five minutes of your time, Mr Lee?"

He reluctantly pressed the buzzer to release the communal door, and then opened his front door. He could hardly refuse, then they might want to search the place, and he had a bit of coke hidden, he didn't want them to find that.

Alan was curious to see him. Anyone who could kill his own child, and then blame it on his girlfriend because she wasn't well enough to defend herself, had to be a scumbag of the highest order. But he wasn't going to go there today, as James was dealing with that.

Lee was standing at the open door, and Alan noticed how he eyed Martha. He was a womaniser all right, probably thought he was god's gift. No doubt women would be taken in by those bright eyes and his curly hair, but there was an air of arrogance about him; he thought he was untouchable. However, it was possible that he could have killed the doctor, so right now Alan would check his alibi.

145

g

They were not invited further than the hall. It was clear that Lee would not be that co-operative, but Alan had the bit between his teeth. His feelings towards this man felt strong. He almost hoped he was the murderer, then they could lock him up and throw away the key!

He nodded at Martha, who produced her notebook and pencil, it wasn't easy to write standing up, but she would do it.

"I would like you to tell me what you were doing on the evening of May 16th."

Ryan looked perplexed. "That was two months ago. Honestly, I have no idea."

"Do you keep a diary?"

"Good point, Tiffany does. Wait a minute."

He disappeared into another room, and they heard a drawer opening, and then he came in with a red diary in his hand, and thumbing through it he found 16th May. Then he read it out: "These are Tiffany's words," he explained.

"IT WAS QUITE HOT TODAY, TOO HOT FOR DOING HOUSEWORK, BUT I WORKED OVER AT MINNIS BAY. DIDN'T GET HOME UNTIL 6. WE HAD PASTA FOR DINNER, THEN STAYED HOME WATCHING TV. I WON'T GET PAID UNTIL NEXT WEEK, SO AS WE ARE BOTH SKINT, RYAN DIDN'T GO OUT FOR A DRINK. HOPE THINGS IMPROVE SOON."

"That sounds very watertight, although we will have to return and speak to Tiffany," Alan reminded him curtly. "What about two days ago?"

Ryan Lee checked the diary again, but it had not been filled in for the last couple of days. He knew, of course, that he had been in the pub yesterday. He had seen that interesting girl who was a bit tipsy, but he wasn't going to mention that. He had been there the day before as well, but he had better get Tiffany to write they had been home again. If he didn't have an alibi, the police could pin anything onto him, or her.

"You do know, of course, that Tiffany was sacked from her job at Eva Scott's house because she stole £20 from her employer?"

"Yes, I know, but Tiffany was desperate. We didn't have enough money to eat that day. It wasn't something she made a habit of."

"Well we need to speak to her!" said Alan, firmly. "Either we come back here, or we take you both down to the station."

Ryan didn't like the sound of this one little bit. What an idiot Tiffany had been to rob the old lady, and then she is found dead only a short while afterwards. The trouble with the law was when you had been inside before, they had a habit of picking on you. No way was he going to go down for this!

"If you come back at 5.30, I will make sure she is here."

"Right, we will return later then," said Alan pointedly. He nodded at Martha that it was time to go, and Ryan opened the door to let them out.

Once they had got back in their car, Ryan mopped his sweaty brow. He was feeling distinctly nervous. He had done his best to avoid the law ever since he had come out, and now, because of Tiffany, they were sniffing round again. What a bitch she was. Not only lost her job, but also brought the law to his door. When she came in he would let her know just how angry he was!

David was pleased that Pamela had taken Holly into the family because she was now less obsessed with herself. Soon she would be a rich woman. The doctor's house was worth over a million, and she had half a share in that, and then there were his assets. David had known he wouldn't be included in the will, but he had stepped up and given Pamela a home when she needed it, and she had told him she was going to give him some money towards rent as soon as she got her inheritance. This was a huge relief to him, as he had a loan to pay back to keep a roof over his head.

When the shock of his brother's untimely death had worn off, it had caused him to re-evaluate his life. It made him realise how precious it was, and the fact that you only get one life. Now that Ian was not around, he didn't have to feel that he was living in his shadow, and that he was such a disappointment to the family. He had found himself a job, so he had his pride back. It was modestly paid, in an office, but it was a start. But more importantly, he had faced up to the fact that he was a gambling addict, and had joined a group of people who were all like himself, and trying to give up. David didn't like living on his own, he wanted his wife and his children back. When he had seen them at the funeral, it had brought back all the memories of when they had been a family, and he realised what an idiot he had been to gamble all that away. Very shortly he would be on his own again, and he was hoping to win his long suffering ex-wife back again. He had managed to resist gambling for a month now, and he had told her that, feeling that if she came back to him, her support might keep him from weakening again.

When Pamela had brought Holly into the family, it had made him want his own family back. She would get on well with her cousins. There was simply nothing about Holly that anyone could dislike. And with a baby on the way, which would be his great niece, this was the perfect time for his own family to unite with Holly and her new baby. He knew he had a long road ahead. There would be days when he would be sorely tempted to gamble, but losing his wife and children had made him realise he really had nothing that mattered any more, just an empty life. But he was alive, and his brother wasn't, and he must not waste a minute of it.

Chapter Twenty

Natalie had been busy planning her next move to bring down Ryan Lee. She realised that to get on his wavelength, she was going to have to assume a different persona. It was important to make sure he had no idea that she was a WPC, as he would obviously clam right up. Her plan was to act a little wild, as if she had no regard for the law. She had even roped in her friend Janice Carter, another WPC, to help her with her plan. Janice thought it was exciting, and Natalie had explained to James that they were going to stage a scene to draw Ryan in.

James felt a bit outvoted by two enthusiastic young women, but he reminded them both very firmly that he would be sitting at a table, in the same room, for their own protection. If he needed backup, he would ask for it. In the back of his mind was the constant thought that Alan would not approve of what was going on, but without Natalie's support, he really didn't know how to get Ryan Lee talking.

Janice was a pretty girl with curly blonde hair, which was cut short. She was tall and slim, and she had a naturally extrovert nature, but this evening she was going to have to play the enraged girlfriend. She had parted company with Natalie before they reached the pub, and was now sitting in the car in a side street waiting for a text from Natalie to tell her it was time to join her.

Natalie was perched on a bar stool, waiting for Ryan to come in. He had to be there when Janice came in to play her part, and she

149

couldn't help the butterflies that were circling around inside her. She prayed that he would turn up, then together with Janice they could put their plan into action.

When Ryan came into the bar, she was conscious of his intent stare. His eyes seemed to bore right into her, and then his face relaxed, and he was all smiles.

"Begorrah, so the angel returns. What are you drinking tonight?"

Natalie had two glasses in front of her. One contained tonic water with ice and lemon in, which she stopped to sip periodically. The other had vodka in which she planned to add to Ryan's drink to get him talking.

"I am OK, thanks. All sorted here." She raised the glass of vodka in salutation to him. So he went up to the bar and ordered his usual Guinness, then perched on a bar stool next to her.

Natalie used this opportunity to text Janice, and got ready for her entrance. She was aware of James, discreetly seated at the back of the pub, hidden behind a newspaper. Suddenly the bar door flew open, and in flounced Janice, determined to put everything into her part.

By then Ryan was sitting on his stool and would be a witness to the little scene unfolding next to him. Janice flounced over to Natalie, hissing in the most venomous voice she could muster.

"You bitch, you couldn't leave him alone, could you? You had to have my boyfriend!" and followed this up with a slap across Natalie's face, which was now reddening. Natalie stroked her throbbing cheek. It really did hurt. Janice certainly was giving it her all, she thought ruefully.

"Why shouldn't I have him? He likes me!" she retorted defiantly, and then she saw the barman stiffen, as Janice loomed menacingly over her bar stool.

"Now now, ladies, take your grievances outside, we run a nice pub here!" he said.

Just to make it look good, Janice raised her hand again. She could see Natalie's cheek was marked. Poor Nat, she hoped she wouldn't have to slap her again. But this time Ryan sprang into action. He liked her, he had hoped their paths would cross again, and he intended to use any opportunity to get to know her. He jumped in front of Natalie, and made a pushing motion with his hands towards Janice.

"Please stop this. Look at her cheek, it's very red!" he said, pointedly.

Janice could see her work was done now. Just one more parting shot before she left.

"You are welcome to her, she's nothing but a tart!" She would have to apologise to Nat later for that one! She turned on her heel after giving them both a withering look, before exiting the pub and returning to James's car.

"That really hurts!" said Natalie with feeling, stroking her inflamed cheek.

"To be sure, it must do," said Ryan, with sympathy. Women were like squalling cats when put together, but clearly this little beauty was no angel, which meant he liked her even more.

"Come and sit at a table over there," he pointed to the back of the room. Luckily it was the opposite side to where James was sitting.

Natalie got up, holding her head high as though she didn't have a care in the world and could face anyone, and picked up her two glasses. After settling themselves at a table, she took a sip of her tonic water, and watched Ryan downing his pint of Guinness.

He went up to the bar to get himself another, and then excused himself. He needed a slash, and she seemed to like him too, so he felt sure she would still be there when he came back.

"Just going to the little boy's room," he said, winking at her, and whilst he had gone, Natalie took the opportunity to tip some vodka into his glass. He swaggered back. There was a certain arrogance in the way he walked, which made her hate him even more. She couldn't wait to bring him down. Now for her turn to do a performance.

"Course you know you have hooked up with a bad girl. Stealing my friend's man was tame to some of the other stuff I have done."

Ryan was enjoying the fact that he was with someone like himself, who didn't care about rules. He was feeling a bit light-headed, obviously his second Guinness had hit the spot. They were sitting in a corner away from anyone else, and he couldn't wait to hear what else this girl had done.

"Well, none of us are perfect. I did a stretch. Why do people leave all their valuables around, and when someone steals them, they try to take him on. Of course I will fight back," he said, proudly pushing his chest out. "Oh dammit!"

She watched with great satisfaction as he became more drunk. He dropped his wallet on the floor, and whilst he was trying to scoop it up, she added more vodka to his drink. He was beginning to slur his words, and the drink was giving him a strange feeling, taking him back fifteen years or more when he had sat with Sheila and got drunk. Up until today he had not allowed any memories to trouble him, but this girl was uncannily like her, and although he had hidden it away inside him for a very long time, he had cared about her, and the baby, and no matter how he tried to pretend, he knew Lily had been his baby.

"Can I get you another Guinness?"

He peered at her, wondering why a couple of Guinness's had made him feel this way. Could the little madam have put something in his drink. Maybe she wanted to have her way with him. He should be so lucky!

"Not right now, maybe later."

Ryan watched her go to the bar, then she came back with another glass of what looked like vodka with ice in it. She giggled and he wondered if she was also tipsy. She acted as if she was.

"So what is the worst thing you ever did?" he asked her.

Natalie giggled again, hiding her nervousness. She was about to make up a harrowing story, but would it be enough to break him and make him confess. She had set her phone to record if he made any sort of confession.

"I told you I was a bad girl. When I was fifteen I got pregnant, but I was still at school, so I had to hide my bump. When I got to seven months, the baby came early. I was alone at the time, my parents were out. I watched my baby struggling to breathe, and I did nothing. When he died, I took him wrapped in a blanket and buried him in the woods."

Even hard man Ryan was affected by her words. She sat there, holding his gaze, not appearing to show any emotion; no tears or trembling lip. But she was causing him to remember just what he had done, and his words came tumbling out, he was unable to stop them.

"I had a baby daughter, but she never stopped crying, drove me crazy, and her mother went all mental. I shook her. Didn't mean to hurt her, just wanted her to stop crying. Then I put her back in her cot, but she didn't look right, her lips were blue and her face was lolling. It's hard to forget."

Natalie felt jubilant. She had got him. Her phone was recording, so she carried on. "What happened to her mother, then?"

"She got locked up. I told you she was mental. I did her a favour, really."

Natalie hated him so much, but the act had to continue, and she mustn't make him suspicious by showing her disgust of him. "Yes, we all have to look after number one in life," she said, forcing a smile. For the benefit of the recording, she pretended to be impressed.

"It was the obvious thing to do, to blame her. Being mental, as you say, she had to be locked up, and you could get on with your life." She pretended to look at him approvingly, and this made Ryan feel better, made him think that what he had done was right, and as he was now beginning to feel less light-headed, his mind naturally turned to sex. This little lady was sexy. She was his type, a bit wild without a conscience.

He leaned into her, stroking her arm, and she hid a shudder. "It's a bit hot in here. Let's go outside and get some air."

Natalie knew she would have to play along with it. He thought she was a good-time girl. Her phone had done its work, and James had previously told her that if she left the pub with Ryan, he would be right on her tail, and, if needed, he would immediately call for backup.

"Why not," she murmured. Inside she was seething, but outwardly she appeared to like his suggestion. Ryan would not have expected her to say no. Women were always drawn to him, and so he stood up, and helped her to her feet.

She knew that all he wanted was to get her knickers off, and this was the part where the job became a risk. He apparently was a violent man, so if he had any idea that she was trying to trap him, he would get angry and might attack her. Inside she felt a bit nauseous, but then she thought about Lisa, and why she was doing this, why any woman would want to do it, so she smiled back at him and got to her feet.

Janice was getting a bit tired of sitting in the car. James had given her his spare key and his instructions had been clear. Never mind that it was July, a nice mild evening, and still light. Instead of sitting in this back street, watching teenagers playing in the road, and racing around on skateboards and bikes, she could have had a walk along the sandy beach, watching the sun setting. It was a beautiful evening, she had done her bit to help, and she was now wondering how long it would take Natalie to get him to confess, if indeed she could. But James being James would want to run them both home. She had been asked not to tell her parents what they were doing. It was all top secret, and she had no doubt if her dad had been aware of it, he probably would not have liked her to be involved. But, she reasoned with herself, she was not in any danger, although Natalie was. That man might look handsome, but he had done a dark deed, and by all accounts had an ugly temper. Poor Nat would have to find a way to fool him and get him onside, because if he had any idea she was out to entrap him, who could know what the consequences might be?

Natalie had kept a clear head this time by only drinking tonic water, but she pretended to be a bit tipsy by giggling for Ryan's benefit. As they exited into the garden behind the pub, she was relieved to see people sitting on a bench, she did not want to be alone with him.

Now they had left the pub, the balmy summer breeze felt pleasant on Ryan's face, and it cleared his head. There was only one thought in his mind, and that was shagging this little tart. She was so tipsy, there would be absolutely no resistance. He linked his arm through hers for the sake of the punters. Her giggling excited him, and he steered her quickly past them, out into the street. It was twilight now, and there was a convenient alley over the road.

154

Natalie felt fear rush through her and she stopped giggling immediately. There was no sign of James, and he wouldn't know where Ryan had taken her. She suddenly felt very vulnerable. Ryan's grip on her arm was strong, and she didn't want to provoke his temper, so how could she escape from him?

But then she felt his hardness pressing against her, and revulsion took control of her senses. She jerked her knee up, and he yelled with pain.

Ryan saw red. This little tart had led him on, and now she was playing hard to get. The spiteful little cow had kneed him in the goolies, but she wasn't going to get away with it. He pushed her roughly against the hedge in the alley, with one hand restraining her, the other one was on her neck squeezing it until she felt tears of pain and fear welling in her eyes.

"Don't mess me about, darlin'!" he said sarcastically. "I might just wring your pretty lil neck."

Natalie was trapped, pushed tightly against the bushes, with Ryan's hand ready to choke her. Absolute terror swept through her, rendering her body helpless, and she felt darkness wrapping itself around her, invading her senses, then she knew no more.

James watched anxiously as he saw Natalie and Ryan leave the bar. She was giggling, and he hoped she wasn't drunk. He had expressly told her not to be, but would she have heeded his warning. It was just starting to get dark, and he didn't trust Lee one bit. He gulped down his last mouthful of the lemonade shandy, and stood up. At that moment his phone rang, but he ignored it. He had to make sure Natalie was all right.

When he got outside, it was twilight. A group of people were laughing and joking by the outside seats in the garden, but there was no sign of Natalie. Surely the bastard hadn't spirited her away in a car? He glanced quickly around him, then asked desperately.

"Anyone see where the couple who just came out went?"

A man who was very clearly tipsy, laughed, and said, "Don't spoil their fun, they went down the alleyway."

James ignored him. The alleyway was just a few yards away, and he ran towards it, noticing it was flanked by thick bushes. When he saw them, shock ran through him. It looked as though Natalie had passed out. Not that it bothered Lee, he was kneeling by her prostrate body, his penis was out, and he was tugging at her clothes, and trying to enter her.

Without even thinking about it, James launched himself at him from behind, knocking him down. He had caught him unawares, and whilst he lay on the ground blinking with surprise, James handcuffed him, then called for backup. "You bastard, you tried to rape her. What have you done to her?" he said angrily.

"She was willing, guv. I didn't expect her to pass out. She must be drunk."

James gave him a look of contempt. This guy was truly the lowest of the low. Two more police arrived, and James read him his rights, and made him pull up his trousers. Then he went to help Natalie, who seemed to be coming round now. Her eyes fluttered open, and she asked, "What has happened, where am I?"

"You are safe now, and he can't hurt you," said James, helping her to her feet. Thank God he had managed to stop the bastard. Whatever would Alan say if he knew about this?

Natalie allowed herself to be led away to the car. She remembered now how scared he had made her, but James had arrested him, and the other officers were taking him away. She felt relief flood through her. She had done her bit for Lisa, and almost got raped in the process. But she had his confession on her phone, so it had all been worth it. Ryan Lee had fallen into her trap.

Chapter Twenty-one

Zoe hadn't been feeling great for a couple of weeks now. She hadn't said anything to Alan, knowing he was so focused on this murder case, but she had done the test, so knew she was pregnant. As Adam was now fourteen months old, he would be just about two when the new baby arrived. She had not been back at work long, just a couple of months, but she planned to go as long as she could before stopping, providing she felt well and fit enough.

Once she got over this morning sickness, things would settle down, and although they hadn't particularly planned this baby, she knew Alan would be delighted, as his family meant everything to him. He would worry about her for the first three months, just as he had before. She found his concern really touching, but right now he did not need any added stress, as this murder case was a particularly harrowing one. The newspapers had reported in great detail how the two victims had died and had now released the name of the second victim. It was not pleasant reading.

Alan was most anxious to find the killer, and she was so relieved that it now couldn't be Lisa, as when the other crime occurred, she had been in hospital. She had met Kate whilst out shopping, and Kate had explained that Lisa would be home soon, and she couldn't wait to have her back. Kate's face had lit up and become very animated, and Zoe felt so happy for her. Now they could go back to their happy life together.

Helen had gone home, so she busied herself bathing Adam. He

now enjoyed having a plastic jug of water, and doing his best to fill up empty yogurt pots on the edge of the bath. Every time he missed and the water splashed, he gurgled with laughter. She was glad the floor was vinyl in the bathroom, as it was much easier to mop it up, and she liked to watch Adam having fun.

She heard her mobile phone ring, so she picked it up. It was Alan.

"I will be a bit late, honey. Last minute interview to do."

She felt disappointment rush through her, but she hid it and kept her voice steady.

"I haven't cooked anything yet. I ran out of ideas today."

"No worries there. I only expect to be about an hour. How about I pick up some Chinese on the way home? "

If he had suggested that in the morning, she wouldn't have coped, as that was the time she felt most nauseous. But it was now five-thirty, so by the time six-thirty or seven came round, she knew she would feel hungry.

"That is a good idea," she said brightly. "Tonight I fancy chicken and pineapple with some special fried rice."

"Honey, is that all? You're not watching your weight again, you know I love every curve of you."

She smiled, hugging the secret to herself that soon he would have a lot more curves to love.

"You know what I like; prawn crackers. Then get what you like as well and I might have a little taste of it."

That seemed to satisfy Alan. He said goodbye, and clicked his phone off. Then his mind switched quickly back to the interview.

"Come on, Martha, let's go back and interview Tiffany Preston."

Lee had told them Tiffany would be home later, and it was just before six when they arrived back at the flat. When they knocked on the door, Tiffany opened it, a young woman with her hair tied back in a ponytail. Her expression was guarded, and Alan saw hostility in her eyes.

"Good evening, we are looking for Tiffany Preston."

"Well you've found her. What do you want?"

Alan showed her his ID. He didn't see fear in her eyes. God she was a tough nut. He smiled pleasantly. "Just to ask you what you did on the evening of 14th July, two days ago."

"Yes, I know when it was," she snapped at him. "The same as I do every evening. I clean houses, and every night I come home and eat, then go to bed. I have to get up early to start."

"Was Ryan at home with you?"

Tiffany paused. "Why are you asking me all these questions?"

"You worked for a lady called Eva Scott. If you read the newspapers, you'll already know she was murdered on the 14th July."

Tiffany went pale; she was in shock. She had no idea the old biddy was dead. Surely they didn't think she had done her in because of £20, as her snidey daughter would definitely have told them about that!

"I don't work for her now," she said, defensively.

"We know," said Alan, watching her demeanour. She appeared to be surprised. "That is why we are asking about your movements so we can rule you out of our inquiry. Was Ryan at home with you?"

Tiffany so wished he was here. She had no idea what he had told the police, or if they had even interviewed him, although obviously they would. She tried to play it safe.

"Yes, he was here. We had dinner together, then I had a bath as usual, and went to bed. He was watching TV."

"But if you were in bed, how do you know if he was watching TV?" asked Martha.

Tiffany glowered at her, thinking what a bitch she was!

"Because he watches a programme that he likes. It's about travel, and yesterday he was telling me it was about the Greek Islands, and he commented that if we had the money, he would love to go."

Alan sensed her evasiveness. These days anything could be recorded, or watched on the hub later, so it didn't prove anything or back him up. He could not warm to her, as she seemed a hard uncaring woman, but, of course, that didn't make her a murderer.

He had an overwhelming desire to leave this shabby flat. It was time he went home and spent some quality time with Zoe. They could enjoy a Chinese meal and a glass of wine. Maybe Adam would be asleep, but he just wanted to leave all the cares of the day behind him and relax. He was sure Martha would want that too, having got married so recently. He addressed Tiffany politely, even though he didn't believe her.

"Thank you for your time, Tiffany, we will be in touch if we need to question you any further."

Martha gave him a strange look, and he knew exactly what she was thinking. With such an unsafe alibi, why was he ending the interview? Once they got in the car he explained.

"I don't believe a word of it, Martha, but Lee isn't there. We will have to find a way to bring them both in for questioning, then put them in separate rooms."

"Yes, and it can't really be for stealing £20 off her ex client."

"Exactly."

He dropped Martha off at her flat, and then continued into Birchington. They had discovered a Chinese takeaway in the square called the New Dragon the other day whilst out walking, so it seemed like a good idea. There was a small queue, so Alan took his place, waiting for it to be his turn.

The Chinese lady who took his order had an inscrutable expression. He was very hungry, so he decided to have sweet and sour pork, as well as crispy prawn balls, a portion of noodles would be nice, and some vegetables. Then whilst he was waiting for it, he sent Zoe a text, explaining he was picking up their supper, just up the road, and to put the plates in the oven to warm. He expected to be back in about fifteen minutes.

He glanced at his watch. Just before seven, Adam might still be awake. He hoped so, as he had missed him today. This morning seemed such a long time past. The lady was calling him over to collect his order; he smiled and thanked her, and as he went to get back in the car, he heard his phone ping with a message from Zoe.

Alan didn't stop to read it, as he would be with her in less than five minutes. The delicious aroma that sneaked out of the paper carrier bag was assaulting his senses, making him feel even hungrier, so he wasted no time in driving onto the garden estate, then pulling his car into the drive.

Zoe must have heard him coming, as the door was open. She knew him so well. Seeing Adam would even take precedence over his stomach, so she took the carrier bag off him, remarking, "Oh, this food smells so good. I will sort it, and if you are quick, Adam might still be awake."

Alan went towards the door that led to Adam's bedroom. It was slightly ajar, so he peeped in. His son had heard him, and he was standing up in his cot with a smile on his face, gurgling with happiness when he saw him. Alan lifted him out of the cot to hug him, and Adam crowed with delight. He held the warm soft little body against himself just briefly. He knew he shouldn't really be keeping him awake like this, but seeing his happy little face after a long day was such a tonic.

"You know I love you son, but it's sleep time now," he said, carefully putting him back.

Adam puckered up his face as if to cry, but Alan was too quick for him.

"If you lay there like a good boy, we have some nice peaceful music," he said, switching the tape on. Adam loved music, and he lay obediently down, allowing Alan to tuck his blanket round him. He blew him a kiss, and then quietly left the room. Just that couple of minutes with Adam had helped him to forget the traumas of the day.

Zoe had served out the meal. Her stomach felt all right this evening, and she did love chicken and pineapple. She had also added a few noodles to her plate, and some vegetables, although she did not fancy the battered prawns. They were dining al fresco tonight, with a tray on their laps. She had also opened a bottle of Chardonnay.

"You are not expecting to go out again, are you?" she asked, before picking up a glass.

"No, honey, I am not. We already did a late interview, and I just wanted to get home."

She poured out his wine, and they both watched the welcome sight of it gurgling into the wine glass. Alan kissed her on the cheek as she passed it to him, and then collected the tray from the table.

"Thanks honey. How was your day?"

"Busy," smiled Zoe. "But it's all good, as the day passes really quickly."

"Yes, it certainly does, but let's concentrate on you and I tonight," he said raising his glass. "To my beautiful wife, who looks particularly glowing tonight."

Zoe was wondering if she should tell him, now that they were having some private time together. But she remembered that last time in the first three months Alan had treated her like a porcelain doll. She wanted to feel her husband's arms around her tonight, as their love life had taken a back seat recently. Her wine glass contained lemonade; he probably would not notice that, and why shouldn't he have some wine and relax?

They ate their meal slowly. She watched Alan drinking his wine, and she then topped his glass up. Now she felt a bit guilty about deceiving him, and she no longer wanted to keep this secret to herself. He picked up his glass and went to fill hers, but she touched his arm gently.

"Alan, no. I have lemonade, I am pregnant again."

She watched his face register surprise, and then doubts crept in. Would he think it was too soon? But then it creased into a big smile, he put down his tray and put his arms around her.

"I should have realised. You've got that same glow about you that you had with Adam. Oh, honey, that has made my day. When is it due?"

"I've done a test, but not seen the doctor yet. I would think about March next year."

"This is crazy. A sibling for Adam, it's great news! All we need now it to sell our flat in Wimbledon, then we can go house hunting."

"Yes, it would be nice to be settled somewhere before the birth. Now eat up before it all gets cold," she scolded him lightly. She knew she was so lucky to have Alan, he might be a tough DCI during the day, but at home he was such a family man.

By the time they had finished and washed up, she was feeling distinctly weary. She was missing her dishwasher, but realised that when they were settled in their new home, they would have all the modern facilities. In this bungalow it was pleasant enough, but certainly it would not be big enough for a family of four.

They settled on the sofa, and then she heard the wail of Adam. He had woken up.

"You stay put, it's my turn. I will switch my phone off. Couldn't drive now anyway," smiled Alan, tucking a rug around her.

Regretfully she knew, that as much as her mind wanted him to make love to her right now, she was just too tired.

When she woke up again, she was amazed to see it was now ten o'clock. They were still on the sofa, Alan with his arm protectively around her. So much for their romantic evening. She woke him up, and sleepily they both moved into the bedroom. Like robots they undressed. Alan only got as far as his pants, but Zoe managed to slip her pyjamas on, then they wearily climbed into bed and were both asleep immediately.

In the meantime, after Ryan Lee had been taken into custody in another car, James rang Alan's mobile. He had conflicting emotions, relief that Lee had confessed to the accidental killing of his own daughter, but also anxiety because he wasn't sure that Alan would approve of the way the confession had been obtained. Lee had almost raped Natalie, and caused her a lot of distress, and he had wanted to confess it to Alan this evening, to get it off his chest. But when his call went into voicemail, he realised that he wasn't going to be able reach Alan tonight.

Alan was usually always available. Such was his dedication to the job, whatever time of the day or night he was wanted, he kept his phone on. But not today, so with Ryan Lee cooling his heels in custody overnight, the only course of action left to James was to run Natalie and Janice home. Natalie appeared none the worse for wear now that Lee had been arrested, indeed she seemed to be particularly elated that she had his confession on her phone. Janice was equally delighted. They had set out to bring him down, and they had succeeded. Job done!

Chapter Twenty-two

Alan woke up suddenly the next morning from a very deep sleep. He peered at the clock; it was six-thirty, only half an hour earlier than he had set his alarm for. Zoe was not beside him, and he could hear Adam gurgling. Then her head peeped round the door, and in toddled his son.

"Oh, so you are awake. We were both out of it last night."

He smiled, remembering that she had told him last night such happy news. He swung Adam into the air, hugging him.

"You, my son, are having a sibling. Your mummy has a baby in her tummy."

But all Adam did was give him a wide-eyed stare, and then gurgled.

"He's too young to understand," said Zoe. "I am going to give him some breakfast now."

"I know. You are an amazing woman, you know."

"Why is that?"

"Well, our love life lately has been a bit on hold, but yet you are pregnant."

"I can't take all the credit, you had something to do with it too," smiled Zoe, then her face changed. "Whoops!" and he watched her rush towards the bathroom, and then heard her vomiting.

When she came back into the bedroom, she looked pale.

"Are you OK, honey?" he said anxiously.

"Yes, it's the dreaded morning sickness. But I am at home today, thank goodness."

"Let me give Adam his breakfast and dress him before I go. You have a rest."

"No, you have to be at work, it's not fair."

"It is fair, I like to care for him, you know I do. Once I leave for work you can take over."

At that moment, Zoe's mobile rang, she pressed the button and spoke: "Hello, Zoe here."

"Hi Zoe, it's James, I have been trying to reach the governor since late last night. Is everything OK?"

"Yes, of course, he was very tired last night, but I will remind him to switch his phone back on." She looked around for Alan's mobile; it was on the dining room table, plugged in to recharge. She unplugged it and took it to Alan, he was busy cooking some scrambled egg for Adam in the kitchen.

"Alan, James just rang my mobile. He's been trying to get hold of you. I explained your phone had been switched off."

Alan felt a bit irritated. "It's typical. Once in a blue moon I have a drink. I best see what he wants."

"Here, I'll dish up his scrambled egg. It's OK," said Zoe.

She handed him his mobile, and Alan felt guilt rush through him. It could be something really important! He switched it on and then rang James.

"Good morning, James. Sorry about my phone being off last night. I hope there is nothing wrong?"

James took a deep breath, good news first. "No sir, last night we took Ryan Lee into custody. He has admitted in a recorded conversation that he accidentally shook his baby daughter to death, and allowed Lisa to take the blame."

Alan was completely taken aback. He had wanted this to happen, but it had seemed a very difficult task to accomplish it. James had done wonders, and he deserved every bit of praise.

"Well done, James. How on earth did you manage to get him to admit to it?"

James gulped, this was it! "Well sir, it was Natalie, she set a honey trap for him. She staged an argument with her friend Janice, then pretended to like him, put vodka in his Guinness glass, and it got him talking."

Alan digested his words. Natalie and Janice were junior WPCs, and being a honey trap always carried a certain amount of danger. He felt a bit aggrieved that no one had told him, but as long as the two young women were all right.

"Well I would have preferred you asked me first, but are these ladies both OK?"

James swallowed nervously. "Yes sir, Natalie was adamant. The women were uncomfortable knowing how Lisa had suffered, and they wanted to bring him down."

"Well, we all did, but I take it they are both OK."

"He did try to rape Natalie. He loosened her clothing, and was just a bit too quick for me when they left the pub. But she doesn't seem bothered by it, and says she is happy to give any evidence against him."

"Oh God, James, he nearly raped her, and she is OK with that? Of course she is not, she may well need counselling. And you acted without consulting me, that is not OK!"

"Yes sir, I know. I am so sorry."

James wished he had been able to talk Natalie out of it, but he knew she would have done her own thing anyway. Nevertheless, he really didn't like being rebuked by Alan, as it somehow took away the pride he had felt at bringing Lee down.

"I am leaving right now. See you at the station, and, by the way, Lee is going to need a solicitor, we have got loads on him!"

"Yes sir."

Alan clicked his phone off. His mind was working fast, then he suddenly remembered he had been helping with Adam, but now he could not. Zoe was sitting at the table, patiently feeding Adam, who also had a spoon. Most of his contents were falling off the spoon, but it kept him occupied, and with the other spoon, Zoe was managing to get some scrambled egg into his mouth.

He strode across the kitchen and kissed her forehead. "So sorry, honey, got to get into the office quickly."

"It's fine. They obviously missed you last night."

"Last night was our night, even if we did fall asleep," laughed Alan. He ruffled Adam's curly hair, and was rewarded with a wide eyed look, and a cheeky smile. Then suddenly he was gone, in what

166

felt like the blink of an eyelid, and Zoe continued to feed Adam. She couldn't help being curious; had the killer finally been caught?

On the way to the police station, Alan thought about what had happened. Maybe he had been a bit harsh with James. After all, women could be very persuasive, and Natalie was a young woman who had a very strong character. Maybe James had thought if he forbade her, she might go behind his back. Of course, he would have to talk to her, and make her realise just how dangerous her job was at times. But secretly he was pleased. After all, attempted rape was another crime to add to the others. Oh yes, Ryan Lee would most definitely need a good solicitor.

When he arrived at the station, he called James into his office. James was looking suitably chastened, but Alan was beginning to feel relief that Lee was now in custody, so he spoke kindly to him.

"James, it's brilliant that we have something on Ryan, but I will, of course, speak to Janice and Natalie. Have you got the recording of his confession?"

"Yes sir," said James eagerly. He had the presence of mind to take charge of Natalie's phone, and he had warned both her and Janice that the boss was not happy about the way it had been obtained. So they were both sitting in another office, waiting for Alan to speak to them. He handed the phone over.

When Alan listened he was pleased that the recording was so clear. Of course, Natalie had to invent a bit of a harrowing story about herself to get him to open up, but it had worked!

"Well that is amazing, James. I have to confess I am delighted." But then his tone altered, "You realise that I have to interview those two young ladies. We are responsible for their safety, and Lee can wait until we are ready to interview him. We need to get his girlfriend in, and they can both be in separate rooms."

"Yes sir, I will be right on it!" said James, preparing to leave the room.

"OK, just send them in first," said Alan.

James went to summon Natalie and Janice to Alan's office. He had warned them that the boss was none too happy, and all the bravado that they had felt the day before had vanished. It felt to them like they had been summoned to the head master's study.

As they entered his office, Alan gestured to both of them to sit down. They were junior WPCs, both barely out of their teens, and he knew if they had been his daughters, he would not have wanted them to take on such a mission. He adopted a stern tone to his voice.

"Natalie and Janice, I understand you took matters into your own hands yesterday, to lure Ryan Lee into a honey trap."

Janice hung her head not knowing what to say, her part had not been at all dangerous, it was Natalie. Even though Natalie had always admired her boss, and secretly thought he was fit, but regrettably happily married, she was not going to take this lying down.

"It was my idea, sir, and I don't regret a minute of it. Lisa took the blame for the death of her baby. She was locked away for it, and it broke her spirit. Speaking as a woman, we could not let him get away with it, so I played on the fact that he was a womaniser."

"Exactly, and you were almost raped by him. People like him do not care about anyone. I don't think your parents would approve of you being put at risk in that way."

"I have already told them sir, and they know it was my own idea. But it's not something I could keep from them."

Alan was startled by her words. It was possible that Natalie would have to give evidence when Ryan was charged with attempted rape, so to know that she had told her parents was a huge relief. He kept his severe expression on.

"Well I hope you have learned your lesson, Natalie, and in future, make sure you come to me before you start doing anything like this again. You cannot act without informing us of your intentions."

"Yes sir," said Natalie. Then she saw Alan's face crinkle into a smile, and his eyes looked kind. Perhaps he was a bit pleased at the result.

"Now off you go, ladies. You both did well."

Natalie exchanged glances with Janice, and they chorused in unison, "Thank you, sir," then they both left the room. As they walked along the corridor, Natalie remarked:

"Well, end of the sermon. It wasn't that bad. He isn't as fierce as

168

he seems, did you see him smile when he had finished telling us off?",

"I did, and he is very fit," said Janice, admiringly.

"Of course he is, and that is why he's spoken for," said Natalie. They both laughed, and continued along the corridor.

James had now taken Tiffany Preston into custody. She had at first refused to come to the station, but James had explained that they only wanted her to help with their enquiries. Knowing that they also had Ryan there had made her very nervous. She had no idea how to answer their questions without making it worse for Ryan. She guessed that she would be interviewed in another room, this was how the police worked, so maybe she should just say no comment to everything.

James and Natalie were going to interview her. There was a special reason for that, as they were hoping that when she found out that Lee had tried to rape Natalie, she might be more forthcoming. Natalie appeared unfazed by the experience, and James secretly admired her pluckiness.

Tiffany felt out of her depth, but she wasn't going to let these coppers know. She was worried about Lee, going back inside was the last thing he wanted, and she didn't want to lose him. It seemed like they were trying to pin the murder of Eva on him. She knew him well enough, she felt, to know that he would not have murdered Eva just because her nosy and interfering daughter had sacked Tiffany. She also knew that if and when they were both released, he would be angry with her, and he became a different person when he was angry. Why was it, in spite of that, she still liked him very much?

She sat defiantly at the table, watching Natalie setting up the tape to record. James sat opposite her, and he looked very serious, and she wondered why this was. She leaned back in her chair, crossing her legs as though she was perfectly relaxed, and hoped that it fooled him.

"Thank you for coming here today, Tiffany, to help us with our enquiries."

h

"Enquiries about what? I haven't done anything, and neither has Ryan."

"Well, I am afraid Ryan has, he tried to rape one of our female officers last night. After chatting with her at the pub, he encouraged her to go outside, and I actually caught him in the act in an alleyway."

This took the wind right out of Tiffany's sails. Jealousy coursed through her, robbing her of any sane thoughts, and, in that moment, her love for him turned to hate. The police would hardly lie to her, and to think she had given him some of her hard earned money to go out and get a drink, then he had tried it on with a police woman; it just beggared belief!

"What police woman?" she asked, angrily. How could he be that stupid, did he have a death wish?

Natalie kept her face inscrutable. She had no wish for this woman to turn on her, and left the talking to James.

"It doesn't matter who she was, but this is why we have arrested him. Clearly you had no knowledge of this."

"Do you think I would still be with him if I did!" she retorted tartly.

"Probably not, but we do know that Ryan has a temper. He has also admitted to accidentally shaking his baby daughter to death when he got angry. Do you know anything about that?"

"Certainly not!"

Tiffany was beginning to realise she knew very little about Ryan, and what James was telling her didn't sound good. She had been the victim of child abuse by her own father many years ago. He had beaten her when he felt like it, and even been imprisoned for it, but it had defined her character, and somehow she always seemed to end up with men who had a temper.

"So, for these crimes we are holding him, but now we need you to tell us if you know whether he stayed in or not on the evening of 14th July, just 3 days ago."

All Tiffany could feel was humiliation that the bastard had been unfaithful to her. She didn't owe him any loyalty at all. She now wanted revenge for yet another failed relationship, and she no longer cared what happened to him. After all, if he had shaken his own baby to death, then he would be quite capable of killing Eva in a fit of pique.

"Most nights he went to the pub for a drink after dinner. As I said, I take a bath and then go to bed. Housework makes me very tired, and I usually get up about six-thirty in the morning. So yes, he would have gone to the pub that evening."

"Thank you very much, Tiffany, you have been very helpful. For the benefit of the tape, this interview is terminated at twelve-thirty. You are now free to go."

Alan and Martha were sitting in the interview room, waiting for Ryan Lee to be brought in. Alan was struggling with his emotions, as everything about this man filled him with anger, but he prided himself on not being heavy handed when interviewing criminals. He had met some nasty types over the years, but he never felt violence was the answer. A lot of these people had already suffered in life at the hands of others, which had made them become criminals in the first place. But Ryan Lee was a huge challenge. First of all Ryan had killed his own child, and then been happy to use the vulnerability that Lisa had because of her postnatal depression to push the blame onto her.

And then, of course, there was Natalie. Ryan had tried to rape her, and she had passed out. It was amazing how she seemed to have bounced back, but she didn't need to be confronted with him, so she was viewing the interview by video in another room. He had expected her to need counselling after the trauma of yesterday, but her euphoria that Lee had confessed seemed to have eclipsed any feelings of horror at her ordeal.

The door opened to admit the duty constable escorting Ryan Lee. He did not look contrite, but very few criminals ever did. He was a handsome looking man, and he knew it, and Alan guessed his looks had probably deceived many women into thinking he was a good man. He had a swagger about him, and his arrogance was apparent. He didn't smile, but curled his lip in disgust.

"Good afternoon, Mr Lee, you have been charged already with attempted rape. . ."

"I want my solicitor!" he said angrily. "It was consensual sex."

"Yes, you need one!" said Alan, pointedly.

"Here he is," said the duty constable, as another man was framed in the doorway. He was tall and thin, and was wearing a pinstriped suit, and carrying a briefcase. He looked a bit shady, decided Alan. Just the sort of person Lee would hire to defend him. The tie that he wore with the suit looked loud, with garish bright red patterns on it, and the suit was a little too big for him. No doubt Lee had got a cheap deal online.

"Good morning, everyone. My name is Patrick Lewis, and I am here to represent Mr Lee.

"Good morning, Mr Lewis, have a seat," said Alan, pointing to a chair next to where Ryan was sitting.

"As I was saying," continued Alan. "Police officer James Martin arrested you yesterday for attempting to rape one of our WPCs."

Ryan was stunned by that remark. He was completely taken by surprise. "She didn't say she was from the police. I thought she was a good-time girl."

"Well you thought wrong," snarled Alan. "We protect our own!"

Patrick Lewis leaned towards Ryan, and said pointedly, "My client will be saying no comment to your charges." Ryan stared desperately at him. He didn't like the way this was going. He had no idea that little bitch was the law. She had fooled him!

Alan then produced Natalie's mobile, and switched it on, allowing everyone in the room to hear Ryan admitting that he had shaken Lily to death. During the silence that followed this, you could have heard a pin drop. Ryan was shaken. He had been fooled by a woman, and now they had him not only for attempted rape, but for infanticide, and perjury. It was useless making anything up, all he could say was no comment.

Patrick wondered what he had let himself in for. Doing a favour for a mate for a bit of dosh had sounded good. But what the hell had Ryan got himself into? He had thought it was a bit of bother over £20. Patrick had been a solicitor before he went inside for falsifying accounts, but he was out now, and had hoped to build himself up a business in a new name to support himself.

Alan put the phone down gently. "I have not finished yet!" he said, pointedly.

172

"Ryan, you went to the pub on 14th, and you were angry because Tiffany had been sacked from her job over £20, which she helped herself to from Eva's handbag. So I suggest in a fit of temper, and we know you have them, you went to Eva's bungalow. You hoped she would forgive Tiffany. You even went to the trouble of making her a cup of tea, and you put a sedative in it, but when she told you she didn't want Tiffany any more, you lost it, and you poured poison down her throat."

"I didn't. I am innocent!" Ryan said pleadingly, looking at Patrick for support.

"Say 'no comment'!" said Patrick, fiercely. He really didn't know how to get out of this situation.

"No comment," said Ryan. All his cockiness and arrogance had melted away. They had three different charges against him, and he felt just like a rat caught in a trap.

Chapter Twenty-three

It was a happy day for Pamela, and she was finally back home again after waiting two months for the will to be sorted out. She didn't like the idea of rattling around in the big house on her own, as Marty only came home at holiday times, so she had invited Holly to live there too. To Pamela, it felt like the baby that Holly was carrying was her real granddaughter. She was certainly Marty's niece, and she was delighted that Holly was so easy to get along with, so it meant Pamela could be a part of their lives.

Holly had her own part of the house. It was undoubtedly big enough, with even her own kitchen and sitting room, plus a nursery for the new baby. Living totally under each other's feet probably wouldn't have worked, and this way they could mutually decide when they wanted to spend time together.

Pamela was beginning to miss having a man in her life, but she had no intention of reuniting with Stewart; he had been such a mistake. Her first priority would be a support network for Holly. She felt that Ian would have liked the support she was giving Holly. It had taken a while for her conscience to prick regarding Ian, but she regretted treating him so badly. It was amazing that he had still loved her, and left half the house and assets to her.

She had given some money to David as promised, and now that Ian was not around to bail him out, he had actually taken some responsibility for his life. He had stopped gambling, and was now in a support group, mainly because he had hope that his wife and children might return to him. They were not going to live in the bungalow, but there was an apartment further down the road. However, David had to hold onto his job for that to happen, because he had to pay his way with the rent. Ian had been his crutch for years, and now he had to show that he could cope without that crutch.

Pamela had celebrated in her usual way by going out and buying a new wardrobe of clothes, but she had not been totally selfish. She had bought Holly a new pram, a cot, a car seat and lots of baby clothes. Holly had been so grateful, it actually made Pamela feel good to be able to help her.

She wondered whether Alan Clarke was going to solve this crime. It seemed very complicated. The police seemed to have had so many people helping them with their enquiries, but no one had been charged yet. She didn't know exactly what had gone on with Lisa. Apparently some sort of accident, and she had been in hospital. In the beginning it had been very serious, but she had pulled through, and was now back at the apartment with Kate, but not back at work.

Now a man called Ryan Lee, who seemed to be someone from Lisa's past, was helping with enquiries, and the local newspapers were very interested in him. But although rumours were swirling around about him, that was all she knew for now. She had not liked Lisa in the past. Lisa had thrown herself at Ian when he was alive, but those feelings of animosity had faded now. Lisa no longer bothered her, so she was glad that Lisa was now getting better. With a new baby granddaughter due in a few short months, Pamela felt more contented than she had for quite a few years, and now she was home again.

Lisa was so glad to be back in her own bedroom. She knew that it had been necessary to be in hospital, first of all for her injuries from the fall, and then the rehabilitation centre. Physically she had needed the physiotherapy, and she felt as though she had suffered a breakdown. Everything in her life had been upside down, and as a person she had felt worthless. That was until Alan Clarke had visited her and explained that her name was now cleared, as Ryan Lee had made a confession, which had been taped. The fact that he had tried to deny it afterwards, and say he was drunk at the time, was not believed, and she had been told that he faced other charges as well. Although she didn't know the details, because DCI Clarke had said that he could not share anything with her at this time, but he hoped her mind would be at rest knowing that she had been cleared of any assault on baby Lily.

Lisa had cried tears of relief at this news, and she had been happy at this time not to share it with anyone except Kate, as DCI Clarke had explained that once the newspapers got hold of it, they would want her story, warts and all. And Lisa knew for sure she did not want to share it, it would only bring back more pain to her. Her relief was akin to someone lifting a heavy boulder from their shoulders. She felt that now she could straighten herself up, and face life again. Kate had been her usual supportive self, and she was so grateful for the way she had supported her. She was the best friend anyone could possibly have.

Lisa was sitting outside in the garden, enjoying the sunshine, when Sally came round to see her. Kate had been preparing afternoon tea and cake, and she invited Sally to join them out in their small garden. Sally accepted gratefully.

"That sounds lovely, Kate. I was delighted to hear that Lisa is home. When I heard she had been hit by a car, I was devastated, but she has made such a remarkable recovery. You must be proud of your sister."

Kate blinked her owl-like eyes, and carried on laying the tea tray, wondering how much of the truth they should tell Sally. It was up to Lisa really, so she took her out to the garden, and found another deckchair in the shed.

Lisa's face really lit up when she saw Sally. In truth she felt ready to go back to work, but would Sally still want her? "Oh Sally, how great to see you, and how is Abby? I have missed her."

"She has missed you!" said Sally, ruefully. "Our temp is not a patch on you, although she does love Abby."

Lisa felt a twinge of jealousy pass through her. Abby had almost felt like her own child. She had always found it difficult to keep

176

things to herself, and she had always been close to Sally, so in that moment, she decided to tell Sally the true story about herself, even if it did mean that she might not keep her job.

"Sally, I didn't have a road accident. Kate just told everyone that to protect me, as she always does," she turned and smiled at Kate, who blinked back nervously. "I had a breakdown."

She saw Sally's eyes widen with surprise, so she went on to explain about Ryan, and their baby Lily. Her voice faltered as she explained how Ryan had shaken Lily to death, and then blamed her, the shock she had felt at the time, and her inability to defend herself. Then she explained that she had been in a secure unit for five years receiving treatment, and when she came out she had been given a new identity to protect her from the public, as it was believed she had killed her own child.

Sally took her hands and squeezed them, scarcely believing what she had just heard.

"So you have spent the last fifteen years knowing you are innocent, with the trauma of losing your beautiful baby hanging over you. How on earth have you coped, Lisa?"

"With difficulty. I know sometimes my behaviour has been erratic, and people think I am a bit strange."

"I have never thought that about you, Lisa. I trust you more than anyone with Abby, and there is no way you could have harmed your baby. I wish I had known about this before. As a solicitor, I would have done my utmost to support you."

"That is kind," murmured Kate. "Luckily the police have somehow got a taped confession from him, and we are told he is being held for other charges also."

Lisa smiled at Sally. She knew she was a good person. "You can imagine the reaction when I vanished with Abby. I panicked when they found out my real name, and my past. At that time they also believed I had killed Lily. This is why I fell out of the window when they caught up with me."

"Well I could have told them different!" said Sally, stoutly. "I never for one moment worried about Abby being with you, and I am only sorry that I didn't get the opportunity to help bring this man to justice. Did you have any idea that Ryan was living as close as Margate now?"

"None at all, until they told me. But any feelings I had for that man died when he killed our daughter!" said Lisa passionately, and Sally put a comforting arm around her.

"The police have done an amazing job," said Kate. "More tea, Sally."

"No, thank you, Kate. Although it was lovely, especially the lemon drizzle cake." Her mind was ticking over quickly about how she could help Lisa. This poor young woman deserved some sort of compensation for all the years of heartache she had suffered. Nothing could bring her baby back but her good name could now be restored, and financial compensation could help make her life more comfortable. She would speak to Don tonight, he was the expert on these matters. She turned towards Lisa.

"Lisa, I am going to put my head together with Don. You have been severely wronged, and imprisoned for a crime you never did. It's turned your life upside down, and I believe we have a very strong case to get you financial compensation."

"The police told us not to speak to the press as they might want a story," said Kate quickly.

"Absolutely, we don't want reporters sticking their noses in and offering you eye watering amounts of money to lay your private life bare. That is not how we operate!" said Sally, firmly.

"Sally, you are always so good to me, and I know you have my best interests at heart," said Lisa.

"To be honest, Lisa, if we win the case, you will be set up for life, and you won't even need to work for me. But as long as we can stay in touch, and Abby can see you sometimes," smiled Sally.

"All the money in the world would not make me want to stop being a part of Abby's life," said Lisa from her heart.

Sally stood up and embraced her. "I must go, but you are welcome to come and visit Abby any time." Then she was gone in a flurry, her stiletto heels clicking across the hall floor, and the faint but pleasant aroma of perfume wafting from her.

Kate shut the door after her. She was feeling a bit usurped. She liked having Lisa relying on her. If she suddenly became rich, Lisa might want to be more independent, she might even want to buy her own home. She was aware that Lisa was beginning to realise her future was not with men, they had let her down in the past so many times, and here she was, Kate, right under her nose, but as yet Lisa had not appreciated that it was Kate who loved her more than anyone else in the world, and a lot more than a sister ever would. When would Lisa wake up and realise that her greatest and most faithful love was living right here beside her? She shut the door, and went back into the garden, but Lisa was not there. Then she remembered, Lisa had a doctor's appointment, just a check to see how she was doing. She went back inside the flat, and knocked at Lisa's bedroom door.

"Are you OK, Lisa? I can give you a lift to the doctor."

"I am fine, Kate, there is no need. I am so much better, and have not driven the car for a while."

"Well if you are sure."

Lisa gave her a spontaneous hug, which was like balm to Kate's bruised spirit. "Kate, I know how much you care, but I need to get back out there and live my life again, maybe even return to work, if Sally will have me."

Kate blinked, her eyes behind her glasses looked confused. "I know she meant well, Lisa, but you don't have to worry about money. Your home is here with me, and we have enough."

"I know that," laughed Lisa. Kate was probably right. Knowing her luck she wouldn't win a case, but just the thought of not having to worry about money, or rely on Kate, felt good. Independence felt good.

Zoe had decided not to say anything at work about her pregnancy until she had passed three months. It was just a precaution, but one of her friends at work had told everyone, they had been trying for nearly ten years, and Tracy had been over the moon when her test was positive. She had even been making a list of everything she needed, and then the poor girl had miscarried, and Zoe's heart had gone out to her.

That had been a few months ago, and Tracy had since told her that the next time, if there was one, she would wait until it was safe to announce it. Zoe knew she was so lucky to conceive so easily, and

179

her age was on her side to. She sincerely hoped that Tracy and her husband would be lucky soon.

The morning sickness was a bugbear, but it had happened before, then settled down at three months, and she was sure it would be the same again. She had a new regime at the moment to help her. She got up a bit earlier, and weathered the nausea, and had dry toast and fruit tea for her breakfast, as right now her stomach couldn't take milk. By the time she got to work, the sickness had usually passed, and she had also found nibbling a ginger biscuit seemed to help her. With all the precautions she was taking, by the time she presented herself on the ward she had her sickness under control, meaning at the moment no one suspected a thing.

She hugged her secret to herself. Only one person needed to know, and she relived the joy on his face when she had told him. Alan was an amazing dad. Even though he had such a demanding job, he still found the time to be involved with Adam, he didn't mind changing a dirty nappy, and he regularly bathed and fed him. Even when she had been breastfeeding, she had expressed some of her milk, and Alan had insisted on taking his turn at night feeding Adam. She had told him not to worry, as in the early months Zoe was not at work, but he had wanted to do it. He wanted to be a part of his son's life right from the beginning, and it gave her a warm glow inside to know that she always had his support.

She could always tell when Alan got important news about any of his cases through the sudden change in his demeanour and the realisation that the job had to take precedence. So when he had taken off so quickly this morning, after the call from James, it obviously meant there were new developments. It would be great if he could solve this double murder, and although she didn't expect him to share anything with her yet, she knew he would as soon as he was able to. His intention had been to feed Adam, but there was some sort of development and he had to go immediately, and she wouldn't have had it any other way. She was proud of how Alan balanced his working life and his home life.

As this was her day off, she had decided not to do too much. In the early days of pregnancy she felt tired. Adam was happily playing with his building bricks at her feet, so she took the opportunity to sit down with a glass of chilled water, and a ginger biscuit, and relax. She bent over to help him build them up, and as soon as it was high, he knocked it down again, chuckling. His happy little face was infectious, and she laughed with him, commenting, "What a cheeky boy you are," which made him laugh even more. Like all babies he was hard work, but he was also a little ray of sunshine in their lives, and she counted herself very lucky that he was healthy and happy.

Chapter Twenty-four

"Honestly, we are just going round in circles. What on earth are we missing?" said Alan, crossly.

"Yes sir, it's very complicated," agreed Martha.

"You know what I think of Lee, and nothing would make me happier than to add the charge of murder to his list of crimes. He could have killed Eva, as his exact times of being in the pub were not really known by the barman."

"But?" asked James.

"What would his reason be for killing Ian Jones? As far as we know, he didn't know him."

"Maybe he killed Eva in a temper 'cos of Tiffany losing her job, and he made it look like the person who killed Ian had done that murder as well," suggested Martha.

"No, too much of a coincidence," mused Alan. "And we established that whoever killed the doctor used the weedkiller in his shed. Now Lee would not have been able to get into there."

"Forensics thought the killer had administered rat poison to Eva, and they also came in and made her a cup of tea. In fact, she let them in," James reminded them.

"You are right, so surely we are now looking for two different people?"

"That's what they want us to think, sir. I still think one person did it. They just did it slightly differently this time. Didn't you say that

Pamela Jones has moved back into the house? That would make it harder to get out into the shed," said James.

"Yes, she got her inheritance, and she's back in there, and by all accounts, so is Holly, Ian's daughter."

"Well sir, I find all that very strange. Pamela suddenly stops being self-centred, teams up with Holly, and invites her to come and live with her. We only have her word that Ian was her father. Maybe Pamela is her mother, and she had her before she met Ian. We only have Holly's word that her mother made a deathbed confession," remarked Martha.

Alan considered her words. He, too, had been surprised at Pamela's character transformation.

But Holly appeared to be lovely in every way, the sort of person that everyone loved. Was he being fooled?

"You certainly have a point there, or she could be a friend of Pamela," he said gruffly.

"She does look like Marty," Martha reminded him.

"Could be a coincidence. Same hair colour and eyes."

"But are you suggesting that Pamela and Holly killed Ian between them?" said James, wonderingly.

"I don't know what I am suggesting. I am just looking into all possibilities. But what I think we should do, is check all the details about Holly. Check her past, and make sure she doesn't have a police record."

"OK sir, I am on it," said James.

"Good man. In fact, because of the proximity of Eva's bungalow to the doctor's house, I think the killer is very close. We also need to interview some of the neighbours again. Surely somebody must have seen something."

"I will arrange some house to house enquiries," volunteered Martha.

"Good, well let's have our lunch, and then maybe meet up again later this afternoon just to see if we have anything new to work on."

Ryan Lee was shocked to know that he had been living so close to Lisa without knowing it. But when they had been together she wasn't Lisa, she was Sheila Black. He had assumed she would stay in the looney bin, as he thought of it, forever.

He bemoaned the day that he had met that little tart in the pub. She had been his undoing. He had no idea she was in the force, he hated being fooled by a woman and he bitterly regretted telling her about when he had shaken Lily to death. And as for Tiffany, she had turned against him, and she had told the law he had gone out that night. If he ever saw her again she would pay for that. What a bloody idiot he had been going round to see the old lady to try and persuade her to take Tiffany back. And she wouldn't listen to him, told him her daughter took care of her, and didn't want a thief in the house. That had made him so angry. For god's sake, it had only been a measly twenty quid!

He hated the law and all it stood for with a passion, that stern DCI who had read him his rights, and charged him with attempted rape and infanticide. He had demanded to see the woman who had accused him of attempted rape, but been told she was going to be kept well away from him, as he had caused her enough grief. If only the bloody constable hadn't come along and seen him with his trousers undone and his dick out, he could have said it was her word against his. The silly cow had fainted, so didn't even know what was going on, but Constable Martin did. And now the swines were trying to pin murder on him. As Tiffany had shoved him under the bus, he was now going to do it to her. He had formulated a plan, and he just needed to talk to his solicitor and then set up an interview with the DCI.

Patrick Lewis jumped when his mobile rang, especially when Ryan's name flashed across the screen. He wished he didn't have to answer it, but he had already been paid, and Ryan wouldn't take too kindly to him not fulfilling his bargain.

"Yes Ryan, how are you doing?"

"I am not doing well, and you need to get me out of here!"

"I am trying, but bail will be difficult."

"I am not talking about bail. I am talking about new information to get me off this murder charge."

"They haven't charged you with murder. There was no real evidence or motive."

"Too right, mate, but there was for Tiffany, she had just lost her job."

"Are you telling me Tiffany killed the old lady? How do you know this?"

"I don't for sure, but she did go out for a while after dinner, then she came back to have her bath. She never said where she went, and I want to tell the police."

"OK," sighed Patrick. He would have to put that suit on again, and use a posh voice to set up this meeting with the DCI. "But it won't change the other charges."

"I know, but I don't want to be in prison for life."

Patrick clicked his mobile off. He then rang the police station to set up a meeting with DCI Clarke. He was told that he was at lunch right now, but would be free around two-thirty, so he booked that time for an interview. He then sent Ryan a text, he didn't really want to get into conversation with him, as his case looked pretty hopeless. Even without the murder charge, he couldn't do much to help him. He knew Ryan had friends who acted on his behalf. Even though he was being detained, he had formed himself a group when he was inside. Patrick did not want to fall foul of them.

He had a shave and combed his hair, and then changed into the suit. It was a long time since he had been an acting solicitor, and nowadays he preferred to dress in jeans and casual wear, but he had to look the part.

He arrived at the station at two-twenty, and was asked to wait out by the desk. He found himself pacing about, and then suddenly he was called into an interview room. Ryan was already in there, slumped like a sack of potatoes over a chair. He greeted him politely, and then Alan Clarke entered the room. He was accompanied by his partner Martha.

"Good afternoon, DCI Clarke. My client has some new information to offer to you."

Alan looked doubtfully in Lee's direction. This bloke could lie for England, how on earth could he believe anything that he said? Still, he owed it to him to listen. He motioned to Martha to sit down, and she set up the tape.

"Interview with Ryan Lee and his solicitor at fourteen-thirty-three, requested by Mr Lee. Well, what new information do you have for us?"

Ryan swallowed nervously, and any trace of arrogance in his demeanour had vanished. He somehow knew not only that this man did not like him, but also he didn't believe him, so he had to make it sound good. "On 14th July, I forgot to say that Tiffany went out after I had come back. She said she was going to see Eva and try to get her job back."

"Why did you not mention this before? You told us that neither of you went out."

"I know, we both agreed to back each other. . ."

"Oh, so now because Tiffany told us you went out, and so did the barman confirm you were there, you suddenly want to throw your girlfriend under the bus."

Alan looked at him with contempt. First he had ruined Lisa's life, now he was trying to use Tiffany to slide out of any responsibility.

"Well, I have got news for you, Lee. A neighbour confirms they saw you coming out of Eva's house that evening, and we have established that, although her body was not discovered until the next morning, Eva did die earlier that evening. We also have your DNA on the door handle, so there is no point denying it."

"Say 'no comment'," hissed Patrick. This whole bloody thing was a nightmare.

Fear rushed through Ryan. Of course his fingerprints were on the door, he had let himself out after the old biddy had refused to listen to him. How on earth was no comment going to stop him being charged with murder? He ignored Patrick. What bloody good was he?

"I only went to see if she would take Tiffany back, but she would not listen."

"And we all know what a temper you have," remarked Alan, drily.

"Not with old ladies. I just went on to the pub and got myself a Guinness. She didn't want to listen to me."

"We only have your word on that. Now I need you to stay here and help us further with our enquiries, and in the meantime, I have a warrant to search your home," said Alan firmly, noting his discomfiture. "Interview terminated at fifteen hundred. Take him back to the cell."

Martha switched off the recording machine, and they both watched the duty constable take him from the room, followed by his solicitor.

"God only knows where he found that solicitor?" remarked Alan, as the door closed behind them.

"Yes, he needs to wear a suit that fits him," laughed Martha. Then she turned towards Alan.

"Did a neighbour really see him go to Eva's house? I didn't know about that."

"I hadn't had a chance to tell you, but James sent someone to do house to house enquiries earlier, and evidently Kate saw him when she was coming home from work late in the afternoon that day. Of course, it doesn't prove he killed her, but it does make him a suspect."

"Does Kate know what he looks like?"

"That is a good point. The description she gave fitted him, so I just took a chance, and as you heard, it worked, because he did go round there."

"But so did Tiffany, apparently. We need to establish who saw her last," Martha reminded him.

"Yes, and as Kate only saw him alone, then it wasn't a put up job between the two of them.

"OK, we have to get Tiffany in again, sir."

"I will send someone to pick her up after five-thirty when she's home."

Chapter Twenty-five

Tiffany was still very angry at Ryan's betrayal. The bastard had been out looking for women at the pub when she had given him money, her hard earned money, to go out and have a drink. She had trusted him. What a fool she had been! She knew he had been in jail, and she was no angel. She had been poor ever since she ran away from home at the age of fourteen, so had to live by her wits.

She had been prosecuted for soliciting. She had thought it would be easy money, but the law had other ideas. She had to pay a hefty fine, and she didn't like any of the punters; some of them had smelly breath, and they didn't wash properly. Tiffany was a sticker for cleanliness, so she had made herself a living from doing housework. Delighted clients often gave her lavish tips, and she had just been getting on her feet when she met Ryan.

Tiffany had fallen hard for him. He was incredibly handsome, but now she realised that all his talk had been mumbo jumbo. And to find out he had used his evil temper to shake his own child to death! Even she thought that was extreme. Her love for him was over, and now she wanted him out of her life. With a bit of luck she could keep the flat, as she would put everything she earned into paying the rent.

After being interviewed again today, she did not expect to hear any more from the police. Ryan was in custody, he had visited Eva, and he had a temper. Those cops would want to find someone to answer for that crime, and they already had him on other charges, so how perfect it would be if they charged him with murder as well. He would go away for life, and she would never see him again. Tiffany would always have a grudge against him as he had blatantly been unfaithful to her. He didn't have to rape anyone, he had her at home, but he just couldn't keep it in his trousers, so she was well and truly done with him!

She put all her anger into her job today. It was a big house at Minnis Bay. She polished every shelf until it shone, and washed the kitchen floor with strong vigorous strokes. She finished at two o'clock, and then went onto her next job. The owners worked all day, so had entrusted her with the key. This was a bungalow at Westgate with a big conservatory. She realised she had been a fool last week, stealing just for twenty pounds, so she wouldn't do that again. The owners had left her forty pounds on the side with a thank you note, so she put that safely in her purse, and left for home. It was now five o'clock, and the evening traffic was building up as she drove her battered old Clio Renault towards the flat.

It was just about five-thirty as she parked her car outside. She was hot and tired, and was looking forward to her evening bath. To her extreme annoyance, she saw DCI Clarke and his assistant just about to press the button for her flat. What the hell could they possibly want now?

"Good evening, Tiffany, we need to speak to you once again about Eva's death, and also there will be officers arriving with a warrant to search your flat. Is that all right with you?"

"No it isn't, but that won't stop you, will it!" she said, angrily. The thought of having the place turned upside down by the law was not a pleasant one.

"We would like to interview you again at the station."

Fear rushed through her. Did they know about her visit to Eva? She shrugged her shoulders, knowing she was beaten, she would have to go with them. She had thought by telling them about Ryan going to see Eva, it would take the heat off her.

She then saw two policemen coming towards her. They must have come to search the flat, so she gave them her key. Maybe it was safer just to comply. Outside was the police car. Silently she got into the back, wondering wildly if she needed a solicitor. But damn it, she had no spare money to hire one. It looked as if she was going to have to live by her wits, and get herself out of this mess without any help from anyone else.

When they arrived back at the station, Alan showed her into the interview room, aware that it was now six o'clock, but this could not really wait. He had spoken to Zoe, and said he hoped he could be home by seven. Zoe had said she would keep Adam up for a bit, as he had fallen asleep about four-thirty, just before his tea, so would not want to go to bed just yet. Having missed out on giving him his breakfast, Alan really hoped he would see him before he went to bed.

Tiffany sat there, her lips tightly drawn. She felt anger, tiredness and fear all coursing through her insides, and she wished this nightmare would just go away.

Alan sat down opposite her, with Martha seated next to him. She had switched the tape on, so he went through the preliminaries. He could see by her face that Tiffany was going to be hostile. He, too, had had enough, and wanted to go home, but he had a job to do.

"Right Tiffany, you told us you were at home on 14th July, but that is not true, is it?"

She had a pretty good idea who had dumped her in it. "I did stay in all evening, but I finished a bit early that afternoon, and as I passed Eva's house, I thought I would see if I could get my job back."

"You did not mention this before. What time was it?"

"Between four-thirty and five, I believe."

"How did you get on with Eva then?"

"I didn't. She opened the door, but did not ask me in. She said her daughter did not want me to work there any more."

"Are you saying you then went home and stayed in all evening?"

"I went home and told Ryan. He then said to leave it to him, he could go round and see her, and he did, after dinner."

"And what did he say when he returned?"

"He said he had called in to speak to her, but not got her to agree to take me back."

"Do you know how long he was with her for?"

"No, neither would he, as he went on to the pub afterwards. But he did better than me, she let him in!"

Tiffany had no idea if what she had just said was true, but Eva wasn't around to discount it, and they possibly might believe her over Ryan.

Alan exchanged glances with Martha. These two were both liars and dishonest. How could they know which one was telling the truth?

"Do you know if Ryan made her a cup of tea?"

She laughed bitterly. "I doubt it. He doesn't know one end of a kettle from the other."

Alan decided he needed to think about the information. Even if one or both of them had killed Eva, it still didn't explain the doctor's death.

"OK, Tiffany, interview terminated at eighteen hours fifteen minutes, you can go for now."

Tiffany could not wait to leave the police station. She was well aware that Ryan was somewhere inside this building too. They had not offered to take her home, and she could not afford a taxi, so she waited for the hourly bus to come. It would take another hour to reach her flat; but she was free, although she had not liked the words he said ". . .for now".

Whilst the bus was bumping its way to Margate, she sat thinking. Maybe she did have the last laugh on Ryan. Nobody knew she had followed him to Eva's bungalow, then waited until he came out. This time she had gone in the bungalow, and as long as nobody had seen her, it was her secret. It was an act of impulse. She had thought of backing him up, but he had come out, not shut the door properly, and then got on a bus to go to the pub. So then it had been her turn. Maybe, after all, she had fooled everyone.

Alan put thoughts of the murders out of his mind as he drove home. Martha's husband had picked her up and they had now gone, so he was hoping that Adam was still up. As he put his key into the front door, he could hear Adam chatting in baby language, and he smiled, convinced there had been a dada mentioned. His son was seated in his high chair, watching the end of CBeebies, and Zoe was sitting on the couch, sipping a glass of water.

He strode across the room and kissed her on the cheek. "Hi honey, I made it then."

"You did, he is not tired right now. He had a late sleep, but if you want you can try putting him down and reading him his story. We have casserole for dinner, so I can dish it up any time."

"Well how about we let him have a special treat, that Sponge Bob video, whilst we eat our dinner, and then I can try him? Another half hour or so and he might be tired."

"Yes, he's happy enough in his high chair. And you must be starving!" agreed Zoe.

They sat down together and ate in a companionable silence. Zoe noted that Alan was quiet, which meant that he was thinking. It was obvious that the murders had not yet been solved, although he had told her that Lisa had been proved innocent of harming her baby, and it had, in fact, been the baby's father. That was as much as he could say right now, but Zoe was so happy, because she had taken a liking to Lisa. She interrupted his thoughts.

"When I took Adam for a walk, we met Lisa. I thought she had been involved in a road accident, as this is the story that had gone around, but she told me everything, including the fact that she had popped into Birchington because the doctor had recommended a bereavement counsellor there. She said her visit had helped her, and she was quite bright and smiling."

"Thanks, honey, it was top secret, of course. Oh, that is good. The poor woman had carried all that pain inside her for fifteen years, and been misjudged by everyone."

"Yes, she also said her employer Sally wants to help her claim compensation, and she has a good case."

"She certainly does. Martha told her that she would probably never need to work again."

"But you know she wants to go back, she says she misses Abby."

"I feel bad now, Zoe, that I warned you off her. I was as bad as everyone else. I thought the worst of her."

"But you could not have known. If you were given information like that, you must not blame yourself, Alan. Nobody knows more than I do what a kind and compassionate man you are."

Alan looked gratefully at her, Zoe always understood. Sometimes he wished he could discuss things with her, and ask her opinion about people, but it wasn't done. He knew his wife was a most discreet person, but it was Martha who sat in the interviews with him, and together they had to analyse the character and honesty of the suspects. There would be time enough to share it with her when these murders had been solved, and the right person brought to justice. He had only shared information this time in desperation when he thought Lisa might be looking after Adam. One thing he could do tomorrow was go and see Kate, and ask her for more details about when she had seen Lee leaving Eva's house.

Zoe went to clear their plates away, and Alan lifted Adam out of his high chair and muted the TV. "Sponge Bob is going to bed, and so are you, my son," he said, kissing him on his chubby little pink cheek. Zoe had already bathed him and got him ready for bed, but as he cuddled his son, an unpleasant odour wafted up.

"You little stinker," he laughed. "I am taking him to bed now, honey. His bum needs changing."

"OK love," said Zoe from the kitchen, smiling to herself. Even the dirty dishes seemed more appealing than cleaning and changing Adam.

She washed the dishes, and left them to drain, then put the kettle on to make them both a coffee. She could hear Alan reading a story to Adam and doing all the appropriate animal noises, and then he stopped.

"I am tucking Adam up now, honey."

Zoe went into the bedroom. Adam was lying still with his blue blanket tucked around him, and he looked really peaceful. "Goodnight little buster, go to sleep now," she said, kissing his cheek.

Alan kissed him too, and then they both quietly left the room, holding their breath. But Adam was not going to fight sleep tonight. His eyes closed, and when they got back into the lounge, they could hear his even breathing through the baby monitor. Zoe heaved a sigh of relief.

"I wish he would go down like that for me," she said. "You make it look so easy."

"I know it isn't," said Alan, putting his arms around her, and holding her close. "That little boy has the best mother in the world."

Zoe smiled. "You say all the right words. I'll go and make our coffee now."

j

Chapter Twenty-six

Lisa felt as if she was beginning to get her confidence back. Kate had welcomed her home with open arms, and from what she had been told, Ryan was going to be punished for shaking Lily to her death. She no longer felt anything other than revulsion towards him, but she had no desire to carry anger around inside her, as it would be forever weighing her down and ruining her life.

She knew she would always feel pain for the loss of her beautiful daughter, but it had lessened, and become a bit more bearable now that she had been exonerated from any blame. She made up her mind she was going to pick up her life again and live it. It had been great to see Sally, and be given news that she might be getting financial compensation; that had improved her mood even more.

When she had met her bereavement counsellor at Birchington, it had been so therapeutic to let it all out. A few tears had actually felt like balm to her tortured soul. Fifteen years of grieving had culminated in finally being free from any blame, and it felt so good. They had both agreed that she now felt free, and Lisa had said it had been such a relief to get it all off her chest. She had been told she could come back any time she wanted to, the support would always be there for her, and for this she was grateful, but already she was beginning to feel emotionally stronger, and life had to go on.

And then who should she meet in Birchington High Street but Zoe, who was so pleased to see her doing well. She had made a fuss of Adam, and mentioned how much she was missing Abby. She really felt that maybe going back to work again might be very good for her. Zoe had agreed with that, and even given her a hug before they parted company. With everyone being so warm towards her, Lisa could feel all her bitterness from the past slipping away. It had felt the right thing to tell Zoe what had really happened. She understood why Kate had said she was involved in a road accident, but now it was time for the truth. She trusted Zoe not to spread it around, as she wasn't ready to be confronted by the press. Sally had said it would happen when she was officially exonerated. In fact, it had been a case that had featured on the national news, but she had been Sheila Black then, and everyone here knew her as Lisa Bryant. Her anonymity would remain to all except close friends, and if it did leak out, well, she had done nothing wrong.

After seeing Zoe she had driven back to Westgate, and whilst she was driving past the Co-op she had spotted Helen coming out. Helen was accompanied by a man with dark hair, maybe a few years older, and she wondered if he was her boyfriend.

Helen had been delighted to see her, and insisted they went in the Beano cafe for afternoon tea and a catch-up. "This is my brother Greg, he's staying with me for a while. Greg, this is Lisa, my nanny buddy."

"How do you do Lisa."

Lisa shook his outstretched hand. He had a nice kindly face, with interesting grey eyes, that lit up when he smiled. And yet she could sense a sadness behind his polite exterior.

"Where do you live usually, Greg?" she found herself asking.

"I have a flat in Chelsea, but I must say it's nice to be here in Westgate, especially with the beautiful weather."

It was not uncommon for people to escape from the hubbub of London, to come to the calm and peaceful Kent coast for a summer break with family. Lisa wondered idly if he was escaping from a marriage breakup or some sad event. She could sense pain in his eyes, and she felt an empathy for him.

She decided not to enlighten Helen on what had really happened to her. With Greg there, it didn't seem to be the right time. Helen said how glad she was that Lisa had made such a good recovery from the accident. "I heard you had to learn to walk again. Thank goodness you are OK," she said. "It must have been a traumatic time for you."

"Yes, it was, but I am fine now," said Lisa quickly, not wanting to pursue the subject. She noticed Greg looking at her. It was almost as if he could read her mind, and she felt herself blushing. Then he stood up. "I am just off to the gents, girls."

Whilst he was absent, Helen quickly explained why he had come to stay with her.

"Greg's wife and baby daughter were killed in a head on crash just a month ago. He is a surgeon at Guy's Hospital, but on leave as he is so traumatised by it. He blames himself for working late, and not being with them when it happened."

In the midst of her own trauma, Lisa realised that she wasn't the only person suffering from bereavement. How terrible to lose his family like that. "Oh, Helen, that is so heart-rending for him. Is there anything I can do?"

"You are kind. He just needs friends right now. He mustn't be left on his own, but don't say anything to him that I told you, he's a bit proud, and will tell you in his own time."

"Of course not. And Helen, whilst he is not here I have something to tell you."

"Go on."

"To cut a long story short, fifteen years ago my partner shook our baby daughter to death. I was suffering from mental illness, so he pushed the blame onto me, and I had to serve five years in a secure unit, and when I came out, I was given a new identity."

She saw the shock on Helen's face. Greg was still not back, so she continued: "Recently my ex-partner came to the area, and the police have managed to get a taped confession from him, so I have now been exonerated."

Greg was making his way towards them now, so Helen spontaneously hugged her, thinking how Lisa must have suffered. "Thank God justice has been done," she whispered. She was still in shock about what Lisa had told her. It would take a while to digest this. She turned her attention back to Greg. "Well bruv, shall we get you home now?" she said protectively.

"Yes, I need to get going too. Kate will wonder where I have got to," laughed Lisa.

"It was really nice meeting you Lisa," said Greg, and she felt his serious grey eyes on her, and he smiled, which lit up his face. There was something really drawing her towards him. Was it because she knew he was suffering, although trying to hide his pain? He shouldn't be blaming himself for his wife and daughter's deaths. Fate was cruel sometimes, but it was its own master, and no one could change it.

As she drove towards home, her thoughts were on Greg, and not herself. His loss was new and raw, poor man, and her heart went out to him. She parked her car in its allotted space, and she noticed the police car outside the building. Were they visiting again?

As she entered the apartment, she saw relief on Kate's face. "Oh, there you are."

Kate was in the kitchen ironing. She was using her steam iron, and standing talking to her whilst she worked was DCI Clarke accompanied by his WPC. They both turned towards Lisa.

"How are you, Lisa?" asked Martha kindly.

"Yes, I am good, feeling much better," said Lisa brightly.

"You are looking very well," said Alan, smiling. "We just popped by because Kate saw Ryan Lee leaving Eva's house on the evening that she was murdered, and we just wondered what time it was. Did you see him as well?"

Lisa glanced at Kate. This was new to her, she had not realised that Kate had seen Ryan that evening. Fear coursed through her when she thought of how close he had been to her that day. She never wanted to see that man again.

"No, I did not see him, thank goodness!" she said, with feeling.

"It was after dinner, about six-thirty. Lisa was taking a shower," said Kate.

"Did you mention it to Lisa?" Alan persisted.

Kate was annoyed by this remark, but she hid it. Putting down her steam iron, she then proceeded to pick up a small glass jug, and poured water from it into the iron.

"Why aren't you using the little plastic jug that comes with the iron?" asked Lisa.

Kate put down the jug, and spoke gently, although she was seething inside. "Detective Inspector Clarke, this man ruined Lisa's life. I didn't even want to mention his name."

"Of course," said Martha, soothingly.

"I have never seen you use that jug before," said Lisa. "We usually put cream in it."

"I have mislaid the plastic one," said Kate. She took her frustration out on the sheet she was ironing, with vigorous strokes of the iron.

"Thank you, Kate. That is all we need now, so we will leave you to your ironing," said Alan.

Lisa showed them out, and Martha and Alan both wished her well. She watched as they got into the car and drove away, and then she returned to the kitchen where Kate was still ironing.

"I am glad you didn't tell me about seeing him, Kate. I never want to see that man again!" she said firmly.

"I knew that. What a stupid question for him to ask!"

"Well, they have to do their job."

Kate folded up the sheet, and then proceeded to dismantle the ironing board. Lisa picked it up, and put it into the hall cupboard where it was stored.

"Let's see what we can have for dinner," said Kate, opening the fridge door.

"I can peel some vegetables," offered Lisa.

They worked together in a companionable silence. Lisa was peeling potatoes, and Kate was shredding a cabbage. Lisa proceeded to tell Kate about her visit to the counsellor, and when she got to the part where she had met Helen and her brother Greg and gone into the Beano, Kate's head shot up, and she looked very surprised.

"Oh, so he is her brother. Has he come here for a holiday."

"He's on sick leave from Guy's hospital. He just lost his wife and baby daughter in a fatal car crash."

Kate's eyes widened. "What a terrible thing to happen to someone!"

At that moment Lisa's phone pinged, and she picked it up to read the message. It was from Helen:

'HI LISA, WAS GREAT SEEING YOU TODAY. WONDERED IF YOU COULD HELP ME OUT.

'I HAVE TO WORK TOMORROW, LAST MINUTE REQUEST FROM ZOE, AND HAD PROMISED GREG WE COULD HAVE A DAY IN CANTERBURY. JUST WONDERED IF YOU WERE FREE TO ACCOMPANY HIM.'

Lisa liked the idea of that, because she was beginning to get bored with being at home. Greg seemed a very nice man, who had suffered a trauma. She knew what it felt like, and if a day in Canterbury seeing the sights would cheer him up, then she was more than happy to do that.

"Oh, it's Helen. She has to work tomorrow, and she's asked me to take Greg round Canterbury."

Kate kept her voice steady, but inside she felt angry. After all Lisa had been through, why could they not leave her alone?

"Do you want to go?" she asked.

Lisa smiled. "Actually, yes, Greg needs friends right now, and helping him will take my mind off my own life."

"It's a kind thing to do," said Kate, but inside she was thinking, here we go again, another man, another infatuation. Would Lisa never learn that men were bad news?

Lisa sent a reply back to Helen. Even though she had only just met Greg, she had felt at ease in his company, and knowing how he must be suffering now, it felt right to want to help him. She arranged with Helen to pick him up at ten o'clock the next morning.

Chapter Twenty-seven

Greg Hunter was so glad of a change of scenery. Since his Chloe and baby Emma had died, the home they had shared in Chelsea was empty, and right now full of memories of happy times. He didn't find it comforting, as he was carrying a burden of guilt inside him that he should have been driving, and maybe then he could have avoided the van that had driven straight into them. It didn't seem right that he was still alive, but their lives had been snuffed out in an instant, and even a month after the tragedy, he could feel the tears forming in his eyes at the thought of it.

He was so grateful that Helen had taken control, and insisted that he come and stay with her. Although she was eight years younger than him, and had always been his kid sister in the past, she had shown a great deal of maturity just when he needed her. When she told him she was working, and couldn't go to Canterbury, he had not really minded, it was hard to focus on anything except the tragedy. Then she had told him about Lisa, and what she had been through, but it was in strict confidence, he must never mention it unless Lisa did. He was shocked to know she had been blamed for the death of her baby, and it had taken fifteen years to put it right.

So, because of this, and only this, he had agreed to let Lisa spend the day with him at Canterbury. There was no way that he was looking for a new relationship. Right now he didn't feel as if he ever could, and probably Lisa might feel the same, but there was nothing wrong in having a friendship. Everyone needed friends in their life, especially through times as dark as this.

He got himself ready for the day out. Normally he wore suits to work, but today he put on some shorts. It was a hot day, and everyone seemed to live in shorts in the summer here. He found a short sleeved blue check shirt and navy blue trainers in his suitcase, that as yet he had not unpacked. In the past Chloe had taken care of all that. She would have unpacked it all and stored it neatly in the wardrobe. Oh, how he missed her!

Lisa turned up exactly at ten o'clock, and he was ready. When he got in the car, she smiled at him, and he smiled back. He knew that life had to go on. "Good morning, Lisa. It's a lovely one."

"Yes, it's hot. I expect Canterbury will be busy, there are lots of foreign students in the summer."

"I think the Cathedral is such an attraction with all its history."

"Yes, have you seen it?"

"Yes, I have, it's lovely."

Greg had been about to say he had visited it with Chloe last year, and she had been pregnant, but he felt the so familiar ache at the thought of it. Was coming here and dredging up memories a good thing? He decided to be honest with Lisa. She was keeping her attention on the road, so he stared straight ahead, it was easier to say it that way.

"Lisa you are very kind to bring me here today. I know you did it to help Helen, but I am not great company right now, and I might ruin your day."

Lisa was just passing the road that led down to Grove Ferry as he spoke those words, and she had a line of cars behind her, but when she found a lay-by she pulled in, switched the engine off and spoke kindly to Greg.

"Greg, if you don't want to go to Canterbury, it's no problem, I can take you back to Helen's."

Greg had expected her to be annoyed, and the kindness of her tone brought tears to his eyes. Before he knew it, the words came tumbling out, and he had explained about the car crash, and how he blamed himself for it.

"No way is it your fault, Greg. Sometimes we just can't change fate, and you were not meant to be with them that day."

"It doesn't lessen my feeling of guilt."

"Not right now, but when your feelings are not so raw, you will see it in a different way."

"I do hope so. Right now it disturbs my sleep."

She could see he was in a bad way emotionally, and could identify with many of his feelings. Although she had not shaken baby Lily to her death, for a long time she had blamed herself for not realising just what Ryan was capable of. So Lisa proceeded to explain to Greg what had happened to Lily, how she had been blamed, and how thankful she now felt that she had been exonerated.

Even though Helen had already told him, Greg was glad that Lisa had seen fit to tell him herself. That meant she trusted him, and he certainly trusted her.

"Whilst you are here, I could certainly recommend a bereavement counsellor in Birchington. I visited her myself yesterday."

He looked at her earnestly. She was so easy to talk to, and she understood how he felt.

"Lisa, you are a brave woman, and I am so glad that justice prevailed for you. Talking to you has really helped me."

Lisa smiled. "You are welcome. Now where would you like to go?"

"I hope this doesn't sound boring, but it's a beautiful day. How about we continue on to Canterbury, and then we go for a walk in the gardens by the river. It's so peaceful there."

"If you wanted we could even get fish and chips and sit on a bench and eat it, just like the students do," laughed Lisa.

"Let's go for it, then!" exclaimed Greg. So she put the car into gear and drove off.

So their day was spent just walking around the gardens, crossing the bridges, and watching the swans elegantly gliding along. There were a lot of people around, many of them from foreign countries, and they were all taking advantage of the beautiful weather.

They ate their fish and chips sitting on a park bench, and Lisa laughed when Greg got tomato sauce down his white shorts. It was a carefree time for both of them. Sometimes the simple pleasures were the best. They did not visit any of the sights that Canterbury is famous for, nor did they look around the shops, but by the end of the day, when they got into the car to travel back to Westgate, they had struck up a valuable friendship. They trusted one another, and wanted to support each other emotionally.

Lisa dropped off Greg just before five o'clock, she had enjoyed her day with him.

"Thank you so much, Lisa, for a lovely day. Helen will be back shortly. Do you want to come in and wait for her?"

"I won't, if you don't mind, Greg. Kate will be expecting me."

"Would you come out for dinner with me tomorrow night? I hear the Swan at Westgate does amazing food. It's a thank you for being such a great companion today."

"Oh, it's my pleasure," laughed Lisa, "why not."

"This time I will come to you, and the hotel is within walking distance. Does eight o'clock suit you?"

"Perfect, see you then."

As she drove towards the apartment, her sense of being free disappeared. As much as she loved Kate, she knew without a doubt that she would not approve of her going out with Greg. If only Kate would understand they were just friends, two people recovering from very hard knocks in their lives. It was not a romance, they were both too bruised to even think about a relationship at this time. They were just supporting each other emotionally.

Alan received a call on his mobile just before he went home. It was James.

"Just reporting back, sir, before we go home. During the search at Lee's flat we found cocaine hidden in the lining of an old mattress."

"Wow, just another crime to add to his list then."

"Yes sir, and also forensics report that at the murder scene of Eva Scott, there is a foreign body caught up in the lining of the chair she was found in. It has not been identified yet, it had found its way into the lining of the chair, and then it's fallen down inside. The only way to retrieve it is to rip the lining apart. Of course, it might just be something Eva dropped herself, but we will know more when we can identify it."

"That sounds interesting. I wonder what sort of foreign body it is?"

"We should know by the morning, sir."

"Thanks for letting me know James, Martha and I are off home now."

"Goodnight, sir."

Alan turned towards Martha, who looked expectantly at him, not knowing whether everything might have changed. Sometimes when she thought she was going home, they had to suddenly go and interview someone, or even arrest a suspect. Alan read her look.

"Relax Martha, we are going home. That was James; they found some cocaine at Lee's flat in Margate."

"Oh, something else we have on him."

"Yes, but apart from that, forensics have reported finding a foreign body lodged so deeply in the armchair that Eva was found in that they will have to rip the lining to get it out."

"I wonder what it is?" said Martha, in a puzzled voice.

"Well, all will be revealed tomorrow. But, right now, we have homes to go to."

"Yes sir, and Clive is in the car waiting for me. He just texted me."

"Off you go, Martha, and enjoy your evening."

"Thank you, sir. See you in the morning."

Chapter Twenty-eight

Kate was laying the table when Lisa arrived home. She noticed her face was glowing and she looked happy, and she felt a wave of jealousy course through her. Lisa had a new man, she always thought she was in love with all of them, and Kate was fed up with the lengths she had to go to in making Lisa realise that none of them were for her.

Kate had never liked men, and it stemmed back to her childhood when her uncle had sexually abused her when she was just seven years old. When she had told her mother, she wasn't believed, and she was sent to her room as a punishment for telling lies. At the tender age of seven she had made up her mind that no man would ever lay a finger on her again, and that she would leave home as soon as she was old enough to get a job and support herself. And she had done this for a number of years, until finally she moved back in with her mother at Faversham, and stayed with her until she passed away.

But she did like women. She found them soft and alluring creatures, and she had enjoyed casual affairs ever since she had left school. She had known Lisa ever since they were at school together, and had fallen deeply in love with her. But Lisa was not gay, and had no idea about Kate's feelings. Kate wrote to Lisa whilst she was imprisoned. She supported and believed in Lisa's innocence, and after her mother died, Kate found herself in a position to offer Lisa a home.

Kate had hoped that Lisa's doomed relationship with Ryan would make her reject men, and even turn to her for love, but then she had developed that ridiculous infatuation for Dr Jones, even though his wife was at that time still with him.

But even if Dr Jones realised how Lisa felt, he certainly never gave her any encouragement. In fact, all the running came from Lisa. Then in the end he had joined the local practice, and Lisa wasn't working with him, and Kate had privately heaved a sigh of relief. But not for long, as Lisa persisted in turning up at any time at his house. She was so incredibly thick-skinned about him.

Kate had been so relieved when Lisa's innocence had been proved. But the time after Lisa had fallen from the window had been harrowing for Kate. She thought Lisa would not recover, and she simply could not imagine her life without her. But Lisa had recovered completely, and just at the time when Kate thought she might turn to her, it had happened again, she had another man!

She made a supreme effort to hide her feelings, and smiled at Lisa. "Did you have a nice day?"

"Yes, we didn't do much, just sat in the gardens in Canterbury and had fish and chips. He needed to talk, so I listened, poor man."

Kate didn't like the sound of that. Talking made people close, and she didn't want them to get close. Lisa was a vivacious and extrovert character usually, this is what had attracted quiet mousy little Kate to her, now she was turning into an agony aunt.

"We have beef casserole. Are you ready if I dish it up?"

"I am, it smells lovely, but your casseroles always are."

The one way to get round Kate was to praise her cooking, although Lisa did mean it. It might be unusual to eat beef casserole in the middle of summer, but Kate's casseroles were really special, and she was a great cook. Lisa was feeling very hungry now. It was six hours since she had eaten fish and chips, and her praise brought a smile to Kate's face.

They sat down and ate their dinner together. Kate had opened a bottle of red wine, which they shared . Then Lisa chuckled when she recounted how some of the students had been having fun and making her laugh when they tumbled around on the grass.

Kate became very serious. "You know, Lisa, now that your name has been cleared, we can apply jointly to adopt a baby. You don't have to work any more. You can be a mum."

"Yes, I know, but initially I would like to go back to work. I miss Abby."

"If we had our own baby, you wouldn't miss Abby, and you could still see her."

Lisa didn't know how to explain to Kate that, right now, she wasn't sure she could cope with being a mum. It wasn't that long since her fall, only a couple of months, and then she had to recover, and she still felt fragile. As much as she loved babies, it was just a bit too early. She needed to be back to full health. As they were living as sisters, she hoped that the authorities would consider them, but right now it was an extra stress in her life that she didn't need.

"Kate, I do want that, but give me a bit more time. Being a mother would be amazing for me and you."

Kate smiled at her. She wasn't really that fussed about having a baby in the house, but it would bind Lisa to her, and that is what she wanted. Of course, she would never tell her that.

Lisa stood up and stretched. Having been out in the sun all day she felt very tired. She cleared the plates from the table, and loaded the dishwasher. Kate offered to make her coffee.

"No thanks, Kate. I am going to take a shower, and then I won't be long out of bed."

"Yes, I am going to bed soon. I have to be up early tomorrow."

As Lisa lay in bed reflecting on her day, she felt glad she had been able to talk to Greg. He was such a nice man, and he didn't deserve what had happened to him. It was so kind of him to ask her out for a meal. She hadn't mentioned it to Kate, but deep down she knew Kate wouldn't like it, she was convinced that Lisa had a new boyfriend, but that simply wasn't true. She plumped up her pillow and turned over, determined to stop worrying about it all. It was time to go to sleep.

Kate was also laying in bed reflecting. The casserole had gone down well tonight, so tomorrow it would be steak and salad, another meal that Lisa really liked. With that thought in her mind, she turned over to get some sleep.

Kate woke up early at six o'clock, and decided to get up, as it was such a bright and sunny day. When Eva had died, she had lost a client, as she always ironed her sheets, but now she had a new client in Minnis Bay. As well as ironing, she wanted her whole house to be cleaned once a week thoroughly, and after that a shopping order would be delivered from Sainsbury's, so Kate would stay to put that all away in the cupboard. The family she worked for were all out at work, and appreciated coming home to a hot casserole, so she had made a big amount yesterday, and put the other half in the fridge. All she had to do when her work was finished was to warm it up, then transfer it into the slow cooker where it would keep hot until they arrived home.

By the time Kate had finished everything, it was four o'clock. She would be home a bit earlier than usual, and the steak would not take long to cook. She usually texted Lisa at least once every day, but today she had got so caught up in her chores at the new house, she just hadn't found the time. But going home earlier was a bonus, so they could have a longer evening together.

When she got indoors it was four-thirty, so Kate sat down with a cup of tea. Lisa was not there, so she reached for her mobile to check where she was. Then she noticed the message, which she had not picked up earlier.

'HI KATE, SORRY I MISSED YOU THIS MORNING, YOU MUST HAVE GONE EARLY! JUST TO LET YOU KNOW NOT TO GET ANYTHING FOR ME FOR DINNER TONIGHT, GREG IS TAKING ME OUT. I AM VISITING ABBY TODAY, BUT SHOULD BE BACK ABOUT FIVE. LOVE LISA X'

Kate felt it, that overpowering rage that was now dominating her body. Although she was only a tiny person, the power of it engulfed her senses totally. Lisa had done this to her once too often, and something inside Kate had snapped. All she could do now was to wait for Lisa to come in, and whilst she did so, her jealousy was festering inside her! Kate had neither the will nor the strength to fight what was going on inside her. It was time she laid her feelings bare to Lisa before she lost her once again to a man!

*   *   *   *

Lisa had enjoyed her day spent with Abby. Although Sally was on leave, she was now pregnant again with another baby expected in the spring of the next year, and had gone to the hospital for a scan. The temporary nanny she had at the moment had a day off, and Lisa had been so happy to be asked to babysit. She had ended up spending the day with Sally, who was now working on how to get her financial compensation. They had lunch together, then Sally and Abby both took an afternoon nap, and Lisa stayed, and when Abby woke up, she looked after her until Sally got up again.

It had occurred to her when she got up and found Kate gone, that knowing Kate as she did, she might well go shopping after work to get some fresh meat for dinner, so she sent Kate the text about going out to dinner with Greg. When she didn't get a reply, she guessed that Kate might be sulking with her. As much as she loved Kate, and appreciated what she had done for her over the years, there were times when she almost felt like Kate was trying to control her life. So going out for a meal with a friend is what she wanted to do tonight, and no matter how much Kate sulked, she would have to accept it.

When she arrived home at five o'clock, Kate was sitting with a cup of tea in her hand. Her face gave nothing away, as she greeted Lisa. "Hi Lisa, would you like a cup of tea? I have more in the pot."

"I'll go and get it, you have been at work all day."

Kate brushed her words aside, and got up. "You have some post on the hall table. I will get your tea."

Lisa could only find a bank statement on the hall table, which was not that exciting, and it was surprising Kate had even mentioned it. She sat down in a chair, and gratefully took the cup of tea from Kate, who watched her carefully, hoping she had put enough sedative in it to make her sleepy. After all, she had to do something to stop Lisa making a fool of herself again.

"Thanks Kate, I will drink this, then I'm off to take a shower. You got my text about tonight I hope."

"I did, but Lisa, I have something I must tell you. It's been kept inside me for too long."

Lisa took a sip of her tea, and then wondered what was coming next. Kate was never a great conversationalist, Lisa was the one who spoke the most, and showed her emotions. And because this was so unprecedented, she gave her full attention to what Kate was about to say.

"Lisa, I have been your friend for many years, and we have been like sisters. I have watched you hurt by men, and I have so much love inside me. The reason why I wanted you to take my surname was not as a sister, but as a wife. I love you, and will always love you."

Lisa was stunned, this was probably the longest sentence that Kate had ever spoken to her, and she had not been aware of her feelings. She felt great compassion for her, but knew she would have to try and let her down lightly. She took a few more sips of the tea before she spoke, but then a feeling of tiredness came over her. She wanted to speak, but it seemed like an effort. She had to pull herself together, it must surely be shock at what she had heard.

"Kate, you know that I love you, but only as a sister. You have been the most wonderful and supportive friend that anyone could have. I do not have those sort of feelings towards you. I can't, because I am not made that way. . ." Her voice trailed off. Extreme weariness was overcoming her, she wanted to get out of the chair and go into the bathroom to take a shower, but she could feel her eyelids were so heavy, and she desperately tried to fight it.

Kate looked at Lisa now slumped in the chair. Those words had cut into her like a knife. Lisa didn't want her! The temper that was waiting to be unleashed was taking control of her, and she was going to let it.

"You don't want me, yet everything I have done has been for you! You are running after yet another man who will dump you when it suits him, and you expect me to pick up the pieces!" she screamed at her. But Lisa had by now become unconscious. The sedative had done its work.

Kate paced up and down in frustration. She knew that she may have stopped Lisa going out tonight, but tomorrow she might leave her and go to him, and she couldn't bear it! The words came tumbling out.

"I killed my mother so I could inherit her money, and give you a home. I hated her really. She let me down badly when I was a child, so she deserved to die. I poisoned her slowly."

210

Lisa moved slightly, and tried to force her eyes open. She could hear Kate's voice coming from afar. It was as if she was detached from her, in another room. It was so confusing.

Kate looked at her struggling to stay awake. She hadn't given her enough pills, but she could soon remedy that.

"Lisa, I want you to listen to what I say. It's important!"

Lisa made a supreme effort to get out of the chair, but Kate stood over her. At that moment, tiny Kate looked huge, and as sleepy as she was, when Lisa looked into her eyes, she saw madness there. This was not the Kate she knew! Although her brain felt fuzzy, she began to realise what was happening. "Kate, have you drugged me?"

Kate pushed her face close up to Lisa's, her eyes were blazing, but all she said was, "Yes."

"Why would you do that?" said Lisa, totally bewildered.

"I am doing it for your own good, to stop you making a fool of yourself."

Lisa felt anxiety course through her, but the shock of seeing Kate behave like that had made her more awake. She only had to look into Kate's eyes to see that she was mentally disturbed. Had she suffered some sort of mental breakdown?

"Kate, you cannot control my life, and drugging me will not stop me going out."

This time all self control had now deserted Kate, and she swung her fist at Lisa's face, catching her on the nose and drawing blood. Lisa gasped with pain, and Kate got a box of tissues from the sideboard and tried to mop the blood which was spurting from Lisa's nose. As Kate mopped the blood she spoke angrily to Lisa.

"Now Lisa, look what you made me do! I have done so many things for you, and this is the way you repay me. I killed Dr Jones to free you from your infatuation with him. Then there was our neighbour Eva, sweet little Eva, she wouldn't harm a fly, but she had to go too. If I hadn't killed her, they would have charged you with the doctor's murder. I did it all for you, and now this time you have pushed me too far."

It was at that moment Lisa realised that Kate was completely insane, and although she was a tiny woman, it felt like there was a giant towering over her. Lisa's face was throbbing from the blow on her nose, but she was now fully awake. She was aware that she was now in grave danger. She would have to try and talk her way out of this situation. It was probably best to humour Kate. She had to get herself out of this house, and to safety.

"It's OK, Kate," she tried to make her voice sound soothing. "I know you didn't mean it."

"I didn't. I love you so much, I would do anything to keep you here with me." She was sobbing now, her body was heaving, and she gently dabbed at Lisa's nose to make sure it was no longer bleeding.

"Kate, could you get me a glass of water. My throat is so dry."

Kate looked at her with pity. Lisa's face was covered in blood, although her nose had stopped bleeding. Kate had now stopped sobbing, and she blinked with her owl-like eyes behind the huge glasses that she wore, and appeared to be calm again.

"Yes, wait a minute."

Lisa's thought had been to make for the door whilst Kate was getting a glass of water, but although she tried to get up from the chair, her legs didn't want to support her, so she sank back against the cushion.

Kate returned with a glass of cold water with ice cubes in, just as Lisa liked it, so she took it off her and quickly drank it down. Kate watched her with interest. She had not given her enough sedative last time, but this time she had. Within a couple of minutes it had worked, and Lisa was asleep. Now there was no way she could go out and meet him!

Kate moved quickly, gagging Lisa's mouth, and then binding her hands and feet together. Then came the difficult part. She was tiny, and Lisa was tall and more powerfully built. She had to drag Lisa's unconscious body from the chair, and she made slow progress towards the hall cupboard.

Opening the cupboard door, Kate managed to drag Lisa into it, although puffing with the exertion. Then she leant against the door to make sure it was closed tightly.

It was now six o'clock and, at some time this evening, Lisa's fancy man would be coming to pick her up. But Kate chuckled to herself when she realised he would never know that Lisa was in the cupboard. After a busy day working, Kate felt very hungry, so she went into the kitchen to prepare her dinner. She even cooked some steak for Lisa, just in case she came to her senses later.

After Kate had finished eating, she took a shower and got into her dressing gown. It was now eight o'clock, and the buzzer went. She spoke into the microphone: "Hello, who is it?"

"Good evening, it's Greg. I have come to take Lisa out for dinner."

Kate felt hatred towards this man who was messing up their lives, but she hid it, keeping her voice calm and in control. "Hi Greg. So sorry, Lisa asked me to tell you she has changed her mind. She doesn't want to come out."

Greg felt huge disappointment sweep through him. He thought he had found a friend, but clearly if Lisa had changed her mind, then she didn't want to spend time with him. He wondered why? Had he poured out his heart a bit too much?

"Have I upset her?" he asked.

Kate felt irritated. Why didn't he just go away? But if she let him in, he would see the apartment was empty. Lisa was not in a position to help herself. He would never know she was locked in the cupboard, so she would do it!

"Come in, Greg. Just for a moment," she said, clicking the communal door open.

When Greg arrived at the door, he was greeted by a tiny lady who had her dressing gown on, but she appeared to be alone. Kate smiled at him from behind her big glasses.

"As you can see, she is not here. She has gone out," she said, exalting at the look on his face, and the knowledge that Lisa was so close to him but could do nothing.

"I am sorry to have troubled you," said Greg, wearily. And then, just as he turned away, there was a thump; it came from the cupboard.

"Oh, it must be my cat," said Kate quickly. Damn, Lisa must be coming round!

But Greg was not convinced. He tried the door, but it was locked. "You lock your cat in a cupboard. That's cruel, where is the key?"

Kate's brain was whirling. He was a tall and strong man, and she was a small and slight woman. How could she get him out of this house? She knew Lisa would have to die, as she now knew too much, but this man was physically much stronger than her. Maybe she could use the situation to her advantage.

"If you don't leave this flat right now I will call the police, and I will tell them that you sexually abused me!" she hissed at him.

Greg was very taken aback. This was the last thing he had thought of, but the idea of a cat trapped in a cupboard disturbed him. This woman didn't seem to be in her right mind, so getting out of there quickly was a good idea.

"Right, I am going," he said desperately, allowing her to open the door for him. Then he sped back to his car, and she watched from the window until he had driven away.

Chapter Twenty-nine

Greg was full of confusion, he felt as if he had just spent a few minutes with a mad woman who locked her cat in a cupboard. Lisa had mentioned Kate to her, the woman who was as close to a sister as one could get, who had supported and stood by her through all her troubles, and this woman definitely did not fit that description.

And then there was Lisa. He had put his faith and trust in her, but to go there and find she wasn't even in, and definitely would not be coming out with him that night, had hurt him. He wasn't looking for romance, and neither was she, and she had not even had the guts to contact him and say she wasn't coming out. He had formed a picture of her and how she would behave in his mind, and now that picture was shattered.

What on earth was she doing living with a woman who locked her cat in a cupboard? Something was not right, and he pondered whether to call the RSPCA or the police. Surely it must be a crime to lock a cat up like that?

In the end he went back to see Helen, who was very surprised to see him. As he entered the room, she tried not to look disappointed. Obviously the evening had not worked out for him.

"I did not expect you back so early. It's only nine o'clock," she said, gently.

"Lisa wasn't there Kate let me in to prove she wasn't there."

"That's not like Lisa, she likes going out. Did Kate say where she was?"

"No, she was acting very strangely. I felt really uncomfortable, and then I heard a noise coming from a cupboard, and when I queried it she said her cat was locked in there. Would you ever lock Bonnie in a cupboard?"

Helen looked at him with astonishment. Kate rarely said two words to anyone. She was a quiet mousy character that nobody ever really noticed. If anyone acted strangely it was Lisa, although recent events explained why. She stroked her sleek black little cat, who was perched on her knee, as she replied to him.

"You know I wouldn't, nor would any responsible cat owner, but Kate and Lisa don't have a cat. Kate is allergic to them."

Greg stared at her, his eyes wide with fear. "Well there was definitely something in that cupboard!"

"OK Greg, do you want to go back there? It's dark and late?"

"As crazy as it sounds, I need to know. Supposing Kate has had an argument with Lisa and locked her in there?"

"OK, let's ring the police."

After Greg had left so hurriedly, Kate laughed hysterically. His face had been a picture! Her mind was gone completely now, and she no longer cared about anything. She would have to kill her darling Lisa, and then she would kill herself. She could lay down beside her and they would be together forever. Having been spurned by Lisa she had nothing to live for now, but she knew she would have to be quick, because that nosy man would be back with the law. But she felt quite proud of how she had outwitted the police, so she sat down and wrote a suicide note explaining everything, then left it by the kettle in the kitchen.

Lisa was awake, her body had knocked against the door, so Kate opened the cupboard door and dragged her out by her feet. Lisa's eyes were full of terror. This was a woman she did not know. Being in that cupboard had terrified her. When she came round it was dark in there, such a small area, and feelings of claustrophobia had engulfed her. As she looked into Kate's eyes, she was full of fear. The gag over her mouth was tight, and the cord cut into her hands and feet, as it had been tied several hours ago.

Kate spoke to Lisa as she untied her gag. "Lisa, our time is up, I have to leave this world and take you with me. But I love you, and I can't bear to see you suffer. I won't poison you. We can both slip away."

All the love and respect that Lisa had felt for Kate was gone. She had been fooled, and the shock of knowing she had been living with a murderer, a woman with hidden depths who had inflicted such painful deaths on others, stirred her to the very core of her heart. Without even thinking about her own fate, her anger came tumbling out.

"You talk about love, but you put our kind doctor through a most horrific death, and dear little Eva, a ninety year old lady, and you did it for me! Don't you dare lay the blame on me. You are out of your mind!"

Kate frowned, even now, after all she had done for her, Lisa didn't have anything nice to say to her! Lisa lay there helplessly on the floor, and Kate once again brought her hand up and punched her in the mouth until blood flowed. "Lisa, you've done it again, and made me hit you. Now we are both going to have a nice drink of water, and finally be at peace."

Lisa tried desperately to turn her face away, as Kate forced her mouth open. Blood was still pouring out, and she tried so hard to resist the water that Kate was forcing down her throat. Then suddenly Lisa became still, and her body slumped back. Kate picked up the other cup. She had put plenty of Valium in both cups, and she downed it very quickly. It wasn't very long before the weariness overcame her, and she lay down next to Lisa to die. But even as she did that, Lisa choked and vomited the liquid that she had kept hidden in her mouth. It projected onto the floor, and Lisa once again lapsed into unconsciousness.

Canterbury police station was closed, and Helen was diverted onto another number when she rang up. She explained that her brother had visited the home of a friend to pick her up to go out for a meal, and found her sister acting strangely. She then went on to talk about the noise in the cupboard, and the reference to a cat.

217

Constable John Cobb listened intently. He was a cat lover. He had two of his own at home.

"So you think there is a cat shut in there?" he asked.

"No, they don't have a cat," said Helen.

John was puzzled. This was an emergency number, and he didn't understand why Helen had rung. It was getting late now, but he tried to keep impatience out of his voice.

"What exactly is the problem, then?"

"My brother said Kate was acting strangely, and is worried she may have had an argument with her sister, and locked her in the cupboard."

"OK, thanks for letting me know. We will send an officer round to check it out."

"Thank you," said Helen, putting the phone down. She turned to Greg: "The police are going to check it out."

"That's good," said Greg.

John sat musing, he was due to finish at ten o'clock, and he didn't for one minute think that anyone was locked in a cupboard. It sounded more like a practical joke, or even that this Helen who had rung up might be a bit drunk. It wasn't the first time that people had made odd phone calls to the emergency number. If only they realised they were wasting valuable police time. But just to be sure, he would make a note of it, and check out this apartment.

By the time he arrived in West Bay it was ten-thirty; not a good time to call on people, and he could see the apartment was in darkness. There were cars parked outside, but he didn't know if they belonged to the people living at that number or not. He pressed the buzzer just once. It lit up, but there was no response. Either the people inside were in bed asleep, or out, so he decided to go home, and, if necessary, someone could go round tomorrow. Having satisfied himself that was the best thing to do, he got back in his car and drove home.

218

Chapter Thirty

"Good morning, sir. This is the foreign body I referred to."

Alan was sitting quietly in his office drinking his first coffee of the day with Martha, when James entered the room carrying a clear plastic bag with what looked like a plastic object inside. He held it up triumphantly.

"Whatever is that?"

"I have one of those. It's a plastic jug that you use to put water in a steam iron," said Martha.

Something clicked in Alan's mind. His last visit to Kate had been when she was ironing. Hadn't Lisa commented that she was using a glass jug, and she said she couldn't find the other one?

"It's been tested, and it was definitely used to administer the poison, then the murderer must have dropped it. It had lodged inside the chair lining, and they had to cut the lining to get it out," explained James.

"Martha, do you remember our last visit to Kate, she was ironing?"

"OMG sir, yes, and using a glass jug, which made Lisa question why."

"Right, you know where we are going," said Alan, briskly.

"Can anyone enlighten me?" asked James.

Martha quickly filled him in about their last visit, and James was amazed. Then he remembered something else. "Underneath the sink in Eva's kitchen, a drum of rat poison was found. Evidently she was terrified of rats, and one was seen in her garden. When Karen found out her mother had bought some rat poison, she took over and got a man in to put it down in the garden."

"Hm, I wonder if Eva told Kate about it when she brought her ironed sheets round?" mused Alan.

Martha rang the desk to explain where they were going, and the sergeant on duty told her about the phone call from John Cobb detailing the incident of the previous night when a lady called Helen had rung the emergency number with a tale about a cat being locked in a cupboard, and when he had gone to the apartment to check it out, the place was in darkness. Martha then explained that they were now going to that same address this morning, and Alan had requested that backup might be required.

When she came off the phone she quickly explained the situation to Alan.

"Oh, my goodness, let's hope we are not too late," he groaned. "If only we had known last night."

"I am coming too!" said James.

They all sped outside and got into the car. As they drove from Canterbury to Westgate, every minute seemed like an hour. Alan was still in shock that he had not even considered Kate as a suspect. Her apparent mousiness had been an act. She was a cold calculating killer, and if Lisa was in the apartment with her, then she wasn't safe.

When they arrived outside, Alan noted that both Kate's and Lisa's cars were in their parking spaces. He told Martha to wait in the car, and call for backup if he instructed her to. Together Alan and James rang the buzzer, but there was no reply. Just then the communal door opened to admit a man, and Alan took advantage of the situation. "I am DCI Alan Clarke, and I need to visit the Bryants. Do you know if they are in?"

"Sorry, no," said the man, relinquishing the door to him. Alan and James walked along the hall until they were outside the door of the apartment. Alan rang the doorbell, but there was no response. Then he looked through the letter box. The door leading to the lounge was open, and he spotted a body on the floor.

"Quick, we have to break this door down!" he gasped to James.

They both ran at the door, smashing it with their shoulders. Nothing happened, so they tried again, and this time the door burst open.

"Oh, my god, no!" said Alan in dismay, spotting the two bodies on the floor.

James immediately called for an ambulance whilst Alan tried to see if there was any sign of life. Kate was beyond help. She had been dead for several hours, and the look of peace on her face after what she had undoubtedly inflicted on others was a surprise.

Judging by the pool of water around her, Lisa had vomited, and although unconscious, Alan did manage to find a faint pulse. He debated about untying her hands and feet, but in the end decided to leave it for the paramedics. As soon as the paramedics arrived, they got Lisa onto a stretcher and carried her to the ambulance. Kate's body was also put in the ambulance, and then they went off with the blue light flashing. In the meantime, Alan had found the suicide note.

Alan called Martha to say no backup was needed, and then went back to the car with James. As he drove towards the station, he remarked, "Well, Kate can't tell us what happened, and we can only hope that Lisa will make it. Of course, this suicide note will explain a lot. Inside him he was cursing himself for not asking to see the foreign body the evening before. Was it too late to save Lisa?

Two days later, after having her stomach thoroughly pumped, Lisa was able to sit up in bed to be interviewed. Alan wanted to hear Lisa's version of events. He had already told himself he would proceed gently with her. After all she had been through, and to end up in hospital again, the poor woman must be feeling very weak. Doctors had said the only reason she survived was because she had vomited a lot of the medication up, whereas Kate had given herself a lethal dose.

When he saw her pale face and tired eyes, Alan felt a great deal of empathy for her. Probably the last thing she felt like was being questioned by them, but he had a job to do, and Lisa's knowledge would more than likely help to wrap the case up.

Martha had her notebook at the ready, and there were two chairs by the bed, so they both sat down. Alan tried to inject some positivity into his voice. "Good morning Lisa, you certainly look better than the last time we saw you. How do you feel?"

"To be honest, I am still taking it in. When you live with

somebody for ten years you think you know them, but clearly I did not know Kate."

"We found a plastic receptacle in the chair where Eva died. It had been used to poison her and then dropped, where it then became lodged in the lining of the chair. We found Kate's fingerprints on it, and also, under the kitchen sink, we found the drum of rat poison."

"Yes, Kate told me she had killed Eva and Ian Jones, she said she did it for me. She wanted me as a partner, and I never realised. She killed Ian because I liked him, and poor Eva just because I was in hospital at that time, so it was obvious it could not be me."

Martha saw the look on her face. Devious Kate had made Lisa feel guilty. So she hastened to reassure her. "Lisa, you mustn't blame yourself, Kate fooled everyone, including us. She was not even on our list of suspects. She did what she did for herself, no one else, and clearly she had some sort of mental condition, to kill people in such a barbaric way."

Lisa felt slightly better after those words. It was just beginning to register with her that the worst of her traumas were over. She had been proved completely innocent of Lily's death, and Sally was right now preparing her case for compensation. She vowed at that moment that she would rebuild her life. She was only thirty-eight. With the money that she got, she would buy herself a new home in West Bay. She now had so many good friends around her.

"Well, Lisa, that is all we need for now," said Alan, smiling at her. "Get yourself better quickly. There's lots of support if you need it."

"Thank you, Mr Clarke. I am going to be fine," she said firmly, and the nurse bustled in to say they had interviewed her for long enough.

"We are going," Alan said, with an ingratiating smile.

As they were walking along the corridor, Alan was surprised to see their nanny Helen, accompanied by a young man, heading for the door to Lisa's room.

"Hi Helen. What brings you here?" he asked.

"Hi Alan, this is my brother Greg, and we are going to see how Lisa is. She's certainly a survivor!"

"I think she'll be pleased to see you," said Martha, noting that Helen's brother was very fit. That would cheer Lisa up.

222

As they travelled back from the hospital, they continued to discuss the case.

"Of course, we have no one to charge, but we have her own confession that Kate committed both murders, and also killed her own mother so she could buy a home to share with Lisa. It also makes sense that she made that phone call whilst Ian was in the armchair after she drugged him, and withheld her number. She had to be certain he had succumbed to the Valium before she could return and poison him. After all, he was a tall strong man, and she was a tiny woman. What amazes me is how she kept her violent side very well hidden for a long time," remarked Alan.

"Poor Lisa. What a shock when Kate turned, but thank God she managed to spit out enough of the poison, otherwise we would have had two dead bodies."

"Yes, thank God we got there in time," agreed Martha, and they were both busy with their thoughts. Just as they arrived back at the station, Alan's mobile rang. It was Zoe. She didn't often ring him at work, so he answered his phone with a certain amount of apprehension.

"Hi honey, what's wrong?" he said anxiously.

"Nothing is wrong, it's all good, Alan. We just got an offer on the flat. It's a cash buyer with no chain this time."

"Oh brilliant! Now we can start house hunting."

"I suppose when the case is wrapped up," said Zoe.

Alan grinned at Martha. "It is wrapped up, isn't it, Martha?" and she nodded happily.

"I am going to book two weeks off. We can go to the beach, have picnics and view houses. Oh, I can't wait!"

Zoe heaved a sigh of relief that the case was over. Alan was taking some leave and they could enjoy being a family, and by the time the new baby was born they could be settled in their new home. Everything was working out so well. In the meantime she would have to wait a few hours until he was home.

Right now Adam was taking a nap. What a good idea! She had got up early, and it had been a busy morning. So she, too, curled up on the sofa for a rest.